Praise for Ella M. Kaye

"I always love the texture, dimension, and perspectives in Ella M. Kaye books. Kaye isn't afraid to tackle difficult subjects, and she especially handles social issues with tact and dexterity. This is a riveting read, packed with words to savor."
Author Maggie Toussaint, about Shadows of Rust & Reels

"The author draws rounded characters, with flaws as well as virtues and is unflinching in showing that some of their injuries and suspicions are self-inflicted. ... Like a ballet, the characters unfold to each other and to the reader and when they come together it means something. Ella M Kaye's eye for detail, description and the 'masks' people wear is telling."
Author Lindsay Townsend, about Pier Lights

"Kaye's characters not only come alive, but will jump out and yell at you, pour their hearts out to you, and you will laugh and cry right along with them. The fun, witty banter and the expressive sorrow will keep you on the edge of your seat."
Liz, Reader Review

"You always seem to suck the reader right into the story, which is a phenomenal thing. Leaves the reader wanting more & more.
Annette, Reader Review

"The first few pages caught me up in their story, and I read almost non-stop until I finished."
Rising Star Reviews, about Pier Lights

Also by Ella M. Kaye

<u>Dancers & Lighthouses</u>
Pier Lights
Shadowed Lights
Pieces of Light

<u>Artists & Cottages</u>
Shadows of Greens & Memories
Shadows of Rust & Reels

<u>Anthology</u>
Music of the Heart from Fire Star Press (2017)
includes the EMK novella *A Melody in the Dark*

Shadows of Blues & Echoes

Ella M. Kaye

Elucidate Publishing
PO Box 1262
Hermitage PA 16148

United States of America

Durango/Silverton Railway, Durango CO

One

"You absolutely can*not* put me on *that* story." Gillian jumped up from the white settee in her editor's office, placed far enough from the glass and black metal desk to announce distance, physical and mental, between the editor and her staff to constantly remind them of her status, and strode right up in front of Karenne, her arms crossed in front of her chest, waiting for the punch line.

"I can. I'm your editor."

"It's not funny." A joke. It was a joke. With that thought, Gillian dropped her arms. "Fine, you got me riled. Now tell me my actual assignment."

"That is your assignment." With a flip of her long fingers boasting perfectly polished red nails, Karenne Wright Jackson, her full name splashed across her name plate in gold on shiny black right at the front of her desk, as though anyone entering her office didn't already know her name, went back to perusing her computer screen. "Your ticket will be on your desk by the time you leave tonight. Call when you get in..."

"You're *not* serious."

"Oh, Gillian, relax. It's just a story."

Her mouth gaped before she pulled it shut again. "There's no such thing as *just a story* and you know it, even if you are totally immersed in your high-brow editor job now instead of being another nobody low-life writer like me. We were friends, you know, when we worked together..."

"Don't get personal. I'm still your friend."

"Then make someone else do it. Kevin or ... or Sally. Yes, send Sally. I'd love to see her wear her $500 Gucci shoes out in the dirt."

From behind the desk, where sticky notes placed in a perfect vertical row over the left edge of the glass boasted a to-do list, Karenne brushed her fingers through wavy brunette salon hair. Professional auburn highlights nearly sparkled as she slipped part of it behind her ear. "Gucci is handbags, dear, not shoes."

"I thought they were shoes, also." Gillian had to pause her rant to think a minute. "They are shoes, also. I know they are. I've heard her say it often enough. Anyway, send Sally."

"Can you imagine Sally doing that story the way it needs to be done? She'd laugh at the whole thing. That's why I have her on pop culture and not on real stuff. You wanted the real stuff, so go do it."

"Real?" Gillian rolled her eyes and stuffed her hands into her beige cardigan pockets. "A big time hotshot went to live in the woods and you call that *real?* He's an attention seeker. So what?"

"I don't think so, not since he goes by a different name out there, which means he doesn't want to be associated with his past life, which means it's a story I want." Pulling a hand mirror, gilt-framed, from her top left office drawer, Karenne Wright-Jackson, newly-promoted to editor, made faces at herself while checking her lipstick, grabbed lipstick from the drawer, also, and freshened it. Never mind it was fine already. "I want this, Gilly. And I want it right." She tossed the mirror and lipstick back in the drawer, shoved it closed, and leaned back in her cushy chair. "That's why I'm sending you."

"But ... but ... he's a *man*. In the woods. Alone. What kind of friend would send a defenseless girl out to find a man alone in the woods who doesn't want to be found?"

"*Defenseless?*" Karenne popped back upright and guffawed. "You? Defenseless? That's the best thing I've heard in years. Come on, Gilly. That's another reason I'm sending you. I never have to worry about you. You'd fall from a skyscraper and end up bouncing off some big fat guy and get nothing but a scrape on your elbow. The poor guy might not be so lucky, but..."

"Real funny." Gillian sighed and paced the white, black, and glass office. Too modern for her taste. Too stringently neat. They'd always fussed about each others' habits that were so opposite, ever since they'd met back in college during their first journalism class. The assignment was to critique each others' stories and find every little thing they could find to criticize. Gillian hadn't found much, and she let a few small things go. Karenne filled the paper with red ink, picking on the tiniest detail even if it wasn't wrong, really, only not the way she would have said it. Somehow that worked into a friendship.

The friendship card wasn't working this time. Maybe Karenne was right about every point she made, but still ... the woods. In the mountains. Where it was cold. And had no convenience stores. And ... and it was dirty. With bugs and ... slithery things.

She shuddered hard.

Karenne leaned over her desk, allowing her navy suit jacket and white low-buttoned shirt to gap just enough to show more skin than was really necessary in an office. "I know you don't want to do this and I know how you hate anything that moves around outside, other than leaves..."

"No, I hate leaves, too. You *don't* know how *much* I don't want to do this."

"Fine. I know, Gillian, but you need to do this. I can't keep you in the 'real stories' department if you keep doing the TMZ kind of things..."

"That's what sells. It's what put my name out there, as much as it is *out there* so far."

"And yet you just complained about this super bachelor millionaire recluse story, which is, I'm sorry to say, a step above your last two pieces."

"You assigned them."

"I wanted you to do more with them, and you know that."

Gillian let herself slump onto the white settee, which she rarely did. She'd learned to hold herself up and look like she *was* someone so people would believe she was. In front of Karenne, she didn't feel the need. "The subjects didn't deserve more time than I gave them, and this won't deserve much, either. So what? He got tired of ... whatever the hell you get tired of when you have a bazillion or whatever dollars and feel sorry for yourself for some ridiculous reason and he went to do a Thoreau thing. So what? It's been done."

"Everything's been done. You know that's not the point. Go find your angle to make this different. Dig deep. Scour him out." Karenne stood. "Not up for discussion. This is your assignment. Go do it. You leave first thing in the morning."

Gillian stood and forced herself not to sigh or slump. She half thought about stomping her foot but didn't allow that, either. She'd worked too hard to become a professional, and stamping your foot at your editor was not at all professional.

Renne was right. Her writing had slipped. Her interest had slipped. It just didn't seem to matter anymore what she wrote about or how she wrote it. No one still read the actual paper and the paper's website got few views, especially the 'real stories' section. People wanted gossip. They wanted scandal. They did not want anything that made them actually think. The headline writers usually made her stories sound salacious, even if they weren't, and that's all that was read most of the time.

Why should she bother?

And yet she had to either bother, and to bother a hell of a lot better than she had recently, or she had to find a new profession. The thought of starting over, though, sent a shiver all the way down her spine to her toes.

Maybe she was in a rut, but at least it was her rut and she was comfortable there.

Comfortable.

In a rut.

What in the hell had happened to her?

She used to feel fire in her soul at the start of every new piece. The research made her near giddy. Going out and grabbing information people didn't want found but that needed to be found was the biggest rush she'd ever had. At thirty-two, maybe that was pathetic. Still, it was something. Something she'd created.

It was something. But it was hardly enough anymore.

And now she had to go out, not only out of town, but way out of town into the middle of nowhere, into a world she'd escaped, to do a fluff piece about a rich guy and try to make it sound like a real story.

Life was just too grand at times.

~ ~ ~

Hank stripped his shirt off, shook out the wood chips, dunked it into the stream a few times, then hung it on a branch. With the warmth of the day, it would dry quickly, he expected. Pulling his jeans down his hips, he paused at the sound of breaking twigs to his right and peered through the trees.

A glimpse of a large brown creature with antlers, a full rack, told him it was only a deer.

With a breath of relief, since he was too tired these past few days to evade some creature that didn't want him there, he pulled the jeans off, then his shorts and socks, shook them out, and hung them beside his shirt. Grabbing his soap, he treaded across the rocks to slip into the cool water.

He shivered at the contrast of his hot sweaty body and the cold stream. In truth, he loved nothing better.

Letting himself unwind before washing, he sat on his favorite bathing stone, a nearly flat smooth boulder just underneath the water at mid-level times, and stretched himself out over its top. The clear water barely skimmed his stomach and thighs. He preferred it a touch higher or even a couple of inches higher so his most sensitive part wasn't sticking out in the sun, but he wouldn't lie there long. He'd worked hard, and late, and there wasn't much daylight left.

With the thought in mind, he sat up again, lowered into a deeper part of the stream, and scrubbed with the pumice soap made with natural oils plus lemongrass for rejuvenation. His stock was running low. He'd have to get into town before long and pick up a batch at the nature store he trusted to only give him what wouldn't hurt the place he lived, the place he loved more than anything in the world.

While there, he'd replenish the canned goods she always held for him, as well. Canned as in home canned, not the commercial sprayed-and-stuck-inside-metal cans processed food that was often on "special" for a dollar each.

Not that it mattered much anymore. While he could, though, he wanted to enjoy the best and freshest of the earth's offerings.

Hank told himself, out loud, to quit whining, since it helped absolutely nothing, and ducked all the way down into the water. Scrubbing his scalp, he came up enough to lather it, and ducked down again to rinse it out. "And now you're talking to yourself. Fine thing if you go nuts before you..." He was not going nuts. He only hadn't talked to another living soul, at least not one that understood him, in ... how long now? Five weeks? Could be. He'd gone far longer. When he first came out to the hills outside Durango, Colorado, got his cabin built, and was settled with his necessities, he'd not gone back into what people called civilization for over two months. It had taken him that long to start to miss it.

It had taken far less time to change his mind again and high-tail it right back up to his cabin.

Donning a pair of old shorts from the backpack he always carried and tossing the rest of his clothing into the denim bag within his pack, Hank set home barefoot and bare-chested. The way he preferred. Like the natives of old.

He'd suffered more splinters and cuts and blisters on the bottom of his feet than he could count after he'd moved to the wild and decided he couldn't bear to wear shoes. Finally, the soles of his feet callused well and toughened and he only wore foot protection when he worked out away from the cabin.

And when he went to town. So he didn't look nuts. No matter what they thought, and he knew they did. Hard to understand something you'd never tried, as he told those who had the guts to say something to him about it. They didn't get it. Their lives or minds were too narrow.

A shame. So many walking around with their noses stuck in whatever device connected them to the world and they used it to show themselves off, often far too much, or to tell anyone willing to listen just how much nothing they did all day long and how they were so bored. They never bothered to connect the two things, though.

Sad. So much knowledge to be had so easily and so few bothered.

Hank shoved it from his head. You couldn't change it. Lord knows he'd tried. At some point you had to throw up your hands and take care of your own needs. The world could do what it wanted with itself for all he cared anymore.

Maybe that wasn't fully true. He cared. He did. He just couldn't risk the stress of worrying about it when he couldn't change it.

Walking past his Nymph Row, as he'd termed it, Hank noticed a patch of termites eating into one of the faces he'd taken so long to carve so precisely from the trunk of a fallen tree.

So be it. Nature would be nature. They had as much right to dig into the dead wood as he did. More, he supposed, since that was sustenance to them and to him it was only a hobby.

Well, more than a hobby, he guessed, as he stood there and watched them devour his work. It was ... sustenance. To him, as well. The act of carving away.

It was life to him.

More than anything else he'd left behind. That wouldn't last, either. Nothing did.

Two

Gillian swatted at a flying insect as she stood beside where the taxi driver meant to leave her and stared down the dirt path. "You're kidding, right?"

"'Fraid not. Want to turn back?"

Yes. Of course she wanted to turn back. She wasn't an idiot. She surveyed the pitted, rocky dirt and the scraggly trees along what looked like a dirt bike trail. He couldn't be serious. There had to be a better way to get to the Dennison place than to walk up and over the hill on a dirt lane.

"Not as far as it looks." The driver tried to sound optimistic.

"Can't you drive down that?"

He snorted. "In a four-by-four maybe. In an ATV, sure thing. Not in this cab, I can't. She'd never make it up that hill and over those holes. Want me to take you back to town? You don't look like you belong up that way."

Of course she didn't belong up that way. She belonged back in Denver where she'd chosen to live after all of the growing up years in the middle of nowhere with dirt floors and an outhouse that always had humongous spider webs in the corners sporting humongous spiders that scared the bejeebers out of her, never mind it was supposed to be "modern times" even back then and plumbing should have been absolutely required in any house where children were being raised. And floors. Real floors.

She swore she'd never go back to that, and here she was in Carbon Junction, Colorado standing on a little road on the edge of a settlement named for being a switch point to somewhere else instead of an actual place of its own, and looking up a path to somewhere even more remote where she was required to go. For work. Work that had pulled her out of that life. How was that for irony?

"Lady? I'm not sitting here all day. Coming back with me or what?"

"No. Thanks. I'll be fine." Fine. Sure, she'd be fine. What else was she *ever* other than *fine*?

Still, Gillian wasn't about to be held back by a little hill, especially after a flight from hell with a little one screaming in her ear the whole way despite his mother doing all she could to gently calm him. And she was fairly sure the sandwich she'd grabbed to take with her from one of the airport shops on the past-security side of the airport hadn't been quite right.

Her stomach twisted and lurched. Her head half thumped and half spun.

Maybe it was only what she'd gotten herself into. She should have walked out of Karenne's office, out of that little pissant newspaper building, to find something that would let her make her own choices, write what she wanted to write ... but then she wouldn't have the paper to pay her travel expenses. There was that. And she did like to travel. Not in the boonies. She'd had far enough of that for a lifetime. But she liked to travel and couldn't afford it on her own unless she found a better paying job. But she didn't want to change jobs. She wanted what she wanted in the job she had.

Someday things would change. Everything changed. She just had to wait and watch for it.

With a deep breath for encouragement, Gillian closed the pulling handle on her rolling bag and picked the thing up by its small handle. The wheels might make it over the dirt okay, but she could imagine the mess it would make of them. It was designed for airports and sidewalks, not the boonies. So was she.

~ ~ ~

Hank tipped his head to a couple who said hello and kept walking. The sooner he finished his business and got the hell out of Dodge, or in this case Durango, the better. Not that it was bad for a city. A decent city. Quaint for its size. Friendly enough. But still a city.

Adding the last of the supplies into his truck, he headed back to Carbon Junction to visit the nature store, enjoyed a leisurely lunch with the owner – you couldn't beat ham from a local pig mixed with local potatoes and homemade gravy if you tried – and stopped to top off his tank before heading to the cabin.

While it fueled, he stood back far enough he didn't have to breathe the fumes.

"City woman, of course. Who else would be foolish enough to walk up over that hill carrying fancy luggage in her city shoes?" The voice beside the truck across from Hank laughed. "And where on earth is she going with luggage out here, anyways? Ole Ernie got her good, I'd say. I'd love to see how she's making out."

Hank rolled his eyes and moved to where he could see the guy who had such compassion for a fellow human. "Over what hill?"

The kid startled. Young kid, barely old enough to drive. He pointed. "Up and over that yon hill through the path to make-out point."

Make-out point. Hank wondered when teens would stop trekking up that mountain pass, barely a pass, for such a ridiculous thing. There were plenty of safer and more accessible places to find privacy. How many had to come down with broken bones first? "A city woman headed that way?"

"Yeah. Hilarious, ain't it? Ernie, the cab driver, told her it was the only way to get where she was trying to go. Laughed all the way home, I'd durn near bet."

"Where was she trying to go?"

"To spy on that guy who wants left alone. Serves her right, I'd say. Whatever the guy did, he has the right to be left alone at his own place, I'd say. Didn't hear he was a murderer or nothing, just something to do with money. Whatever, she has no right to spy..."

Hank sighed and ducked back out of view, finished filling the tank, and headed out faster than he usually drove. A city woman in "city shoes" walking that excuse for a path? Insane. He'd have to have a talk with Ernie.

Three

"Stupid, stupid, *stupid!*" Gillian cursed herself for the umpteenth time and again thought of turning back. But she didn't quit. Ever. It was against her nature. Even with blisters on her feet from sand inside her shoes and on her palms from carrying that stupid pretty suitcase up the stupid dirt path along the stupid mountain trail, she wasn't giving up.

She had to be about there. The driver said only a couple of miles. She walked more than that all the time, every day. Around the city. On sidewalks. Not on dirty bumpy windy trails that felt like a full vertical incline by now.

Stopping for a minute again to catch her breath and wipe sweat from her forehead – she was going to be one heck of a wreck by the time she got to her story subject – Gillian startled at a loud crash in the nearby brush. An animal. Bear, maybe? They had to have bears out here in the mountains of nowhere, right? Reaching slowly into her pocketbook for her pistol, she pulled it out but didn't let it show. Silly, she thought. A bear wouldn't know what a pistol was. And even sillier, her little pistol was only enough to stop a man long enough to get away from him. It would do nothing against a bear. Unless she hit it in the balls. Could you see a bear's balls? She supposed if it stood up, she could, unless it was female, and she'd heard female animals were more dangerous than males.

Her father had always said as much, but she was never sure whether to believe him. Ever. At least half of what he'd ever said was a joke, but it sounded like everything else he said, so it was impossible to tell the difference. She had a boyfriend once who did too much the same, joked with a straight face. Gillian had bid him adios fast. She'd had enough of that for one lifetime.

With the thought that a bear would only be more angered by a small pistol, she tucked the thing back in her handbag, grabbed her suitcase, and picked up her pace.

"The hell with it." She put the thing on its wheels, pulled out the long handle, and dragged it behind her. "Let it scratch. Let it fall apart for all I care." At least the grating noise of plastic wheels against dirt and rocks should scare away any creature small enough a pistol would actually work on it. She'd never had to shoot a snake or any other slithering, crawly thing before, but it didn't mean she wouldn't if needed.

The drag of the case against the rough earth was nearly as bad as carrying it. She was winded. Beyond winded. She was exhausted, sore, bone-weary, sleepy from the early flight, thirsty, and ... and totally pissed the hell off. "Karenne, this is it. Never again. Just wait until I get back. I swear I'm going to knock you down."

When she regained enough energy.

Coming to a clearing at one side, Gillian was nearly overjoyed. She was there? Dragging the bag, she went off the path onto ... an overlook. It was nothing. Only an overlook. But there were boulders flat enough to sit her tired ass on while she looked out over the mountain. Which mountain? She should know for her story. Right now, she couldn't care any freaking less. She only wanted to be home in her cozy bed with her plush pillows and her shower.

So the overlook boasted a nice view of trees. Yeah, she saw trees all the time. And the little river they'd driven beside was just a river. Gillian didn't get what the big deal was about. She'd grown up in it. They were just trees, which had meant a whole hell of a lot of sweeping leaves out of the house, the nasty falling down wind-rattled excuse for a house, every day during fall. And looking out the jalopy's windows through bird poop since they just loved the trees, especially the chokecherries that added some red tint to the poop which just made it all the more disgusting.

"You're not going to get done with the job by sitting here. Get up." Gillian had told herself the same many, many times. It was her own personal pep talk. It worked, again, and she cringed at every movement.

If she'd been prone to tears, they would be streaming down her face by now, but she wasn't and she wouldn't allow it. Slapping at a mosquito pushed thoughts of tears aside and returned them to anger. She was good at anger. It fueled her.

"Fine, Karenne. Just wait and see what kind of story I get. I'll make it so magnificent, editors from really big papers will be banging at my door, it'll be so good. And then you'll have to send Sally out on your ridiculous missions for stories you want. If you want them, get your ass out of the office and you go do them…"

"Talking to someone you think is there?"

Gillian jumped at the deep male voice and looked up from the dirt and rocks in her path to see … um … not what she would have expected to see out in the boonies. A polished and proper looking man, despite the Wranglers and T-shirt. Blue. Dark. Like his eyes. His wavy hair was neat, not too short, not long, and shiny dark blond. He reminded her somewhat of the archangel warrior, what was his name?, with that hair and that build, his strong facial features…

"Hello?" He tilted his head and approached slowly. "You okay?"

He thought she was nuts. Gillian nearly let herself laugh hysterically. Or maybe he was a mirage. She'd heard of those. Too much heat. Not enough water. She'd nearly do anything for a cold glass of water…

"Here." He stepped close enough to hand her something, barely close enough, and studied her face.

Gillian thought about her pistol but forgot all about it at the sight of a canteen, an actual metal canteen covered with some kind of heavy fabric. She didn't know they made the things anymore. "Please tell me that's water and you're not some maniac I shouldn't be this close to. Be warned, I defend myself well…"

"Good thing, but you're not much of an outdoor type, I'm guessing."

"Why would you say that?" Stupid pride. Of course she wasn't, but only because she didn't want to be.

He scanned her outfit. Her chic new pants in their oh-so-soft fabric in a luxurious dark green that flowed around her legs as she walked, usually, were dirt-stained and wrinkled and stuck to her moist legs. Her cream blouse showed sweat stains and was all kinds of catty-wompus from switching her handbag to one side then the other. Luckily she had a dark green cami underneath so nothing else showed through.

And her shoes. Not close to $500 Guccis but expensive enough and usually comfortable enough to tread the city sidewalk all day long if needed. Now scuffed and dusted in dirt. And it was hard to argue through her pounding heart from being startled.

"Okay, so I didn't expect this. I generally take cars when I travel such distances and the guy said a couple of miles, an easy walk. Idiot. I'd like to squeeze his thick neck. He could have told me the truth and I'd at least got a hotel and put better... Anyway, can you tell me how much farther it is to ... um..." Darn, she couldn't for the life of her say the name of the homestead, even if it was her subject matter.

Shuffling through her handbag, she was careful not to show the weapon and careful to keep it close to her hand. "Here." She pulled out a pink neon post-it note. "The Dennison ranch. You know of it?"

"Dennison *ranch*?" He said it like it was the most ludicrous question on earth.

"Well, whatever Mr. Hank Dennison calls his home base, his land, house, whatever. Do you know it?"

"Why do you ask? Have relatives who work there?"

"Out here? If I did they'd have to visit me if they were interested. No. It's..." Maybe she shouldn't say. Would the area help hide their recluse? It was possible. If so, she'd never get any information.

"It's what? Why are you looking for it?"

"I want to talk to its owner, if it matters to you. Can you help me, or not?"

He shrugged. "Another three miles or so that direction. As a warning, there are two ridges you'll have to cross that have less of a path than this one. Bring a compass with you?"

"Compass?"

"That little thing with an arrow that points north so you know what direction you're heading?"

"I *know* what a compass is, thank you. He said it was just over this hill."

"He?"

"The taxi driver."

"His name happen to be Ernie?"

"How should I know what his... Oh. Could have been. Why?"

The man scratched the back of his head through the wavy hair. Beautiful hair, if not terribly thick. Beautiful eyes. Friendly. But wary.

"Ernie doesn't like outsiders buzzing around."

"Neither do you, I would say."

"Not terribly, to be honest."

"Then why should I believe you?"

He shrugged. "Don't. Have a good day. Make sure you check for ticks when you bathe tonight. You'll want someone to check your scalp for you. At least take a good swallow or two before you go on, and don't say I didn't warn you."

A swallow. He was holding the canteen toward her.

She tried to lick her parched lips. What if it wasn't water?

With a light shake of the head, he tossed his head back and poured what looked like water into his mouth, then poured a bit into his palm and held it out. "Want to check?"

"Put my hand in yours so you can grab me? I told you..."

"If I'd wanted to, I could have easily enough before you even saw me. Do you want a drink or not?"

"Yes." She hated to give in, but he made too much sense and he looked okay. Water. It tasted like cool clear water, but better than any she'd ever had. "That's wonderful."

"You're parched. Most anything would be wonderful."

"Yes, but ... it is..."

"Pure spring water straight from the earth."

Gillian started spitting to her side. "From the earth? Unfiltered?"

"Pure. As I said. You won't get better anywhere or any that's better for you. But have it your way. I can't stand here jabbing all day. Have a good one."

She stared when he started to leave her. He was *leaving* her. Alone. On the mountain. Ridges? Three miles? No, she didn't think so. "Hey."

He paused and turned.

"Okay, I'm sorry. I'm not usually so rude. It's been a bad day."

"Not my fault."

"No. You're right. And I apologized. Could you tell me if there's a faster way down this thing and back to civilization than the way I came?"

"Civilization. Interesting choice of terms for what I figure you mean the city."

"Of course. Hotels. AC. Sidewalks. Cars. Roads."

"Yes, well, I would have taken the road. It's just over there. Where I'm parked."

"Parked?"

"My civilized truck is just yonder. If you can make it that far, I'll give you a lift back to town."

"Bless you. Seriously. I didn't want to be here in the first place, but my boss..." She stopped at his raised eyebrows. "Anyway, yes, please. I'll give you gas money..."

"Not necessary. Let me take that." He nodded at her bag.

"Oh, I couldn't ask you to..."

"Bottle up that pride, lady. You're too worn out to argue."

Hank admired the spunk, but he was glad she closed her mouth and decided not to argue. For her own good. She was getting a step too close to heat sick. He could see it.

Insisting she carry the water, he bade her to drink it slowly but to drink it. Not only hadn't she argued, she obeyed. He never would have guessed it.

Settled in his truck, she introduced herself as Gillian Hart from Denver and asked his name.

He hesitated. If she was looking for him, she'd know his middle name which he used as an alias along with the last name of an old friend. Around Carbon Junction and Durango, he was known as Aaron Forrester. So far she didn't seem to realize who he was and he planned to keep it that way, so he gave her his childhood nickname. "Henry. You need to drink more of that water. Slowly."

Again, she obeyed and took a couple of swallows. "First name or last? Do you only have one?"

Sarcastic thing, she was. "Didn't figure you needed more than that since I'm only giving you a ride to town. Henry Franklin, if you need to know." Again, he stole Gia's name, this time, her married name. Just in case Ms. Hart had more going for her than he could see so far and would figure it out. Of course, could be her head wasn't clear enough to think about it yet. Dehydration did horrible things to the body, and to the brain.

He was glad he'd found her so fast and was parked close. Carrying her suitcase was no problem. Carrying the woman along with her suitcase would have been.

Putting the AC on low, which he never did for himself, or almost never since he liked the heat and liked to stay within close range of the outdoor temperatures as much as possible until it got too cold, he stopped at a crossroad and checked the canteen. "Not enough. Drink more."

"Sure you don't have something in it to make me ... well..."

"Don't flatter yourself. I don't want to have to take you to the emergency room in Durango. I have better things to do. It's nothing more than that."

"I'm fine."

"You're starting to splotch. Danger sign. Drink that water." He headed the truck back the way he'd come, into town. "Where are you staying?"

"Just drop me off in that little town where the path starts. I'll call a taxi."

"Only one of them comes to Carbon Junction regularly. Want to spend more time with Ernie?"

"It's only a few miles into Durango. You can't tell me none of them will come out here."

"For a price."

"I have money. I'm not exactly a beggar."

"Have it your way." Hank took his time driving back the county line road. He wanted to at least be sure she was okay before dumping her off to wait for a taxi that would likely take an hour coming out. Too few people had use for the things. They all drove. He had to wonder if she'd never left the city before. "This your first time traveling?"

Her back stiffened. "I travel all the time. Usually to places worth traveling to, however."

"And this isn't?"

"No." Her shoulders relaxed. "Sorry. I guess that was insulting, wasn't it? Were you raised here? Haven't you wanted to venture out elsewhere, see bigger and better things?"

Hank had to force himself not to laugh. "Lady, if you'd ever stood up at the top of that mountain you had only started to climb and looked out over the incredible expanse of mostly unspoiled land, you would realize how ludicrous that question was."

She stared a moment then turned to watch out the window. At least she drank more water when he ordered her to do so.

Pulling into the gas station, Hank put the truck in park and looked over at her. "This good?"

"It's fine. Thank you. Are you sure I can't pay for your gas?"

"Wasn't enough to bother. Sure you're okay here and you feel well enough to be left alone?"

"I do fine alone, thank you. I'm not needy or dependent, even if I was unprepared to hike a mountain I didn't expect to hike today. I could have done it if I'd been prepared." She opened the door and nearly fell out, and he reached over to grab her arm, but she caught herself. "I'm fine. It's just farther down than I expected."

He forced himself not to grin. And while he did get out to pull her bag from the back, he forced himself not to follow her in and sit with her until the taxi came. He had supplies to get home.

Four

Gillian gaped up at the Strater Hotel when the taxi finally pulled in front of it, paid what was probably an exorbitant rate for the drive that he probably made longer than necessary, and heaved her scuffed dirty bag up the few cement stairs into the reception area.

At least it looked like Karenne had accommodated her well. She'd expected a near bottom rate hotel, as usual. This... This was the old west back a couple of centuries. It was all dark wood with heavily textured dark red and light green carpet and wallpaper, accented by heavy curtains and old-time chandeliers hanging from the ivory tiled ceiling. A grandfather clock told her it was nearly dinner time. Gillian was almost surprised to see the clerk use a computer to check her booking when she said she had a reservation.

"Bad travel day?" The young girl gave her a sympathetic smile.

"You have no idea. And I'm sure I smell. I'm so sorry. I usually don't."

"I didn't notice, and I'm sorry you've had a rough day. I hope you'll enjoy the hotel and its comforts. Feel free to wander around..."

"I'm far too tired tonight, but thank you."

"Of course. I'll call someone to help with your bag."

Generally, Gillian argued she didn't need help. She always packed light. She could handle one bag. But it wasn't rolling well anymore and she was deep down flat-out exhausted. She might have just keeled right over out on that trail if that man hadn't shown up...

And why did he? She hadn't thought to ask why he was there. Anyway, how ironic would it be if she'd ended up face down in the middle of nowhere while rodents and other crawly things took advantage of the free lunch of her decaying body? Karenne would feel bad if she did.

A shudder made her force her thoughts elsewhere.

Signing the paperwork and following the young man assigned to escort her, Gillian gaped again at her room and the antiques he pointed out while he set her bag barely inside the door and asked if the room was all right. "It's beautiful. Thank you." Overwhelmed by the opulence, western style opulence, but still opulence, she gave the guy a bigger tip than she normally would.

Starting to strip off her clothes while she found the bathroom, unable to resist the sparkling welcome that would lead to feeling human again, she decided to call Karenne real quick and give her hell first.

"Gilly, where have you been?"

The worry in her friend's voice diffused her somewhat. "I'm here working. You realize cell phones do not work well in the mountains of nowhere, right?"

"You were supposed to check in when you got there."

Gillian explained she'd wanted to at least check out the ranch or homestead or whatever it was before she bothered with her hotel, and explained what she'd gone through and how she would have died out there where her editor sent her if not for the man...

"Man?"

"Oh Karenne, just some local Don Juan or whatever..."

"Don Juan? He's exotic and came on to you? Was he gorgeous and..."

"Okay, wrong Don, I guess. Not gorgeous. Not exotic. Just a plain man. I'm exhausted. I'll call in the morning."

"But he went out of his way to help you? How chivalrous. Don Quixote, you mean?"

"I guess." Gillian rolled her eyes. Her friend never stopped looking for a man for her although she wasn't looking for one herself. She didn't want that until she was more settled where she wanted to be and doing what she wanted to do.

"You were polite, I hope. And you got his name."

"Polite enough, and what does it matter? He gave me water and a ride. In his truck. Nothing more. I offered to pay his gas..."

"Oh, you didn't."

"Of course I did. Anyway, it doesn't matter. I'm here and still alive and badly in need of a long, cool shower. Thank you for this hotel, by the way. It's just gorgeous."

"I figured it was the least I could do. I'm sure I'll have my head in the wringer for it. No fear. I'll smooth talk them out of it. Have a good shower, Gilly. I can't wait to hear what you think of Mr. Hank

Dennison. Let me know as soon as possible."

"Hell." Hank banged his palm against his steering wheel, slowed to nearly a halt, and turned around at the entrance to his private road. He had to check on her. If he could find where she'd gone.

Of course he could find out. Ernie talked easily. Hank had no doubt he was the one who'd picked the woman up to take into Durango. As tired as she was, he assumed she'd go straight to her hotel, so Ernie would know.

He was crazy. There was no need to make the trek back into the city. He'd dropped her in a place she could find help if needed. She looked smart and capable enough outside the fact she was a city girl in the mountains. He had no need to check on her.

He nearly let himself turn right around again, but she wasn't well. And she was in from Denver for work. Likely didn't know a soul in the area. He knew that feeling. It used to fill him with anxiety. A ludicrous thing to think back on.

Either way, he had to check.

Needing to piss and hating to use convenience station toilets that always smelled of piss and sometimes worse, he slowed again to a stop, jumped out and walked around to the other side of his truck just in case someone might come along and not want to see it, and let out a breath of mental relief to go along with the physical relief. Good thing about the boonies, as she called it. Couldn't do that in the city without threat of arrest. Or much else, either, these days.

Didn't matter to him anymore.

Zipping up, he returned to continue his ridiculous quest.

It didn't take long to find out, either. Ernie was, as he often was, sitting at the station leaned against the back of his taxi sipping coffee from a Styrofoam cup talking to a couple of guys who were also there a lot. Hank didn't know their names and he didn't care.

He pulled in a couple of spots away and motioned for Ernie to come over as he stepped out, purposely leaving the truck running as noise interference to their conversation.

Ernie strutted over as though he was king of the gas station parking area. Probably, he was. "Hey, guess what I found trying to wander your way today? Look there, I rhymed."

"Yes, I know what you found. Not smart to send her up there on foot. She was nearing heat stroke..."

"Stupid dame has no right stalking you. From a paper, I'd reckon..."

"Still not smart. How about you don't do that again? I don't want that on my conscience."

"You didn't do it..."

"But it was on my account. I appreciate the thought, but tell them you don't go that direction and leave it at that. I can deal with interlopers as needed. Without harm. Got it?"

"Yeah. Just trying to help." He hunched his head into his shoulders like a child who got told off.

"And I appreciate it, as I said. Tell me something. Did you pick her up again and take her into the city?"

"Yep." Ernie snickered and scratched at his beer gut. "Took my time getting back here though I wasn't far away or doing nothing and then took the long way around to her hotel." He snickered again. "She didn't even suspect nothing. Those city women who think they run everything..."

"You realize that's not ethical?"

Ernie shrugged and scratched again.

"Which hotel?"

"Why? She's not bad looking. Got the hots for her?"

Hank forced himself to hold his tongue and just get the information he needed. "She was nearly sick from the heat. I want to make sure she's okay. How did she seem?"

He shrugged again. "She walked in and out of the cab of her own accord, with her bag. Guess she's okay enough. If not, she's staying in a fancy enough place they can manage if she needs help, I'd say."

"Which hotel?"

"Strater. Staying there, I figured she had enough dough my detour wouldn't hurt her none."

Hank sighed. "Not very gentlemanly of you."

Ernie laughed and this time scratched at his balls. "Never said I was. Damned heat. Sweat makes me itch."

"Try a shower now and then. You smell, too." Hank turned away from the image of the man with his heavy arm raised and his nose beside the big sweat stain under his armpit and got back in his truck to head to Durango. To the Strater.

Five

Gillian wrapped in her robe and nothing else, luxuriating in the soft silky fabric after the long tepid shower. She considered staying right there in her room all night, ordering room service, and kicking her feet up on the bed.

But after the trying day, she wanted civil company. Even when dining alone, she felt part of everything when she was in a room full of people who paid no attention to her but who she paid attention to well. She'd always studied people. It was what made her interested in journalism. Their stories.

She'd fallen away from that lately with pieces that had more pull, more interest. Fluff really, but interesting fluff. She could make almost anything sound interesting when she tried. The right wording. The right emotional slant. A bit of distortion here and there.

Easy enough.

Maybe she'd go back to her interest in the real story, no slant, only what he said that she would keep in its context.

Or she wouldn't. Depended on him.

Maybe that was why she'd gotten away from real stories. Too many people were just rude asses and she delighted in getting even with slant.

Bad form, she knew. She hadn't been sleeping well. Her conscience yelling at her, she supposed. But a good belt of rum and water helped to an extent.

It sounded good about now, too.

Giving in to her wish to be around people, asses or not, Gillian found the most comfortable clothes she ever let herself wear in public – old faded jeans that fit her just right, with a bit of stretch, and a clingy soft burgundy sleeveless blouse that hit just above her belly button in front and scooped down to just below her belt in back that felt even better than it looked, over the barest bra she had – and made her way down to the hotel restaurant. That would have to do. She had no interest in going back outside.

~ ~ ~

Hank sat in the parking lot for some time before he took a deep breath and walked into the Strater. Must be a big time paper she worked for. Nice, he supposed. He used to think it was nice. He still did to an extent.

As he opened the big wooden doors, he had to wonder if the woman realized the paradox of choosing an old west style hotel while basking in her precious "civilization." He would have guessed she'd be at the Hilton instead, with its indoor pool and contemporary amenities. Could be she didn't choose it.

Asking for her room at the front desk, he waited while the clerk called up to say she had a visitor.

"I'm sorry. She's not answering. Would you like to leave a message?"

"Thank you, no." Did he wait around and see if she'd be back soon? He decided, as Ernie said, that she'd be fine in the hotel and could easily get help if needed.

He knew that. He did.

So why did he hesitate to go back through the double doors until he'd seen her?

"Hello again."

Hank turned at her voice and found himself scanning her curvy fit figure, more fit than he would have thought earlier in the day, topped by faded snug jeans and a dark red somewhat lacey barely there blouse that made him think he should have gone on home.

"You know someone staying here?" She was watching him, waiting for an explanation for the unexpected second meeting.

"Only you. Not that I know you, exactly. You clean up well, Ms. Hart."

Luckily, she smiled. "Gillian, and thank you. I'm also a lot more together than I'm sure I appeared earlier. I don't usually frazzle so easily." She slipped a short strand of light brown hair behind her pale lobe. "So should I ask why you're here?"

She wore no earrings. There weren't even holes for earrings. Unusual. He had to force his thoughts back to his mission. Why was he there? Good question. He gave her the simple part of the answer. "I came to make sure you were all right. That heat when you're not used to it can be tough, and you were looking rather rough. No rhyme intended."

Another grin accompanied a slight shift of her arm. Her fingers caught the thin strap of a small handbag. "I'm fine by now. It's a wonder what air conditioner and a nice shower can do for you. Thank you, though. It was sweet to check. Can I ... um..." She glanced behind her. "I was just going to find something to eat. Can I show my appreciation by treating you to dinner?"

No. Just say no, Hank. You know better... His gut overruled his head, easily, while he tried very hard to keep his gaze only on her face. "You don't mind if I join you? I'll buy, though."

"I won't hear of it. Least I can do. Please."

He gave in. A stupid thing to do. He knew better. So much for finally having control of himself. She'd ruined that. Not a woman in three years had ruined his control. When he was with one, in any way, it had been his choice, his doing, a measured decision, not an uncontrolled ... desire or need. After dinner, he would go right back to his cabin and stay there.

Gillian was enthralled by the Diamond Belle Saloon which Henry suggested as a nice casual setting. Casual wasn't how she'd describe it. The place was a full-out old time west saloon, at least what she knew of them from movies. It could have been a movie scene with the bartenders in their old-style white and black elasticized shirt sleeves and black hats, and serving girls in bustiers of shiny red, purple, and green with matching short lacy skirts.

He'd asked for a balcony table where she could look down at the long ornate wood bar with its top so heavily varnished it reflected the lights and the shelves of alcohol, the big piano and its costumed male pianist, and across at the heavy dark red drapes lined with gold tassels. Even the ceiling was intricately detailed in textured gold bordered by blue that reached down over the bar and was speckled with stars. Chandeliers made to look like old candelabras provided most of the soft light, and ceiling fans slowly turned to circulate the air.

She had to ask what he'd said three times so far while she was tuned into the ragtime music and dance hall girls. She was far more interested in watching the girls than he was, amazingly, with as beautiful as they were in their exquisite costumes. Maybe he didn't lean that way. Although the way he'd looked at her made her think he did.

So far he hadn't talked much about himself, but that was fairly typical of men, that she'd found, at least of those she'd dated. Over dinner, he asked about her job and how she liked it and she had to admit mostly she did. She had maybe said too much. He could possibly know Hank Dennison and repeat what she said, but what did it matter? She expected trouble from the hard-nosed business exec turned mountain hermit, anyway. By her guess, the man was nearing sixty, although records were unclear on that point. And all reports called him ruthless and self-serving.

Not a story she wanted. And not a man she wanted to deal with. Gillian preferred talking with struggling professionals who were often arrogant through their struggles. She found that endearing. Maybe because she was the same. Struggling. And arrogant. Maybe too much so. At least she understood it. You had to be just arrogant enough to believe you could make it into big time in order to make it into big time. Many very skilled and capable people never would only because they lacked enough arrogance. She refused to apologize for trying to get where she wanted to be, no matter how it made her appear.

"Do any dancing?"

She startled at his voice and met his amused expression. "No. Not at all. Why would you ask?"

"You're studying those girls pretty hard. Figured you had a reason."

"Because they're talented and they're good and ... well, I love their costumes. I'm always intrigued by people who can do things I can't."

He leaned slightly forward over the table. "I'm guessing that list is fairly small."

With his deep blue eyes taunting her, Gillian took a good swallow of her martini and tried to decide what he meant. "What list?"

"Things you can't do. Other than mountain hiking in heels, that is, even low heels. Not sure I could do it in those shoes or that outfit carrying that bag, either, so it's not a criticism."

"That again? How long are you going to rub it in?"

He grinned and leaned back. "That's it. I'm done. How's your steak?"

"Luscious. How's your chicken?"

His eyes sparkled. "Luscious."

"Really? It's chicken."

"You don't like chicken?"

"Sure. In salads. Not much on its own. Kind of bland, isn't it?"

"Not with this bourbon sauce, it isn't. Put the right kind of sauce on it..." He glanced down at her blouse. "And anything is ... luscious."

"You're making fun of me again."

"Sorry."

"No, you're not."

He gave her a shrug and swallowed a gulp of tea.

"So you're on some health kick or something? Chicken and iced tea while I'm doing it all out with steak and a martini?"

"I have to drive."

"Doesn't explain the rest."

"Yes." For a second, he looked the slightest bit vulnerable, but he bounced right back. "Something like that."

"You don't look like you need it." As a return compliment, or insult, however he meant it, she let her eyes roam his frame, the part she could see above the table. He had a good build. Sturdy. Not too thick. Not too thin. It went perfectly with his masculine and handsome face, not gorgeous, as she'd told Karenne, but nice. Well taken care of.

"Looks can be deceiving, can they not? As a journalist, you should know that. It's like putting sauce on chicken. Or on a story. It's pretty easy to make things look the way they aren't."

A story. Gillian set her martini down, pulled her shoulders back, her chin up, and met him face to face. "Okay, enough cat and mouse. Why are you actually here tonight?"

"I told you why."

"Uh huh. There's more to it. Why are you here? And don't lie to me. I will know if you are."

He stared a moment, studying her. "I know what story you're

on."

"Of course you do. Small town news travels fast, which is why I don't live in one." She sipped her drink but kept his eyes. This was not a man to let her guard down against. Or to show one tiny ounce of weakness other than what he'd already seen.

"And why I do. I find the openness far more comforting than the crowd that smiles to your face in public while stabbing you in the back behind walls. At least you know where you stand in a small town."

"At least we mind our own business."

He nearly choked on his tea when he laughed. "Coming from a journalist down here to flush out a man who wants to be left alone?"

"Different. That's my job."

"That you chose. No one in this country is told what work they have to do. You chose it. Don't use it as an excuse to hide what a busy-body you are. And no offense, but facts are facts..."

"I am *not* a busy body." At heads turning, Gillian realized she'd raised her voice too much. "I am a journalist. I uncover stories that need to be uncovered. For the good of society."

"That so?" He leaned forward again. "What good would it do society to flush out Hank Dennison and tell people what he's doing and how he lives? What good could that honestly do for anyone?"

"You know him." It dawned on her that he must be a friend of the man's, or an employee, maybe.

Henry sat back again. "I know him. Answer the question."

"I don't have to answer anything."

"Right. Because you ask the questions and expect them answered, is that it? If you don't get what you're looking for, you'll write what suits you."

"I don't need your approval for my job, Mr. *Franklin.* And I assume that's a false name, with the way I had to ask you for it. I read people well, just so you know. What is it, really?"

"Do you?" His glance, thrown over his glass of tea, said he didn't believe her. Tea maybe to keep his head clear, to be careful? Had his employer sent him to flush her out?

"I do, actually. So?"

"Doesn't matter if it's real or not. I don't care to be part of your story. Can't stop it, but I won't help it, either."

"Typical." Gillian raised her martini at him in a salute. "Everyone thinks they're important enough to be put in an article just because I'm doing one. Don't worry, Henry. I don't find you interesting enough to bother."

A flicker of amusement flashed through his eyes. "I'm glad. Since that's out of the way, feel like dessert? I'll buy since you're doing dinner. There's a little place..."

"No. Thank you. It's been a long day and I'm ready to be in for the night. So maybe we could just finish the meal with civility, shake hands, and go our own ways?"

"If you'd rather, although I didn't see that it was getting uncivil. However, you might answer yourself what I asked before you go further with this."

"You're not going to stop me from doing the story."

"Figured I wouldn't. At least stop fooling yourself that you have any interest in helping society and admit it's only for ... the fun of it or for your own needs. Not a criticism. We all do it some way or another. But we should at least admit when we're being self-involved in the guise of *helping mankind.*" He stuffed a piece of chicken in his mouth.

Gillian didn't want one more bite of her steak. He'd soured it. Civil? The man called that civil? Obviously he hadn't lived right here his whole life. He had a whole different feel about him. Well-traveled. Successful. Obnoxious and arrogant and very much self-important. But smart. And learned.

The less time spent with this man the better, as far as Gillian was concerned.

"Lose your appetite?"

She met his pointed stare. "No. I'm full."

"No, you aren't. Don't be a diva with me. Eat like a real person. You've got to be hungry after your adventures."

"My stomach isn't terribly happy, after my *adventures.* And I am not and have never been a *diva,* thank you very much."

"In that case, tea would have been a better choice than a martini.

You're going to feel like hell in the morning."

"And you would know?"

"I would. And I do."

"You're a doctor."

He laughed. "Not close."

"You haven't said yet what you do."

"You haven't asked. And don't bother. I wouldn't want you to find me even the tiniest bit interesting enough to mention in your story."

"Most people want to be."

"I wouldn't dare argue that, but, Gillian Hart, I am not most people."

"Thank the Lord." She muttered it under her breath, but he laughed and toasted her comment with his raised glass of iced tea.

Six

Hank lugged a bag of ice from his ice cellar up the narrow stairs. Should have made them wider. Better to keep the cold where it belonged that way, though. He shoved the bag up through the square door onto the plank floor of the back porch, crawled up behind it, and lowered the square back into place. Then he stopped to catch his breath.

He was tired today. Unusually tired. He should have come right home after grabbing his supplies instead of worrying so much about that woman who was doing just fine in her fancy hotel with her restaurant food...

It was the food, the refined sugar in the bourbon sauce and in the salad dressing. He wasn't used to it anymore. He'd be tired the next couple of days.

With a sigh, he heaved the ice into his arm and took it to the kitchen cooler. If he wasn't afraid of losing his ice and having to haul more in the back of the truck with half of it melting on the way, he'd open the floor again and let the cool come up into the cabin.

It was hot. Dog days of summer. The end of July was the worst time of the year in the mountains, as far as he was concerned. Winter, he didn't mind much. It was a nice reprieve from busy days outdoors and constant well pumping to keep enough fresh water on hand to replace all of the sweat he lost.

Sweat was good, though. It cleared shit out of his system.

Maybe that would make two days of fatigue one instead. He'd go work outside. Sweat it out. Then bathe in the cool stream.

The thought comforted and revived him and he filled his chilled canteen with cool water... Hell. He'd forgotten to pull venison out of the ice cellar to thaw for supper. Tempted to make do with vegetables and not bother with the meat, Hank changed his mind quick on that one. He needed the protein.

Are you on some kind of health kick?

Gillian's face drew back into his thoughts. Yes, something like that. Although, like their different definitions of *civilization*, he called it *real* eating. Not a health *kick*. Pure. Natural. Constant. Not off and on when he thought maybe he should try to be healthier for a time and then fall back into the easy and convenient trap. Like too many things, easy and convenient food was a trap. It took him far too long to catch on to that, but at least he had.

On days, though, he did think he'd gone too far.

When he had to change his mind again, he would. For now, he was fine without ease. And he was nearly fine without daily companionship.

Refilling the ice box and dispensing with a breakfast of oatmeal and a fresh peach – best thing about going into town was having fresh, unfrozen fruit for a few days other than what he grew – Hank pulled into his sturdy boots, grabbed his tool pack, and headed to explore a spot he'd seen a couple of days earlier.

Too early to call Karenne, Gillian figured. The worst thing about traveling for stories was doing it alone. It was also the best thing, in a way, since she could make her own schedule.

She lounged in her robe with a cup of sweet, milky coffee and a huge muffin she'd bought from the restaurant before heading up to her room the night before, after she'd gotten Henry what's-his-name off her back. Blueberry. It was ... luscious. Even if he would laugh at her term, it was. A man who ate chicken at such a nice place was too reined in. He had no idea what he was missing. And he was wrong; she felt fine this morning, other than her arms being a bit sore from hauling her suitcase. Of course, she'd also picked up a sports drink to rehydrate before bed. She was smarter than he expected, which would work to her advantage if she ran across him again.

Eat like a real person. Her eyes rolled at his phrase. Okay, so she'd finished her steak and potatoes in her room rather than putting them in the little mini-fridge. She would pay for the rich food later, when she got home, on her treadmill. While she traveled, she let herself indulge. Too much strictness ate at your soul. She did that enough without depriving herself of food. She loved food. It was her one true comfort. Her treadmill kept it from showing on her. If she was willing to pay the price, she saw no reason not to enjoy a bit of forbidden fruit at times.

Especially when she had to go do something she seriously did not want to do.

The thought of trying again to hunt down Hank Dennison weighed her spirit to the bottom of her... well, to her core. Why had she agreed to do this? Henry's comment refused to be banished. How would it help society to out a man who didn't want outed, who had been out and wanted ... what?

What did Hank Dennison want after he'd already had it all?

That was her angle for the story. Not why he wanted out. Or maybe that, too. Why on earth would someone be on top of the top and be able to live where he wanted and go where he wanted and buy what he wanted without worrying about budgets and counting pennies to buy groceries and fill his tank want to be away from ... anything?

To stop working, yes. She got that much. If she had what he did, she wouldn't be told what to do or worry with a schedule or take assignments she didn't want. She also wouldn't want to keep track of ... whatever the hell he kept track of as CEO in charge of thousands of people if she could simply choose to settle in a nice house with people to take care of it.

If Gillian had that kind of money, she would travel often. When tired of traveling, she'd sit at home and ... and what? Work on her novel, maybe. The one that had been sitting in the far depths of her file cabinet for years that she rarely thought of anymore.

A quote she'd read once told her she probably wouldn't. *If you can give up writing, you should.* Probably true. And she had. So she should. She'd even given up on doing those decorated journals she'd started years before.

Apparently she didn't want it enough. What she wanted was a major story. She wanted to write an important news story everyone would read because it would spread everywhere and get shared on social media and get a zillion hits...

Her fifteen minutes of fame. Everyone wanted it. Why shouldn't she?

What good will it do society?

The question haunted her while she showered and dressed in

fresh jeans, still soft and fitting, a tight cami of dusty blue to blend with the jeans, and a gauze sleeveless blouse to look professional-ish, as well as she could in jeans, but lightweight enough she wouldn't get overheated again, with any luck.

Shoes would be a problem. She didn't have hiking shoes. Her Keds would have to do. Her dusty blue microfiber Keds she just loved. And dusty would be too correct after wearing them to track down a CEO-turned-mountain-man.

Trying to force herself out the door, Gillian stalled by looking out over the mountains through the hotel window. It was pretty from the window. She preferred to see it that way than up close.

Nope. She couldn't do it. Just the idea of going out there kicked in her sinking feeling, as though a fifty pound weight was pulling her under the waves of a dark greenish brown murky pond. She couldn't go back into the mountains.

Gillian pulled her cell from her front pocket and speed-dialed her boss, pacing until she heard the greeting.

"Don't even say it, Gilly." Karenne threw her best warning tone.

"I didn't even say hello yet."

"No, but I know why you called. Yes, you're doing the story. No, I won't listen to arguments."

"But Renn…"

"Nope. I won't hear any buts. I want this. Go do it."

"I can't." She slumped onto the foot of the bed. "Seriously, I … I just … can't even walk out of my room right now."

"Don't do this now, Gillian." Her voice softened.

"It's not like I schedule it. Something about this story just… It's getting to me. I can't do it."

"You can, Gilly. *Can't* isn't a word you use."

"Sometimes I do." She stood again to pace the room to try to fight off the sinking despair. She did. She often said it, at least to herself. Sometimes she scolded herself for it and changed her own mind, but this…

"Pull it together. This is important to me."

"I know. I don't know why, but I know…"

"Okay. You want to know why?"

No. Gillian didn't honestly give an ounce of a shit why it mattered to her friend. Not right now she didn't. She was a bad friend. No wonder her boss was the only one left. But she just...

"Still there?"

"Yeah." She stood in front of the window. Those mountains were so immense. So strong. So wild and unforgiving. And too much like home. Way-back-when home. Not the home she chose. She didn't want to go back there.

"Want to know why?"

"No." Gillian ran her fingers along the bottom edges of her eyelids, trying not to bother her eyeliner while she rubbed away the dampness.

"That bad?"

"Yes. I want to come home." At a long silence, she sighed. "Okay, I sound like a five-year-old, but you don't get it. Henry... the man who rescued me yesterday, he said something that made me second-guess ... everything. Again. And..."

"Ignore him. He's not your story. Gilly, I don't care about this story personally."

Her jaw dropped. And she dropped her ass back onto the bed. "Then why in the hell..?"

"Because I have this huge hunch that you need this story. You know how my hunches are, right? I can't ignore it. You need to do this."

"You're crazier than I am." It was nearly a whisper.

"Maybe I am. But do this."

"Renn..."

"Do this and I'll let you pick and choose your own assignments from now on as long as I'm editor. Okay? Enough sauce for the bitter duck?"

Sauce. *Anything was luscious with the right sauce.* Maybe Henry was right. "Promise?"

"Absolutely."

Could she? The huge black pit in her soul said she couldn't, but her brain answered. "Okay."

Seven

Unwilling to trust the taxi driver again, or anyone else, Gillian rented a car, bought a map since the rental place warned her not to trust GPS in the mountains, and clenched her teeth as she headed back into Carbon Junction.

Someone would tell her how to get out to the CEO hermit's place. She only had to use her charm and her wits and an offer of being included in the story. She was always careful with that. Being included didn't mean she had to use a name. A simple "with a nudge the right direction from a local" worked fine. She imagined those who got that kind of mention weren't real happy about it, but it was part of the job. She had to keep focus on the story.

Of course she was also unwilling to trust the first person to give her general directions, so she asked not two, but three willing sources, disguising herself as an old girlfriend who wanted to check on him to be sure he was doing well. She was a decent actress. If she ever had to change careers, acting was always possible. She had a believable face, Karenne always told her. It would help her go far as long as she kept her name clean enough.

It was maybe not clean, exactly, but it was clean enough.

With the map, directions from locals, and a case of bottled water in the trunk along with a tall bottle beside her, Gillian felt almost willing to do what she had to do. She felt almost human instead of like the misty gray thing that had come over her in the hotel. Action always helped it. She knew it did.

It was hard as hell to move herself into action, though, during those times.

Her mother told her to get help. Her father told her to get over it and be an adult. Her brother ... hadn't talked to any of them in she didn't know how long. Gillian decided to walk away from them all and do things on her own.

And look where it had her: on an old thin bumpy road on a mountain going who knew where to see a man she didn't want to see to write a story she didn't want to write.

Suddenly, she had to check her handbag to be sure her pistol was there. A sigh of relief took over when she felt the cool metal. And then the deep dark pit swept in and Gillian had to pull over. In the middle of nowhere. She didn't dare stop in the middle of nowhere. What if... What if what? No one was around. She'd keep the car running and if anyone pulled up behind her she'd get moving again.

Decided quickly out of necessity, she slowed, stopped, put the car in park, and dropped her head over her arms crossed on the steering wheel.

She should have asked Henry for his cell number. Just in case. Even if he didn't like her, or trust her. He'd come to check on her because she got too hot. Or so he said. Maybe he was only trying to get information...

And it had worked.

"*Idiot.*" Gillian raised her head and banged her fist against the steering wheel. "He probably warned the guy by now. He probably came right out here after he left me and told him to..." To not answer? To not be home? To sic dogs on her? Or wolves, maybe, out here. He'd have protection. She was an idiot to have said so much to a stranger.

And she could have just blown her chance to have the control she wanted with her stories.

If so, she'd quit. Walk away. Go ... back to ... to what? Grocery store clerk? Scanning stuff and putting it in bags while surly people who hated to spend money on the convenience food they loved to eat barked at her because someone had a ton of coupons or...

She'd promised herself she wouldn't go back. Only forward. No matter what.

"Just keep going. You've gone this far. Just go." With a huge breath that hurt her lungs, Gillian put the car back in drive and determined to find out whatever she could. As Henry said, she could make up the rest if the guy wouldn't cooperate. What did it matter?

Hank sat back on his haunches and studied his work. So far so good, he supposed. Swatting at a mosquito, he grimaced at the pain in his shoulder from the sudden movement after two hours or so of nearly immobile intense tension to keep his hand steady. Time for a break to get his circulation moving.

Obviously he'd sweated enough to lose much of the anti-pest effect of the tea tree/lemon balm oil he relied on to deter bites. It was hellraciously hot. His canteen was too low already. He wanted to get more work done, though, before heading all the way back to the cabin. It had to be a good two miles away. On a good day, he'd walk it in thirty minutes or so. This morning it had been nearly double that. On the way back, it could be more than double. He was still tired. And now his joints were stiff.

He stifled a moan as he stood and stretched his arms as high as possible, then leaned down to stretch his spine. In his younger days he could put his palms on the floor with his legs straight. These days he was happy when his fingertips brushed the ground. Today, his shins were as far as his fingers went, but then, he wasn't a youngster anymore.

"Quit thinking like an old man, Dennison. Does you no good whatsoever." And forty-nine was not old. Not these days it wasn't. On days, it sure as hell felt like it.

With a deep cleansing breath, Hank left his tools and paced back a ways to find the little stream he'd crossed.

He'd walked too far by the time he realized he'd gone the wrong direction and had to turn back. If he'd taken his tools with him, he would have just trekked back to the cabin and called it a day. Maybe he would call it an early day. Let himself recuperate. Get back at it earlier the next morning.

Why not? He set his own hours now. He could do as he pleased.

And yet he'd found he was a worse slave driver to himself now than he'd been when he was technically working. Even then, he was harder on himself than on anyone else. Despite what was said about him.

"Let it go, Dennison. Just let it go."

There it was. The stream. But by now his adrenaline was fueled by his constantly returning anger that he kept trying to push aside, to release into the dead wood.

As Hank filled the large canteen he carried when he worked, he thought about the reporter woman's words and the look on her face at the thought of drinking "unfiltered" pure water instead of that chemical-treated fluoridated excuse for city water she likely called "clean," and shook his head. He took a good swallow or two, capped it, and cupped his hands to pull water over his head and let it rush down into his shirt, front and back.

Along with the adrenaline, the cool water was enough to encourage him to get back to work.

Gillian let out a frustrated yell at no one but her steering wheel. Where was the road that was marked on the map? The one she had to take to get where she wanted to go? It had to be there. It was in print. She couldn't have passed it all three times she'd been back and forth, not with as slow as she was driving, at least the first two times. By now her speed had increased. Her patience was nearly gone.

She was hot. Frustrated. The AC was running but only on very low so stepping out of the car to trek wherever she had to go on foot wouldn't be too much of a shock. As it was, the back of her shirt was sweat-plastered against her where it touched the fabric seat. Good thing she hadn't splurged on a car with leather interior. To drive it out here? Not likely.

Why couldn't he have become a hermit somewhere exotic? On a houseboat on the coast somewhere or on a deserted island? Did it have to be so damn difficult?

"Okay Gillian, just calm down and *find* the effing road already." Slowing again, she retraced her treads and nearly gave another frustrated yell when she found the stupid road barely beyond where she'd started looking for it. The map was drawn badly. It shouldn't have been that close.

She wanted a pizza. She wanted to just go back to Durango, shower, put something more comfortable on, and order the biggest pizza she could find. Sausage. Pepperoni. Ham. Maybe a couple of veggies, as well. And double cheese.

That would be quite a long run on the treadmill.

It would be worth it.

The road was far more narrow than the one she'd just left and she hoped like heck she wouldn't pass anyone coming the other direction.

They'd have to go around. She wasn't about to take the rental into the brush just because Mr. CEO Hermit wanted to frustrate the hell out of her by living way out here. Just because. Of whatever. And who cared, anyway? Henry was right. It didn't matter. He was probably a loony bird. Probably looked like Grizzly Adams by now and acted just as gruff. Who would care?

Karenne did.

Or she didn't, actually. It was for her own good? Was it really? Talk about a loony bird. Karenne had to be top of the flock for thinking *this* would be good for her in any way, shape, or form.

Okay, Gillian. Just take it easy. It's an actual road, whether or not it resembles one.

She glimpsed what looked like a cabin ahead and to the right. Was that it? Couldn't be. Too small. But maybe the owner would have directions and be willing to help. Maybe he'd be as gruff as Grizzly Adams, or as Henry, and tell her to turn back.

It was a free country, still. More or less. She had journalistic rights. And she was getting this damned story if it killed her.

Which it could, she supposed. But by now she'd put far too much energy and aggravation in it to quit.

And now she was getting curious as to why he chose *here*. Was he from here originally? Had he grown up the way she had and decided to come back to it of his own free will? If so, he was indeed a loony bird. She'd have to be tied and dragged back here to live, or anywhere similar.

<h1 style="text-align:center">Eight</h1>

Hank chiseled the final stroke into the dead stump and sat back to study it. Not bad for a morning's work. And he was starving by now. His watch told him it was way past lunch. He'd pay for that.

At least he could help it somewhat by munching on the trail mix he always carried while he started back to his cabin. He'd have a good lunch and then a good soak in his stream. Maybe the other way around so he didn't drop sweat beads into his food. With enough trail mix, he could take time to bathe first.

He'd let himself take the rest of the day off, maybe read a book, write his buddy. When he came to the stream, he crossed barefoot, his jeans rolled up, set his tools safely on the side of the bank nearer the cabin, and stripped down to the skin. He'd walk back naked since he hadn't brought dry clothes out this time and wouldn't put the sweat- and dirt-caked outfit back on his clean refreshed body. One thing he loved about being out here: only the bugs to worry about if he decided to walk around natural.

He shivered when his thighs touched the cold water, as he treaded into the deepest spot of one of the mountain streams that fed into the Animus river below, the river locals and some tourists used to fish or jet ski or raft. The river was public. This stream, unnamed as far as he knew, was his alone. It was on his purchased property. Not that anyone would know as much since he had no property lines drawn or marked in any way other than his cabin, but it was his all the same. Legal and binding at the courthouse.

He could sit naked in it as often and for as long as he wanted. And today might just be a good long soak between his fatigue and the heat.

While he soaked, lying on his back gazing up at the way the sunlight filtered airy streams of dust and pollen through the tall pines and assorted deciduous trees, he couldn't help but wonder how Ms. Hart was doing with her story. Was she out looking for people to interview? For leads? Had she given up? He figured it was pretty unlikely she'd given up already. She had a bit of a shark nature in her; it was what pulled him to wonder about her more than he knew he should. But there was more. A hell of a lot of defensiveness topped the list of what he could see. Curiosity, which was no surprise, given her profession. A good bit of cockiness. But more. Something deeper she tried to hide, maybe even from herself.

She read people well, so she said. Hank thought she might think a bit too highly of her ability to do so. Her story subject sat in front of her, had dinner with her, taunted a bit, even, and she still believed he was only Henry, an acquaintance. So she was naive, as well. And yet, she wasn't.

An odd mix. Made him want to get deeper, to find out what she was all about behind the defensiveness.

Or, she could just go on back to Denver and leave him be. That would be okay, too.

Gillian parked a little ways from the cabin, wary of its occupant and aware she'd have to hightail it back to the car fast if he was more than only gruff. But she had doubts anyone out here would shoot her just for walking into the yard and knocking on the door.

The place wasn't quite as small as it looked from a distance. There was a decent back porch from what she could tell without walking around, which she didn't dare do, at least without checking for occupants first. Couldn't be the right place, though. The Dennison ranch or whatever it was called would be far bigger than just this cottage. Was that little side building an outhouse? There was no plumbing out here? She figured that could be true.

Looking up around the trees, she spied no electric lines and shook her head. Why, in this day and age, would anyone choose to not have electricity? Gillian would live in a one room shack with electricity long before she'd live in even a mansion-sized cottage without it.

She made her way to the door and knocked, lightly at first, then louder when there was no reply. Someone lived there. It was obvious between the open windows and tire tracks that led around the back. She knocked harder. No stirring. No sound other than the raucous crows swirling above the trees that gave her a creepy feeling.

She didn't like birds. Well, canaries in cages were fine. They were pretty. Small. Non-threatening. She could deal with canaries. Those were no canaries. They were crows. Gillian had read that crows were smart. Not a comforting thought, as far as she was concerned.

She shivered. In the heat.

No one home. Lovely. She'd have to continue up the small-ass road and see what else she came across. For all she knew, it was just over the hill.

Cursing inwardly, Gillian made her way back to her car, clenched her jaw when the tires skidded on gravel, and eased out onto the road, such as it was.

After what must have been five more miles, she shook her head and turned around to go wait for someone to return to the little cottage and ask if she was in the right place. With any luck, they'd at least be as friendly as Henry and wish her well, at least in health. Everyone she'd met in the area, other than that cabbie, had been very friendly. Polite. Well-mannered. She figured it would extend decently up into the mountains.

This time she pulled in front of the cottage and walked boldly to the front door. Only a fool thought just because something was safe the first time, it would continue to be so, but she expected it was safe, anyway.

Again there was no answer, and she hadn't expected there would be. Gillian wasn't about to sit in the car that by now would be hot again already, so she wandered the front yard, noticed the large stack of wood, considered walking around to the back but thought better of it. No use offending the owner by nosing about. It would be hard to ask for assistance that way.

Instead, she wandered away from the place, just a bit into the tree line, and hesitated at a rustling until she found a couple of squirrels chasing each other. Mating, she supposed. At least something didn't let the heat bother them, other than the crows, which now circled to the side of her, to what she thought was northeast. Who needed a compass when you had instinct? Gillian should have told Henry that when he asked if she had a compass...

The thought of crows circling stopped her in her tracks. Crows circled dying things while waiting for food. Was the owner out there? Injured? Surely anyone living out here would be well prepared and capable of taking care of himself.

Still, maybe she could return the favor of Henry's rescue by helping someone else. Not sure what on earth she would do if it was a man who would likely be heavier than she could handle, Gillian realized she could be on a fool's errand, another one, but she could at least could run back to the car and drive to town for help and hope he'd last until it arrived.

Either way, she had to check, so she headed the direction of the crows, fighting her own fear of them, and hurried her steps in between watching for crawling slimy or hairy things around her feet.

It was a rough patch of land. A couple of times one of her Keds got stuck and pulled off her heel and she had to stop long enough to get it back on. Several times she jumped at a noise in the brush, her hand on her pistol in case she had to keep the critter from getting too close. A couple of times she lost her balance and scuffed herself. As long as she didn't break something, she could deal with scuffs. She was never low on scuffs and scratches as a child. If needed, makeup would cover them well enough when she returned to Denver. But she did have to be able to drive back to...

Water. She heard what sounded like trickling water. Slowing her steps and hanging onto saplings as she made her way down the small but somewhat steep ravine, she saw the water. A little stream. Not terribly little. But beautiful, nestled beneath the trees where it was shaded. A soft wind rustled the leaves above it and harmonized with the trickling sound. Pine scent filled the air. Not a smell she enjoyed.

Gillian decided to treat herself for the punishment of the last couple of days by soaking her hot feet in the stream and resting a bit before continuing. Her break. Everyone got breaks at work. She might as well allow herself the same.

When she hit the sandy bank, she pulled off her Keds and held them in one hand while she treaded toward the water. It was deep there. Rugged. She'd try a little farther upstream where it looked smoother.

The cool sand and rounded stones beneath her feet made her almost think she could live next to this. Almost. But the damn mosquitoes and flies said she wouldn't. And the crows. She'd forgotten the crows and the possible rescue.

They were easy enough to find again. Upstream farther. She headed that way, looking up at them and down at her footing, unwilling to put her shoes back on until she had to, and came face to ... naked body the crows were circling. Male. Very obviously male. His face was turned, his head atop his crossed arms, at an angle that showed mainly his jaw. She couldn't tell if his eyes were closed, or open and non-blinking, but the body wasn't pale or distorted. It was healthy flesh, very well in shape flesh and toned muscle. He didn't seem at all in trouble, unless the crows decided to take the plunge or a fish decided he was bait with the way he bobbed...

Gillian looked away. He was fine. No help needed. Just napping on a large flat water-logged rock. Or was he only napping?

Hell. If he was naked and needed help, she would scream in frustration for sure. This was not her forte, and not her responsibility. She could quietly slip back and pretend she'd seen nothing.

That's what she would do. If he was naked and didn't need help, Gillian did not want to get too close. If it came down to his well-being or her own, she would in no way choose his.

Stealth-like, using every bit of her trained balance from yoga classes, Gillian moved part backward and part sideways, watching her step, alternately watching the man to be sure he didn't notice her, and she had to admit, at times, leering at his solid lean tanned form with the thick patch of dark blond hair streaking down from between his pecs, straight down in a heavy line to his stomach where it scattered and thinned. The sun cast highlights where it managed to filter through the heavy trees and made the hair glow.

Almost angelic.

Stupid thought, Gillian. Knock it off and get away from him, already. He could be... She wouldn't let the words form in her mind. Other than *dangerous.* He could be dangerous, as she'd told Karenne. But why would a man like that be out here on his own? Hiding?

Or maybe he wasn't on his own. Her heart raced at the thought. Maybe there was a wife or girlfriend nearby watching Gillian leer at her man. All she needed on top of the past two days of hell, including sharp words from Henry, that obnoxious ... well, not obnoxious.

Honest. Straight-forward. But too straight-forward and not enough. He was smart. Too smart. She couldn't quite tell his angle and she wasn't used to that. It bugged her. It intrigued her. Mostly, it...

Her ankle wrenched and she felt herself falling...

No. Hell. Her palm hit something sharp and hard. She was in the water. She'd actually fallen *into* the damn *water*. This wasn't happening. Had she yelped? She didn't yelp. She didn't scream *like a girl*, as they called it. She didn't... She didn't...

Gillian could only sit there in complete shock as the realization of the cold wetness spread over her up to her waist. Her ankle burned. And her palm. A streak of red ran down her wrist and she stared...

"You all right?"

At the male voice, she pulled her gaze from the blood to the ... outrageously in-shape man in all his glory. Her face grew hotter than the sun burning down on her back, her wet back...

"Didn't get enough adventure in the woods yesterday? Had to try again?"

She finally saw his face when he crouched in front of her. Henry.

Gillian laughed. She laughed until her guts hurt and her head pounded as much as her ankle throbbed. It wasn't funny. She saw not one thing funny about the situation. The coincidence of looking for Hank Dennison and again finding Henry whatever his name was and...

Suddenly it dawned on her. "You're Dennison's ... lookout of some kind, aren't you? Let me guess. He lives down the road and you screen people out with your ... your ... mountain knowledge and ... and..."

"Let me help you up."

"No. I can get myself up and you're ... you're..." She let her eyes skim him again as he crouched the way a man always crouched, his legs wide open.

"Naked. I was bathing. I do that. Not usually with an audience."

"I wasn't... I wasn't looking at you... I mean, looking for you. I was looking at ... for..."

Henry chuckled. "Yeah, I get what you were looking at. Or rather, who you were looking for. Sorry to disappoint you."

"No. You didn't." Damn. Her face got hotter than hell. Or hotter than the Colorado mountainside in the three hottest damn days of the year which of course were the days Karenne sent her on a wild goose chase just to find ... a wild goose.

"Would you rather sit there until I go put my pants on or do you want help now?"

"I don't need help."

"That's debatable, I'd say." He stood. "Just put your hand out. You can keep your eyes turned away if you'd rather."

"Wouldn't you rather I did?"

"Doesn't matter to me. Except I don't want you to lose your footing again, so maybe just keep your eyes on your feet."

Her feet. Gillian picked her soaked Keds out of the water and set them on a rock to rub her ankle. "You live out here to be a nudist?"

"I'm only nude while bathing. Aren't you?"

"I'm not... Oh. And sometimes when I sleep, but..." The heat in her face spread to her ears as she realized she'd said far more than she intended.

"Relax, lady." He crouched again, this time turned from her. "We're not fifteen. It's no big deal. Come on. Let me help you. How bad is the ankle? Can you walk on it?"

"I guess I will. I'm not crawling out of here."

"Not with that puncture in your hand, anyway. We have to get that cleaned out. Let me see it." He grasped it without her permission and pulled it into the water.

"Don't. The water's dirty..."

"Not here, it's not. Let it soak a minute. The cold should help numb it, too. Are you doing okay? No shock, right?"

"What?"

With his other hand, he tugged her eyelids up one at a time. "Looks okay. Where's your car?"

Her car. "Um." She looked back toward where she came. "Over there. Somewhere. I ... followed the crows. They were circling. I thought someone was hurt and..."

"More likely an animal, and you'd best stay away from a hurt animal unless you're trained for that and have protection."

"I have a gun." Damn. She didn't tell people that.

"Tucked into that outfit somewhere? Why? Do you plan to shoot the horrible Hank Dennison when you find him?"

"Shoot him? Of course not. I'm not... I want a story, not... I'm not..."

"Where's your gun?"

She met his eyes; hers widened. Her heart pounded again.

"Oh, calm down. I am not going to hurt you. If it's in your bag, it's drenched with the rest of your things by now." He nodded at her handbag. Her leather handbag. Now on a rock just out of the water, dripping.

She reached for it and cursed when her ankle twisted. "Just use it on me now, why don't you? This damn mountain is going to kill me, anyway." She dropped her head on the knee of the good leg that was somehow propped up in front of her and closed her eyes.

"This?" His voice showed amusement and she looked up again. He held her pistol in his hand, pointed away.

She grabbed it.

"What on earth good do you think that's going to do you in the mountains? Afraid of the crows? Might work on them if you can get it to shoot accurately enough, which I doubt."

"I'm a good shot."

"Good for you, but... All right. Let's get you out of the water. Take my hand..."

"No."

"My hand is typically naked. Nothing to fear from it. And if you keep your neck turned that hard very long, you'll have one more aching spot."

"Would you just go put your clothes on, please?"

"I'd rather not."

She met his eyes, careful to meet only his eyes.

"Took them off because they're soaked in dirt and sweat. And like I said, I was bathing. Don't want to have to come back and start again."

"So ... you're just going to walk around like that?"

"Long enough to get home to fresh clothes. I didn't plan on

anyone being out here."

"Go on ahead, then."

"And leave you?"

"Yes. My car…" She forced herself up, realizing he put a hand on her elbow to steady her, and cringed when she put weight on her foot. "Holy hell."

"Sure you want me to leave you like this?"

She tried again. Her eyes clenched with the pain but it held her weight. "Yes. I can manage."

"Don't be ridiculous. Just come out onto the shore where it's dry. I'll run back to my cabin and return. Dressed. With something for that foot. Going to be okay for a bit by yourself?" He was helping her get to shore.

She didn't have much choice but to let him. "My car is that way." She pointed the direction she thought she'd left the car, at the little cottage. His cottage?

"Okay, but you drive with that foot, right?"

Her right foot. "Hell." She stared at her foot. At the water now beside her. At her clothes, muddy and soaked. At the trees. The crows. Anywhere but at him. "I can't just leave it."

"I'll take care of it."

She shivered. It was hot. Too hot. Her face still felt like it was about to burn up. But she shivered. "I just want to go home. I'll work retail again. I don't care anymore." Shoving her hands against her face, she cringed again, this time at her palm, and she looked at it.

"Sure you do. You only need to get out of this sun and into something dry. Water and food. You'll be okay, then."

His soothing voice annoyed her. "Don't be nice to me."

"Why shouldn't I be?"

She tugged her soaked shirt down and shook it to try to get it to hang loose rather than stick to her. "You wouldn't believe the nasty thoughts I've had since dinner last night."

He laughed. "I'm very well used to that, usually expressed. Don't worry about it. Come on, Gillian. Just put your weight on my arm and keep as much as you can off that ankle. My place isn't far. Or sit over there in the shade and I'll come back. Your choice."

Crows still circled overhead. She could see them diving around the trees and her body shrank from them involuntarily.

"You're actually afraid of those birds?"

"Don't make fun. I'm not in the mood."

"But you have your ... uh, gun, such as it is."

"And I'm not regretting even one of those nasty thoughts by now."

The smile accompanying his chuckle was ... too cute. Really. Still, she was pissed. Too pissed to care how effing naked he was or wasn't. "Just let go. I'll get back to my car. I don't need your help or your laughter at my expense."

"Fine." He released her, walked over to where a pile of dirty clothes lay in a huddle, swooped them up, and headed away, into the trees. His taut backside was nearly as tanned as the rest of him. So he did this more often than he wanted her to think, did he? Why should she believe a word he said?

With anger fueling her, she ignored the sharp pain in her ankle as she forced her sopping shoes back on her feet and headed toward her car, in a slightly different direction than he took.

By the time she got well into the trees, she was nearly biting her bottom lip off to fight the pain, and stopped, breathing hard and ragged. Maybe she'd just sit down and let the crows have her. Who in the hell would care? Karenne could get her own damned story if she wanted to come out here and hunt for it. But she wouldn't. She'd never in her life done anything harder than ... than give birth, apparently, since she talked about it so often like it was a curse or something. Except she did it, willingly, two more times after the first "horrific" experience, so Gillian figured it wasn't all that horrific. She'd like to see her boss out here now.

She had to grab a sturdy branch to catch herself with the next step. Her ankle gave out. "Oh, come on. Just get me to my car." She looked at her foot as though it had a mind of its own. "I'll sit in that hotel and do nothing and make the damned paper pay for it. Just get me to the car. I'll figure out how to drive with my left foot. It's gotta be doable."

"Talk to yourself often?"

She started at the voice behind her and nearly fell over while trying to balance on her one good foot.

"Sorry." He had pants on. Dirty, nasty jeans. But at least his lower half was covered. "Can I help you now?"

She wanted to plop down onto the rocky dirt and sob. But she wouldn't. She stared at him. At the thick line of hair separating his chest...

He came over and picked her up.

"No." She pushed at his shoulders...

"Don't worry, princess. You won't owe me anything."

"Don't call me that. And I'll walk. Put me down."

Damned stubborn woman. Hank was far too tired to carry an average sized woman, even one as fit as she was, all the way to his cabin, particularly in his dirty jeans that tugged at him.

But the ankle was swollen. Above her pretend sneakers that were more stylish than practical, there were no socks to cover the roundness pushing up over the sneakers. What he was going to do with her, he didn't know, but she needed to stay off the thing and let it rest.

Was he Dennison's guard? Hank nearly laughed at that one. At least she hadn't pursued the question. She could think he was. It was close enough to the truth, it wouldn't be a lie to let her think so if she wished.

Two-thirds of the way back, he found a place to sit, set her on it, and stretched his arms and shoulders.

"I told you I could walk." She eyed him as he took a swallow from the canteen and then offered it. "No. I'm..."

"Don't argue, lady. I'm close to out of patience."

"I never asked for your help."

"What was I going to do? Let you hobble back to your car with one good foot and one good hand?"

"Yes."

He shook his head. "Probably should have. Might have taught you a bit of humility that wouldn't hurt anything."

"Humility? Don't act like you know me. And don't think I don't have…" She stood and started walking, limping, in the direction they'd just come.

"Just stop with the false pride, would you? I'm tired today. Normally carrying someone your size would be no problem. Today it is. But I'm still better fit for it than you are, even with…" He bit his tongue and stepped in front of her. "Take a drink of this."

She glared, but she held still.

Hank shrugged. "Fine. Then don't. Like I said, I'm out of patience." He capped it, released it to fall to his side, and picked her up again, against her struggle. "Just stop. Trust me, I'll get you out of my hair as soon as physically possible. Got a friend not far away…"

"Do you?" She stopped flailing and eyed him.

"Would you put your arm around my neck and make this easier?" He stopped and gripped her tighter until she obeyed. "Think I don't have friends?"

"Yeah, I think you have a pretty high-powered friend. Close by, right? Gonna get his help for me?"

"That would make it far too easy for you to do what you shouldn't be doing."

"Why shouldn't I?"

"Because it's not your business, or anyone else's, either. Everyone has a right to privacy, no matter who they are."

"If people wanted privacy, they wouldn't make themselves so publicly visible just for a buck, would they? And don't bother to argue, because you'll never convince me otherwise."

Hank shook his head and stayed quiet the rest of the way, ignoring her attempt at questioning him. Soon, luckily, she got that he wasn't answering and fell silent.

By the time he reached the cabin, he was not only out of patience but also out of strength, and he had to go back for his tools. Damned woman should have stayed in Denver where she belonged. If he'd wanted that kind of annoyance in his life, he wouldn't have moved out here.

Nine

Henry's cottage. The one she'd been nosing around. Gillian supposed it wasn't much of a coincidence since there weren't many up here in the middle of the woods.

"Want to open the door?" His voice showed strain, or annoyance. Maybe both.

"Isn't it locked?"

"You're kidding, right? Why would I lock it when, A, as I said, there's no one around here generally, and B, the windows are wide open?"

"Okay, don't be snippy." She turned the knob and ducked her head in to make it harder for him to knock it against the door frame if he'd had intentions of doing so. Surprisingly, he was careful not to even rub her shoulder against the frame while carrying her inside. He set her down in front of a cushioned wood chair, helped her lower onto it, and stepped back, breathing hard.

"You should have put me down. It wore you out..."

"Don't bother." He walked away, to a kitchen area, where there was a small wall oven and what looked like a large hotplate along with a couple of heavy cast iron pans hanging from hooks. The place smelled of ... lemons and wood and outside. The outside, woodsy smell made sense since it was a log cabin with the logs showing inside, not even flattened cut logs, but still round. Almost nothing hung from the logs that served as walls. No calendar. No paintings or photos. Nothing but a couple of wood shelves with only a couple of knick-knacks on the shelves that also looked made of wood. Miniatures of animals and ... something human. She couldn't tell from where she sat. Definitely a man cave if she'd ever seen one. Even so, it was actually pretty cozy. Clean. Neat. There was a small stereo on a wood stand, and a large ceiling-to-floor bookcase. His sofa looked more utilitarian than comfortable, covered in what she expected was corduroy. Light green. With baby blue pillows, not terribly plush.

A fireplace donned the corner beside the door. At least the thing had real floors, not dirt, and they were clean as much as she could tell.

"Water from the well. Good enough for your taste?" He pushed a glass at her. It had a couple of ice cubes and she was grateful.

"Thank you."

"You're welcome. Now to figure out..."

"I mean ... for more than the water. I'm sorry I was such a pain, but I hate to have to have help. I try hard to avoid that and..."

"We all need help at times. Like I said, drop the fake pride. Never liked it before and I don't now, either. Your car's a rental, I'm guessing."

"Yes. If you could help me over to it, and I mean just a helping arm, don't pick me up again, I'd be grateful."

"How do you expect to drive it?"

"With my left foot." She gulped cold water and tried not to look at him more than was polite, but the contact of her skin, bare other than her lightweight blouse, against his bare chest and arms had distracted her a little too much. He did look awfully fit, which made her wonder why carrying her had been such a struggle. She wasn't all that big. Scrawny, really. Tall and thin, well, more gangly than thin...

"Ever try that?"

She met his eyes, trying to figure out what he meant. Pointless. Too distracted with him still half nude. She'd have to ask. "Try what?"

"Driving with your left foot. Do you feel okay?"

"Oh. Yes. And no. I mean, yes, I feel okay, and no, I haven't tried it, but I'm sure it's possible. I can get myself there if needed, also."

He stared a moment as he drank from his canteen. "I'll get you there. Before I can do that, though, I've got to go back to the stream. I won't be long. Here." He pushed another chair close to the one where she sat. "Elevate that foot." Helping her raise the leg, he gently pulled off her shoe.

She winced at the pain. "No, leave it. I'm not staying long enough..."

"It'll feel better if it's not pushing against the swelling." He set the wet, dirty Ked on the floor and examined her ankle. "Can't tell if it's broken, but there's nothing protruding. Good sign. Sit still until I get back." Again he went to the kitchen, poured something in a bowl, brought it to her, and reclaimed her glass to refill. "Pistachios okay?"

"My favorite."

His head tilted as though wondering if she was telling the truth. "Wouldn't have guessed that."

"And what would you have guessed?"

"Chocolate covered cherries or something similar."

"Oh." Her mouth watered. "Now I want those. But strawberries, not cherries. I don't suppose you have any."

"Sure. Under the cabinet next to the invisible espresso machine." His tone was even but his eyes sparkled a touch. "I'll be back..."

"Wait. You said you were tired. Rest a minute."

"Afraid of being alone here? If you are, I have a shotgun I'll leave with you. Wouldn't use it unless you have to since it has a heck of a kick, and I'd want you to make sure it's not just me coming back..."

"I don't know how to use a shotgun."

He walked over to the bookshelf, grabbed a key from inside a book, opened a tall, thin cabinet beside the shelf she never would have thought about being anything except the shelf's end piece, and grabbed a gun from within. Checking for a cartridge, he pointed it toward the door, showing her where her hand should be, with a warning to keep her finger off the trigger unless she actually intended to shoot. "If a person should barge in on you, which is extremely unlikely, point it and act like you know how to use it. Bears don't open doors, and I'll shut it tight so a snake won't come in for the cooler air."

"Snake?" Her eyes widened and her heart thumped.

"They don't come in often. If one does, toss some pistachio shells between you and it and scare it off. Don't shoot a hole in my floor or wall due to a snake. Unless it's a rattler, then you have my permission, but try to aim well. With this, you only have to aim somewhat close." Henry propped it against the chair her foot was using and headed to the door.

"Are you going to be okay out there alone?"

He looked back, his eyebrows raised. "Are you serious?"

"But, doesn't someone live here with you? If they come home and..."

"I live alone. Purposely. My friend down the way does stop by at times, but she won't be up here today. If she does knock for some reason, don't shoot her."

"She?"

He tossed a grin her direction, went to a room she couldn't see from where she sat, came out with a pair of jeans and a towel, again said he'd be right back, and walked out the door.

Gillian nearly panicked at the thought of being alone in that cottage with no one around but ... but ... bears? Was he serious? She couldn't tell. She supposed there would be...

She jumped when the door opened.

"Just me. Not a snake. Forgot about your hand." Henry treaded over to the kitchen, opened the full-door cupboard, and pulled out a bottle of peroxide. After pouring a splash of it into a metal bowl, he added water and brought it to her along with a hand towel. "Soak that a while. Might burn a bit, but that's better than infection. Back soon."

"Wait."

"Lady, it's going to get too late to do what I need to do before we can get you and your car into town. I have things to do."

"You don't..." She didn't want to argue anymore. "Forget it. Fine." Clenching her jaw against the burn, she stuck her palm into the disinfectant. Another shiver ran all the way from her hand to her spine to her toes.

"You okay?" He waited with the door open.

"Fine. Just... You are coming back?"

"I live here."

"Yes, but..." The sun behind his body made him look like a silhouette instead of a real person. Maybe this was all a nightmare.

"What are you so afraid of?"

"Nothing."

"Don't lie to me."

She focused on the bowl, on the billions of tiny bubbles fizzing up from her palm to burst at the top of the water. But she couldn't deal with the thought of why it bubbled, so she looked around his place instead and tried to ignore that he'd come back over and stood close to her, still with no shirt.

He set the back of his hand against her forehead and then her cheek. "Are you okay?"

"My ankle is killing me. My palm burns. My brand new Keds and leather handbag are ruined, not to mention I'm sitting here out in the middle of nowhere with bears and snakes and crows circling, soaked up to my ribs. Yeah, I'm good. Go frolic in the woods or whatever you need to do. I'm perfectly fine and dandy."

With a shake of the head, he went to the room she couldn't see that she surmised by now was his bedroom, and came back with a bundle of blue, two different colors of blue that didn't particularly match. "They're too big for you, but they're dry if you want to change while I'm gone. Do it right here so you don't have to walk on that foot. I'll knock before I come in, but you'll have plenty of time."

He stood far too close with his bare hard sun-tanned chest as he checked her head again and pressed his fingers against her neck, feeling for her pulse. He reeked of some awful scent she didn't recognize. Apparently satisfied with whatever her pulse was, even if she knew it was beating far too fast, he lowered his hand. "Sure you're all right?"

"I'm great. What is that smell?"

"Tea tree oil and lemon balm. Bugs don't like it."

"Neither do I."

A flicker of a grin graced his face. "I'm more afraid of them biting." Reclaiming the jeans and towel, Henry returned to the door, his strong back apparently used to hard physical work just as tanned and muscular as his front.

"Maybe you shouldn't be." She spoke under her breath, but he turned around.

"You should know your voice carries well. And you know what they say about biting the hand that feeds you, right? No biting, Gillian."

Through the renewed heat in her face, she met his eyes. Deep, deep blue eyes. "Don't worry. Glad you remembered my name, though. I'd rather you didn't call me *Lady*, like I'm some kind of nuisance..."

"Aren't you? And think about that before you answer."

She couldn't answer. She had been a nuisance. It was the last thing she wanted. When he stood there staring she told him to go on with whatever he needed to do and she'd rest her foot a bit and head to her car on her own so he could go on with his business.

With a deep sigh, he returned and crouched beside her. She thought immediately of the last time he did, naked, unashamed … and she flushed hot enough she had to wonder if she could get sunburn that way.

"Sure you're not in the wrong line of work?"

She stiffened, her chin raising on its own accord. "I'm good at my job."

"Yes. Probably are. Doesn't mean it's right for you. You don't seem terribly happy with what you're doing."

"Happy? My hand hurts. My ankle hurts. My ass hurts, in case you need to know, from falling on that rock. I lost my cell phone somewhere along the way, probably in that stupid stream with fish nibbling on it, and it'll cost and arm and leg to replace even though it was a cheapy thing in the first place. And I hate the freaking jungle with its crawly, slimy, hairy things everywhere. That doesn't mean I don't like my job or shouldn't be doing it. It only means I shouldn't be out here in this hell-hole."

"Okay." He stood and walked out.

When the door closed, she shoved her hands to her eyes then cursed herself for the sting in her eye. Peroxide. Stupid. Stupid. *Stupid.* She just wanted to go home and crawl into her bed and stay right there until she could convince herself it was fairly safe to come out and … and that she wasn't quite as fully stupid as she felt sitting there in a strange man's cottage, wet and muddy and hurt and … and scared to death that he'd left her there alone.

"Get a hold of yourself, Gilly. You're a big girl now, unlike the last time you had to be out here in the wild. You can do this. Just change clothes. That'll make everything worlds better. Just get dry. One step at a time. Just one step…"

She couldn't do it in the living area, though, even with the door closed and light-filtering curtains floating over the open windows. She couldn't. So she hobbled, half hopping and half cringing with a few well-placed curse words, to the room he'd gone into, and paused in the doorway. A modern bedroom for such a simple cottage, and far bigger than she expected. With a shower beyond a small open door. He had a shower. Why on earth did he bathe in the dirty outdoor water when he had a shower?

Deciding to help herself, Gillian hobbled over, dropped the clothes he handed her onto the dark and light blue striped comforter over his perfectly made bed, and made her way into the bathroom. Only a trickle came from the shower head, even when she turned it all the way on. Barely more than a trickle. And cold. Maybe it would warm up and strengthen as she stripped out of her wet things.

It didn't, though. After a few more valid words she didn't let herself use in public, some banging on the faucet and shower head, and sweating more with the effort, Gillian nearly screamed in frustration. It took forever for the trickle to barely wash off the grime. If her foot didn't hurt so badly, she'd go get a couple of glasses of water from the kitchen sink and dump it over herself. How was there running water in the kitchen sink but not in the shower? Finagling back out of the shower, she took a couple of hops over to try the bathroom sink. Water came out normally. Cold water, but it would work.

There was a small glass beside his toothbrush holder. She could use that to grab water and dump over herself, but it would be a hell of a lot of hopping from sink to shower and she wasn't up to that.

She did at least wash her face by cupping her hands, and ran some behind her neck, leaned forward so most of the water went back into the sink rather than on the floor, and considered using the hand towel to soak and wash her underarms... The water fizzled down to nothing. And stopped.

"*Holy hell!* Who *chooses* to live like *this?*" Frustrated beyond anything she'd known in a very long time, Gillian grabbed the bath towel from the bar behind her, scrubbed herself dry, taking what she could of the remaining sweat with it, and hobbled over to the bed to put his clothes on. Hers lay in a wet heap on the bathroom floor, and she left them there.

She was hot. Hurt. Miserable. Too much to hobble anymore right now. So she sank down on his bed. Just for a minute. No more.

But the pillow case was luxurious. And the sweat pants were too thick, too big. She slipped them off and slipped under the sheet and thin comforter, not bothering the blanket folded at the foot of the bed. Gillian knew she shouldn't intrude so much, but after as much as she'd seen of him, she didn't figure it made much difference.

The sheets were as luxurious as the pillow case. They were absolutely heavenly, with as tired as she was. Just five minutes. Then she'd get up…

Hank dropped the two sturdy saplings he'd cut down and shaped, and stored his tools in the shed beside the cabin, one of the few things he kept locked.

As he promised, although she'd had far more than enough time to change clothes, he knocked on his own door and opened it … to silence, and an empty chair, the bowl still on the table with untouched pistachios.

Where'd she go? A sinking feeling in his gut said she'd gone off to look for her phone to call for a taxi. Damned stubborn woman. Now he'd have to go after her, again, and he was too damned tired for that.

He had to at least eat something first, since he wouldn't do her any good if he collapsed. Heading first to drop his dirty jeans in the bathroom and grab a shirt, he stopped at the doorway. She was in his bed, under the covers. Almost afraid to check, he approached slowly, calling her name.

She turned, sighed heavily, and kept her eyes closed, her hands gripping his sheet firmly in front of her chest. Only asleep.

She couldn't stay there. He didn't share his place. Ever. With anyone. He'd already stretched that to let her in, against his best judgment. She couldn't stay.

And he couldn't make himself wake her.

He'd take her back to the hotel when she woke and deal with the car later. In the meantime, he went to find food. Real food. He was glad he'd set meat out to thaw. Vegetables alone wouldn't cut it after all of that annoying, exhausting, and he had to admit slightly embarrassing, adventure.

Her laughter hadn't helped matters at all. Hank had thought about mentioning he'd just been in a cold stream, but he figured it would sound too much like the fifteen-year-old he said they weren't when he was trying to act adult, so he'd kept his mouth shut.

She was a good bit younger than he was, judging by the smooth unwrinkled skin and light brown hair cut short and stylish, with no gray to be seen. The girl was still in her prime, while Hank was ... well, past his prime and had little to offer anymore. Not that it mattered.

It didn't. He was only hungry, as he'd told her she was. A man couldn't be in his right mind when he was hungry. It didn't matter in the slightest that she had a figure well taken care of and an independent nature, which he actually appreciated more than he would let her know. No use making it worse.

Gillian woke with a start at a noise. In the cottage. She'd fallen asleep. Jerking herself up to sitting, she forgot about her ankle until it hit the floor and she cursed out loud. Then she silently cursed at the fact she'd revealed she was there to...

"Hey." Henry looked in. "You okay?"

She caught her breath and let it out in relief. "I fell asleep."

"I noticed." His glance fell to her bare legs. Only for a second. "Couple of rough days you've had. How's the ankle?"

She pulled the sheet over her thighs and raised her bad ankle over her good leg. "I think I can't walk on it. It's worse than before." And swollen. Super swollen. Her stomach lurched.

"I was afraid of that. Hold on a minute." He disappeared again and she quickly wrestled into the sweats he'd given her. Gillian wanted to tell him to come back and not let her be alone until she got a grip. Either that or pull her car up and let her get in it and get to the hotel and be alone and stay that way...

"These might help." He returned with crutches in his hand. Kind of. Not the kind she was used to seeing...

"Had to guess at your size. Hope they work."

She accepted his help to stand and slid the things under her arms.

"Careful of your hand, though. Can you use the top of the palm instead of the bottom? Ever use these?"

"No. Where'd they come from?"

"Trees. Just needed some shaping. Try them out. I tied leather around the bottom for traction, but it's not like rubber, so be careful."

"You made them? Or ... someone you know. Is that where you went?"

"Gillian, just try them out. I have a very late lunch ready. My guess is you're hungry..."

"Starving."

"Then come on."

She managed to hobble out to the main room, unsteadily, and with some pain in her hand, but it worked well enough and Henry stayed right beside her with a hand ready in case she needed it.

He helped her to a chair and held the roughly shaped sticks as she lowered to the table and inhaled the aroma from the pot on the stove. Rich, meaty, tomato...

"It's only stew, but it's thick and should fill you. Want cornbread with it?"

"Yes. Please. It smells..." She was going to say luscious but stopped herself.

"Luscious?" He set a bowl in front of her and grinned.

"Yeah. And go ahead and laugh. Guess I can't even bitch at you for laughing after everything you've done for me."

"Don't worry about it. Eat. Then we'll talk about the next move."

"Next..? Oh. Yes. Hey, does your shower always just trickle? You actually get clean that way?"

"Shower?"

"I helped myself. I was muddy."

"You turned the shower on?"

"I did, but it didn't work well and it didn't get warm. Don't tell me you don't have hot water."

Henry shoved a hand through his hair with a grimace.

"What did I do wrong now?"

He shook his head as he took a big bite of stew.

"Tell me. I won't give up until you do."

"Too tired for that. Just eat, all right?"

"Henry, really. What did I do?"

He studied her a moment, then sighed. "The shower runs on a special pump that heats the well water. The pump runs on the generator. I keep the pump off during most of the summer so it saves propane and I don't have to call them out here but once a year. Running it while it's off screws things up and I have to fix it manually."

"A bad screw up?" She felt sick.

"Not all that bad. Relax. Like I said, I'm just more tired than normal today and the last thing I wanted... Doesn't matter. Eat."

"I'm sorry."

"Apology accepted. Maybe when I drop you at your hotel, I could use your shower and unwind nice and long in return."

"Of course." She tensed as she said it, and he met her eyes, questioning whether she meant it, or maybe how she meant it. "Only fair. Really. It's fine."

"I wasn't serious."

"No? You sounded serious, and it would be fair."

"Thank you, but no." He stabbed a piece of the cornbread and shoved it in his mouth.

"Why not? It's not like, well, like I'd have to worry by that point, since..."

He swallowed and looked at her like she was a complete moron. "All I need is for someone to see me go into your room with you. I'm local even if you aren't. I don't want or need that kind of..."

"Publicity." She fished a bit. Someone who worked for the CEO hermit wouldn't want publicity, she supposed.

"Invasion of privacy. I'm a big believer in privacy."

"So am I, but..."

"Are you? Just your own or other peoples', too?"

"Fine." Gillian was absolutely not having that discussion again. Not with him. "It was only a friendly offer in return for what you've done. Nothing more. In case you were wondering."

"I wasn't." He caught her eyes for just a second, then continued wolfing down his food.

They were silent for some time and she scoped his place more in the silence. Gillian hated silence. She hated it with a passion. She always had something on, even the radio very low in the background. Or she talked to herself. Since he was right there, he'd have to deal with being her target instead. "Nice little cottage you have here."

His eyebrows raised. "Cabin."

"What's the difference?"

"I'm a male and it's not a little vacation hideaway and I don't have it covered with lace and doilies and cutesy things. It's a cabin."

"Well, excuse me all to heck. And yes, I do know you're male. That has been made perfectly clear with plenty of evidence."

Instead of shocking him and throwing him off guard as was her intention, he raised his glass of water in salute, with a light twinkle in his eyes. She felt her face get hot and ducked it behind her own glass of ice water.

Silence filled the *cabin* again and it drove her nearly crazy. "Doesn't the quiet out here drive you crazy?"

"I like quiet. Want more stew?"

"No, thank you. It was wonderful, though. Should I ask what was in it?"

"I doubt that you should."

"Wait. If you don't have electricity, how did you cook?"

"The stove runs on wood or propane, whichever I choose. Special made. Most often in decent weather, I use the wood-or-charcoal grill out back on a screened porch. Keeps the heat out of here when I don't want the heat."

"Can I see it?"

"See what?" He eyed her as he swallowed water, from a glass this time rather than his canteen.

"The back porch. And whatever else you have way out here."

"No." He got up to grab the dishes. "Go have a more comfortable seat and we'll talk about our plans before it gets dark."

No? Why couldn't she see the back of the house? Was he kidding with all of this rustic stuff? Did he have more out there? Actual electric and a real shower and ... and she had to know. But if he had a real shower, why would he bathe in the stream?

This guy would make a far better story than some CEO. That could be it. Gillian considered the option as she hobbled over to the chair he'd placed her in before that now had a towel over it. Her wet, muddy clothes. She'd messed that cushion up for him, too, she imagined.

To distract herself from everything she'd done wrong the past couple of days, Gillian thought about her story. She could use the angle from Dennison's ... bodyguard or mountain guide expert or whatever he actually was. At least she'd met him, had talked to him, had seen his cottage ... cabin. Whatever. She could handle doing the story that way. Through a real person. An everyday person.

Of course she'd have to try very hard to forget just how much she'd seen, which wouldn't be so easy to do. Maybe she wouldn't try to forget. She only wouldn't let it carry into the story. Or she'd let it into the story as a hidden metaphor. Or she'd open the story with her running into him that way and...

No. That would be unfair. Very unprivate. She couldn't quite do that. Not after how helpful he'd been. Still, it would make a hell of a good start, a good eye-catcher so to speak, for an article. *That*, people would read.

She couldn't do it to him. But maybe she could use it as fiction somehow. If she ever went back to that.

Instead of just sitting in the quiet while he went somewhere she couldn't see – to wash the dishes in a bucket maybe? Horrid thought – Gillian hobbled over to the bookshelf to peruse what kind of things he read.

Nothing like she'd expected. *War and Peace. The Iliad and The Odyssey.* More recent fiction of historical nature. Some non-fiction contemporary history. She never would have guessed it. She expected to see *Call of the Wild* or *Moby Dick* or *Kidnapped* or other adventure-seeker books. Maybe even Zane Gray or John McDonald.

"Always nosing about, no doubt."

She jumped at his voice, at the accusation in it. "Just looking at your books. Is that not all right?"

"Do I have a choice?"

"Why do you have them here where anyone can see them if you don't want them seen?"

"Not just anyone comes into my home." He wandered over and sat on a small couch. "Go on and look if you wish. For a minute. Then we need to get you back to the hotel. My thought is I'll drive you back and arrange for someone to come pick the rental up in the morning."

"I can't leave it out here overnight."

"Why? Afraid a bear will get in and drive it away?"

"Don't be obnoxious. What if ... if it storms and the road washes away..."

"None expected and it hasn't yet."

"Or if ... well, I found my way out here. Someone else might and..."

"Not likely."

"But they could and it's sitting down there away from everything."

"Then I'll go bring it up here next to the cabin. Better?"

"No. Yes. But it still... I can't just leave it. My name's on it and..."

He leaned forward. "You always do that?"

"Do what?"

"Find as much as humanly possible that could go wrong even though none of it is very damned likely?"

Gillian frowned and pulled her shoulders back. Did she? Maybe she did. But it was better to be prepared. She had to be prepared. You couldn't just leave everything to fate. Maybe mountain man, here, could, but not a city girl like herself. She had to think of the what ifs. Besides, her job taught her to think of the what ifs. It made a better story than "just the facts, ma'am." Plausible what ifs made people think. And plan. And...

"All right. You win." Henry stood. "Let's go."

"And do what, exactly?"

"I'll drive you into town and we'll pick up someone to drive back out here with us and take your rental back to wherever you got it."

"You're going to just ask someone to do that? Someone you know, right? A good driver? I don't want to pay for..." Her head spun.

"Unwind just a touch, lady, or I'll never make it through the rest of the day."

"Well heaven forbid I should want the car back in one piece."

His head slightly tilted, he came to her. "You know, if I were you, I'd worry more about getting yourself back in one piece."

"I am in one piece, and..." The spinning magnified and she tilted on the makeshift crutches.

He caught hold of her arm. "Are you? I'd say the heat got to you more than you expected. Sit." He guided her to the couch and helped her down. "Do this often?"

"Never. I don't know... I'm fit and together and healthy and... I don't know what this is."

"A long couple of days. Low blood sugar. Heat you're not used to. Hold still and I'll get you more water. It's dehydration maybe, too."

"Or something alive in that water. You don't have bottled or ... or..."

"Nothing's wrong with the water. If something's off balance inside you, you brought it with you. You didn't get it out here."

"My hand. Infection?" She peered at it. It looked clean as far as she could tell, but she was woozy...

He took it in his own. "Your hand looks fine. And it wouldn't do this, not this fast, anyway. Hope to hell you didn't bring some virus out here to me."

"I'm not sick." Although at the moment, she wasn't terribly sure.

"I hope not. You've been a pain in my ass enough. Drink this."

It was useless to argue. And he was right. She had been a pain in his ass. In his cute, tight, bare ass she still saw although she tried not to. Though she didn't want to. Not with him or anyone. No. She wouldn't even think about it. And she wasn't staying any longer.

Gillian gave the glass back and stood, but the dizziness slammed in and she felt herself tilting.

Henry picked her up. Several steps later, she was lowered. Onto his bed. The silky soft sheets. They smelled like him. Like his naked shoulder her head was against earlier. Like ... like fresh stream water.

It was kind of nice, actually. She had to admit it.

He was kind of nice, too. Annoying. Frustrating. Far too immodest. But kind of nice. The story had to center around him. She would do it that way. She would be comfortable with that.

Ten

While she lay there in the quiet, far too much quiet, Gillian's mind swirled with thoughts that were as bad or worse than the dizziness. Why was she dizzy? She never did that, even with her worst bouts of depression. Did the man have her that riled? What if something happened to the rental? What if she did all of this and never got to Hank Dennison to do the story to make it worth it? Almost. She wasn't sure it would ever be worth all of this. Especially if she was sick. What if...

It started after lunch. Did he put something in it? He'd called her a pain in the ass ... well, he said she'd been a pain in his, and she couldn't argue, but ... was he trying to keep her away from his boss? Was it worth enough to him to put something in her food?

She had to get up. She wouldn't let him win. If she kept moving... But why would he make her crutches if... He... He had them already. Or someone did. There hadn't been time to make them. Had there?

Where on earth would she go if she left, with her car so far away and hobbling and ... and in his clothes. The pants were rolled twice and barely stayed around her waist if she was careful. Part of his plan? But he hadn't pushed her in the water. She'd done it...

She'd done it all herself.

Unless he was a master manipulator, and maybe he was. Who else would a super powerful CEO hire to watch his back? Not Johnny-off-the-street. That was for darn sure. Was he ... an ex Navy seal or something?

Too much news, Gillian. You watch too much news. Just stop now. He's been nothing but helpful even if he shouldn't be...

A trap?

With her heart racing, she pushed herself up. Where were her crutches? He'd left them in the other room. Part of the plan. Of course he had...

"*Stop* it, Gillian. Just *stop it.*" She shoved a hand through her hair, glad it was short enough not to be too much of a mess, and debated whether she was paranoid or smarter than he thought.

"You okay?"

She jumped at his voice. In the doorway. "Why?"

"Heard you talking."

"What did you put in that stew?"

"Why? You have a food allergy I should have known about?"

"No. No allergies, and I never get dizzy. What did you put in it? If it kills me, will it be worth it to keep me from writing a stupid story?"

His eyes rolled. "Lady, you are seriously disturbed. Again, maybe find another line of work."

"Do you tell everyone that when they come up to find Dennison? You make them think they're nuts and ... and..."

"Right. If you're nuts, you brought that with you, also." He took a step closer, eying her like she was a cougar about to spring at him. "I think I should take you back to town. Your clothes are nearly dry. I put them in the sun. Not clean exactly, but wearable. Want me to give them a few more minutes to finish drying or do you want them as they are?"

She stared. Her clothes. Almost dry? Why would he do that if ... if... She was nuts. "Okay."

"Okay, what?"

"Okay, I give. You win."

He frowned. "Are you on medication you've forgotten?"

"What? No. I... Hell. Okay, I'm sorry. It's been a horrible, maddening two days and I didn't want to be out here and I hate my editor right now for forcing me, pretty much, and myself for letting her, and this is the absolutely last place in the world I want to be. I'm usually very together. Bright. Witty. Charming. Really, I am. I'm not nuts. I'm ... exhausted and ... and I give. If it's that important to you that I don't do the story, I won't. I can't fight this much. It's not worth it. So if there's an antidote to this dizziness, because I hate being dizzy, too, just give it to me and I'll get out of your hair and quit being a pain in your ass. I may not quite get the image of it out of my head, but that's another story and that doesn't get shared..."

"The image of what, exactly?" He ambled closer.

Realizing what she'd just said, she felt her face get hot. "No.

Nothing. I mean... Nothing I saw ... um, nothing ...”

He crouched in front of her with a very much too amused expression on his face.

“Don't do that.”

“Do what?”

“Crouch. Get up.”

“Crouching bothers you?”

“No. Yes. Now it does.” She turned her head.

“I'll get up when you answer me. What image?”

“Uggghh!” She rolled away from him, half crawling to the other side of the bed, and stood. Cringing when her foot hit the floor, Gillian sat again, and looked back when he chuckled. “What in the hell is so damned funny?”

“You have seen a naked man before, am I right?”

“Well, of course. I'm not...”

“Is that the image you mean? Still thinking of me in the buff?”

“Just stop.” Gillian dropped her elbows to her knees and her face to her hands. Karenne was going to have hell to pay when she got home, *if* she ever got home.

“Relax, lady. I'm only teasing. Okay, so I'll admit it was somewhat embarrassing for me, as well. I cover with humor. I didn't mean to make it worse.” Hank sighed when her shoulders shook, and he walked around to the other side of the bed. “There was nothing in your food that wasn't in mine. The only way I would try to stop you from doing the story is by asking you not to do it, to consider the ethics of it, because I think you're far too ethical a person to give in to this only because someone told you to do it. I think that's what's making it so hard for you.”

“I have to ... to eat, you know. I'm down to... to instant noodles once a day by the end of the month when the paper's not buying because I can't... My apartment rent went up. Gas is crazy ridiculous and so is traffic. Food ... is nearly as bad as my rent and I'm only feeding me and...” She looked up, her eyes moist and desperate. “You keep protecting Mr. Dennison if you feel the need, and I understand it, I do, but maybe consider that others of us need things, too. And I can't feel sorry for some super rich guy who got *tired* of being rich when I'm ... when so many of us are...”

“Maybe it wasn't being rich he got tired of. Ever think of that? Maybe it was people like you who assume a hell of a lot you don't know or understand.” Hank paced away, not quite out of the room. “I'm getting your clothes and I'll take you back to your hotel. And yes, I'll get your car there, too.” He paused at the door and lowered his voice. “Maybe you ought to look harder at your own choices if you're this miserable instead of blaming someone who took steps to make his life better. Maybe it's *you* you're upset with and not some guy you don't even know.”

Damned woman. Hank had let it go. Mostly. The envy. The greed while calling others greedy. The misplaced hate and distrust. She didn't get it, and she thought she was capable of writing about it?

He stormed outside and shook out her clothes to soften them a bit after being stream washed and sun dried. He'd come out here to get away from everyone wanting something from him every fucking minute of the day and night, and what lands on his remote hand-built doorstep? Another one who couldn't manage her own affairs well enough and had to screw up his peace and quiet.

Well-earned peace and quiet. He deserved it. No one got him through his own mess. No one got him to the top. He got himself there. And then he got himself out...

Maybe she had family she could call. The idea of putting her in that hotel with a bad foot and whatever was causing the dizziness, not knowing if she'd be smart and go on back home or continue her attack article quest, didn't go over well with him. Although he shouldn't care. Hank knew he shouldn't give a damn one way or another. Giving a damn, though, was what eventually got to him, what made him have to get away.

He stared up at the blue sky past the forest green leaves swaying in the barest breeze that didn't make its way down to where he stood, and rubbed his chin. He could tell her who he was and then tell her to get out and not let himself worry about what she wrote. Or he could tell her to stop buying name brands and manicures and probably expensive haircuts if she was having such a hard time paying bills. He could tell her where he started and what he'd been through to get where he was.

Not that she'd buy it. Or even if she did and if she wrote that, it would get skewed during editing and he'd still come off as ... as greedy. Unsympathetic. Hard. Or like it was easy for him.

He hated that the most. People assuming he was lucky to have what he had or that it was far easier for him than it would be for them. He truly hated that assumption with every bit of passion he could still muster.

Although that wasn't much these days.

"Are you bringing my clothes in here or are you just going to stand there and hold them?"

Hank rolled his eyes and turned to where she stood, propped on the porch, on the crutches he'd made. "Come get them." He held them out.

"It would be a lot easier for you to take a few steps this way than for me to get down those steps."

"I made you the damned crutches. Want me to use them for you, too? You're going to have to get used to them, I'd say. Might as well start. Here. Want your clothes? Come get them."

"Fine." She stuck her chin out, finagled the saplings down the steps with only two near falls – better than he'd expected – and hobbled over to grab them.

"You're welcome."

She turned back only a second. "Thank you for drying them. As soon as I change, I'll be out of here. I'm using your room. For privacy."

He almost laughed at the privacy comment, but Hank preferred her snooty hostility to the feeling sorry for herself attitude. Anger was useful to a point. Self-pity was not.

When he made sure she got back up the three steps without falling on her cute little ass that looked far better in her jeans than in his sweats, Hank went down to get her car to pull it up to the cabin. Otherwise she'd more than likely try to get down to it herself, and he'd have to worry about whether she made it.

Gillian fumed while she pulled into her own things that felt like sandpaper. Didn't the man have a dryer? Couldn't he run a small one off his generator? Maybe he didn't mind having his clothes stiff, but she did. Of course, maybe he didn't wear them much and he only was now for her sake. She was half surprised the man didn't stay naked just to frustrate her since he seemed to delight in trying to frustrate her.

And help her. Both. Why would he do both? When she liked someone she did anything in the world for them she could, including trying hard not to annoy them. When she didn't like someone, she would annoy the heck out of them and not think twice about it. No back and forth. It was one or the other. She liked someone or she didn't, and how she acted reflected that.

Except she wasn't at all sure whether or not she liked Henry ... Henry who wouldn't even give her his real last name. Did he have it written somewhere? There was a desk out in the main room. Maybe it would be there. Or in a drawer? His medicine cabinet.

The bedroom door was closed. She could go look real quick. Did she dare? Of course she dared. She was a journalist. Snooping was part of her career. He knew her whole name. Why shouldn't she know his?

Her heart raced when she snuck in and quietly opened the one little cabinet opposite the sink. Toothpaste. Toothbrush. Comb. No prescriptions. Deodorant, which almost surprised her. It looked like homemade deodorant, which was even more surprising. If he ran around naked, why bother with deodorant?

A few tiny bottles were on the top shelf. Essential oils. Peppermint. Frankincense. That was an oil? Gillian only knew of Frankincense from the Wise Men story. Curious, she opened it to take a whiff and grimaced. It smelled horrendous. Did he use it to help keep people away? Replacing it, face forward, as it was, she picked up the lemon oil and cleansed her palette with a couple of whiffs. That one, she understood. Tea tree. She'd heard of that. He'd said he used it for bug repellent. Deep Woods Off would work better, she figured. Lavender? The man had not only essential oil, but *lavender* essential oil? There had to be a girlfriend nearby. Why else would a man like him, a full nature kind of guy, have lavender oil? Men didn't use that. But then how many used oils at all instead of Off or something similar?

There was nothing with his name on it. Most of the small cupboard was full of towels and toilet paper. At least the man didn't use leaves. He didn't buy cheap towels, either. They were thick and lush, good quality. The kind she would buy if she could.

Deciding to just ask his last name since it was fair enough to know it, Gillian borrowed his comb to neaten her hair, thankful it was short and didn't need more than a comb after years of keeping it long and having to fuss with it constantly, used his toilet in case she took a detour and it took too long to get back to her hotel, and headed back out to the insufferable man.

She paused as an afterthought at his dresser. Curious about what he might have other than jeans and the large sweats she left on his bed, Gillian pulled the top drawer open. Snooping way too far. But she was curious. And he didn't talk much.

There. In the back corner underneath his boxer shorts – at least he wore underwear, which she was slightly comforted to know – was a little amber bottle with a white lid. She nearly left it alone. But she couldn't quite.

Turning it to find Henry's last name, which was really all she wanted to know, she was taken aback by what it was. Valium? Why would he need valium? What on earth could he be so tense about out here by himself? By his choice? Maybe that's why he was...

Hank A. Dennison

Gillian saw the name and felt her fingers squeeze the little bottle nearly until her hand went numb. Henry ... was Hank Dennison? Karenne said he used a pseudonym, but ... but ... Henry was ... about forty-ish. Or so he looked. Hank Dennison, big shot CEO Hank Effing Dennison was in his sixties, she thought. Wait. Was that right? Or did she again mix up what she expected with the facts she'd read? No. Henry was too young to be a big CEO. He was too down-to-earth. Too mountain boy.

Maybe he'd borrowed them from his boss. Gillian started to breathe again. That was it. Illegal as it was, she knew it happened. Still, why would Henry, smooth calm grinning teasing Henry need Valium?

Of course, almost no one realized she suffered with bouts of severe depression, either. Only her boss and a couple of ex boyfriends and that was why they were both exes. They couldn't deal with it when she didn't want anything to do with them for weeks at a time. Not that she blamed them.

But not Henry.

Hank. Henry. Not much of a pseudonym if it was him. He was smarter than that. He wouldn't...

She had to know. One way or another.

Holding the bottle, she couldn't hold her crutches, so she stuffed it in her front jeans pocket just enough to stay in and mangled getting the bedroom door open enough to get through it.

He wasn't there. "Henry?" No answer returned, so she mangled getting out the front door, also, and stood on the porch for a few minutes. No sign of him. He would have told her if he was leaving, wouldn't he?

Cursing not-so-silently, Gillian hobbled down the three stairs and carefully made her way around to the side of his cottage. Cabin. Not cottage. He was not a female with lace and doilies on his tables. She rolled her eyes. Male chauvinist, maybe, though.

"Henry?" She called out loud, then again, louder. Her palms burned from the hard wood of the crutches, but she continued around to the back. If he could just leave her that way, she could darn well look around in case he was there.

She spotted his truck. At least he hadn't gone far.

Another step and her right crutch slid on a soft spot and she landed on her ass with a thud she heard as well as she felt it. "*Really?*" She slammed the ground with her best hand, neither was good but the right was at least not rock-punctured. Except now it was. Where there should have been dirt and grass, a rock protruded.

"*Really*, damn it? *Really?*"

She couldn't just sit there until his highness of the woods decided to come back, so she mangled the job of getting herself up with two sore hands and a sore ass while trying not to put weight on the ankle...

And she laughed. Hysterically. On her knees which were now

dirty again and on the better hand which was the worse hand a minute ago, Gillian knelt right there and laughed. Before long it turned into sobs mixed with laughter and then just sobs.

And then it stopped and she sat. On her sore ass with her sore hands pressed to her head that started to thump from the emotional outburst. "Okay." She looked upward, at the soft wispy clouds ambling along in no hurry, squinting at the brightness. "Okay, I give. This time, I mean it. I'm done. Can I just go home now?"

Of course she had sense enough to know she had to get herself there, so she clenched her jaw through the pain and got back on her crutches and ... and spotted a row of wood carvings that made a kind of fence line down the hill toward a shed.

She had to look despite the pain, despite knowing that if she managed to get down the hill, she'd have to manage to get back up, and headed toward the nearest.

Exquisite. An exquisitely carved mermaid protruded from the base of the tree, her tail wrapping around as though to hold herself onto it.

The next was a leprechaun. He had a pot but it was upside down and coins were falling out and sinking into a river. Or a stream.

Fairy. Unicorn. Pegasus. Some kind of sea creature. A dragon and a winged lion. Even a phoenix.

Gillian found herself transfixed in studying the carved tree trunks and running her fingers along the detailed grooves of the smooth wood. They were all the same height, all cut off evenly at the top, as far as she could tell. They were taller than she was by several inches and had a dark stain in some of the grooves to show up the accents, still the natural color of wood in other places, covered by some kind of sealant. She alternately moved close to touch them and hobbled backward to look from a distance.

"What in the hell are you doing?"

She about jumped right out of her skin before she recovered to find Henry staring from the top of the little hill. "You scared the shit out of me."

"Good." He stormed down the hill and stood between her and the phoenix. "What are you doing back here?"

"Looking for you. Did you do these? They're magnificent."

"Your car's here. If you can manage well enough to nose around my property down here where you don't have permission to be, I assume you can get yourself back to the hotel and jump on a plane home. Now. Go."

A plane home? "I'm not done here." She'd just told herself she was, but now she couldn't. This was definitely a story worth doing.

"Yes, you are. I've been nice up to now, but unless you want me to charge you with trespassing, you need to leave. Now. No more questions."

"Trespassing? You brought me here. How is that trespassing?"

"Because now I'm asking you to leave." He turned his back to her and walked away, up the hill.

"Wait." Gillian pushed herself part way up the hill which was physically much harder than she expected with the way she had to angle the crutches and with as much as both hands hurt. He was nearly out of sight by then. "*Hey*. I'm going. But tell me one thing." Breathing hard, she paused to catch her breath when he turned, a thumb in his pocket, and waited. "Hold on. I don't want to yell."

"Doing a good job of it so far."

With a frown, she hoped he'd stay right there as she pushed herself to the top of the hill. Not quite there, she had to stop a minute to catch her breath and rest her hands.

"Need help?"

"Absolutely not." She spat the words at him and kept going, non-stop, until she was face to face.

"Well?"

"Did you carve those?"

He started to turn away but lowered his eyes. To her pocket. To the prescription bottle. "So much for not being on meds. For what? Feel better now that you took them?"

"They're not mine."

"That so? Then..." He lowered his eyes again and before she could react, he grabbed the bottle. His body straightened, stiffened, as he read the label. His eyes pierced hers. "*This* ... better not be part of your story, lady. If it is, I will sue you and your paper for wrongful search, for trespassing, and for anything else I can come up with."

"*You're* Hank Dennison." It came out a whisper. She didn't want to be right.

"Get off my property. And if you have anything else of mine, leave it when you go. Keys are in the car. Along with your phone. It was beside the tire. No, I didn't nose through it. Someone in this damned world has to have some kind of scruples, no matter what little good it does them."

Gillian stared at his back as he walked away. Scruples? Hank Dennison was lecturing *her* about scruples? After what *he* did?

Sue her? For what, exactly? She'd already told him she had nothing he could get out of her. But her paper... She would never get hired again if she brought a lawsuit onto her paper. Except she wasn't... No way would she bring that into the story. The one she wasn't writing.

Maybe. And maybe she would.

Henry ... *Hank* ... stormed up his front steps and slammed the door.

Gillian stood and let herself have time to think. He didn't admit he was Dennison. He did, though, act like he had plenty of power. But who carved those trees? She couldn't fit the two images together: CEO with a lack of concern for his employees and artist with a penchant for fantasy. They didn't fit.

Maybe he was family. A brother? Was that why he didn't say his last name? Henry and Hank Dennison. Possible. A lot of couples gave their kids names all starting with the same letter. Far too cutesy for her taste. But they did. It would explain a lot.

If Henry was Hank's brother, she could very well understand why he'd need a mood control prescription to deal with that fact since he was ... an artist. Gillian just knew the carvings were his. He'd made her crutches. He had the tools. He lived out here ... among his canvases.

She'd need medical help, too, if she had to live out here, even not being related to Hank Dennison.

With a long sigh, Gillian knew she couldn't leave things as they were. Forcing herself to the cabin, up the stairs, she knocked. Of course he didn't answer. She didn't expect he would. His windows were still open, so she hobbled to one of them.

"Henry? Just so you know, I won't mention it. To anyone. Okay? I do have scruples. And I won't bother you again. I'm going home to do ... sports stories or something. Either way, you don't have to worry about me coming back." She stood still a moment then ducked her head, took a deep breath, and hobbled to the car.

Driving with her left foot would be interesting, especially down the narrow bumpy road and then through Durango traffic. But she'd manage.

Eleven

Hank watched through the window until she opened the car door, got in, and tossed the crutches aside. On the ground.

He shook his head, sighed, and went to stop the damned stubborn nosy woman. When he got to her window, she was looking at her feet, shifting them around. "Let me drive." He picked up the crutches. "And you'll need these until you find better ones."

"You said to leave anything that belongs to you."

"I made them for you. They're yours."

"No. Thank you. I want nothing from you. Move, please, so I don't hit you." She shifted into reverse.

Hank backed up a couple of steps and watched while she fumbled, lurched, stopped, lurched again. With a shake of his head, he approached as close as he dared. "Let me drive."

Her chest rose and fell and she turned a glare at him. "I'll get it. Besides, how would you get way back out here again?"

"I'll manage. And you're going to send yourself right off the edge of the road trying to drive that way. Can't have that on my conscience."

"Your conscience? Really?"

"Just put it in park and move over."

"I don't take orders."

"Ever hear of foolish pride?"

She tossed her head. "Ever hear of women's lib?"

"And you're one of those who take it to mean you should never get help from a man, despite his fully honest intentions, I suppose. Again, foolish pride."

"Is that so? And you'd take help from a woman if you needed it?"

"Gladly. If I could find one I trusted. Same with men, by the way. I'm an equal opportunity distrustful highly experienced human being. For good reason, which you just proved again. Still, I don't want you to run yourself off the road and bring a bunch of people up here asking questions. So if you would, please move over and let me take you safely into town and then you can write whatever you damned well please about me, as you know you can and I know you will."

She stared a moment while thoughts crossed her face, differing thoughts, differing expressions. "Tell me who you are."

With some hesitation, he figured he had little choice by now. "Hank Aaron Dennison. My father was a big time baseball buff. He wanted to add a couple of other names in the middle somewhere but my mother put the kibosh on that, thankfully. I was raised small town blue collar, worked my way up, found out I was giving too much of myself for too little in return that actually mattered, so I got myself out of it again. Good enough?"

"They say you trampled a hell of a lot of people on your way up, and even more on your way out."

"I know what they say."

"Is it true?"

He leaned forward, his hands on the base of the car window. "Doesn't matter if I say it is or isn't. You'll believe what you want and write what you want. So be it. I can't let it matter anymore." He stood again. "Now, are you going to let me drive or do I follow you all the way in case you run off the hill?"

Her eyes moistened and she turned away; a hard grip on the steering wheel made her knuckles white.

He almost felt a little bit sorry for her. "I have never in my life tried to hurt anyone. Okay? Just move over, Gillian. You're in no condition to drive."

"What in the hell do you care?"

"I don't want your family to sue me for letting you leave my place impaired."

"My family doesn't give a shit about me. And vice versa. It's the paper you're worried about. But don't. They're a small paper and they don't have half the resources I'm sure you have to attempt a frivolous lawsuit."

"Frivolous? You going over a hill would be frivolous?"

"My own carelessness. Doesn't affect them. Karenne might care. My editor. Otherwise..."

"You have more than your editor back home." He studied her face, her determined stubborn hiding-something face.

When she didn't answer, her gaze out in the trees somewhere,

Hank grabbed a deep breath. "Okay, Gillian. I'm not actually worried about being sued and I'm not worried about people coming around asking questions. I'm worried about you, your safety…"

"Why?" Her light brown eyes pierced his. "I'm nothing to you but a pain-in-your-ass reporter, and I don't blame you, but don't pretend like it's anything but covering your own ass when I know better."

"You don't know half what you think you know." Against his better judgment, again, he touched her face, sliding his palm against her soft, warm, pale cheek when she didn't draw back. "And I know more about you than you think. You're a spunky, stubborn, determined go-getter who will do what you need to do in order to get where you want to be."

"No, I'm not."

"You are. Maybe not every day. But you are. I admire that. I see a lot of my younger self in you. I think you'll go far once you head the right direction, whenever you find what that direction should be, which you don't know yet. And despite your … minor ethical shortfalls, you do seem like a decent person with a lot of potential. So yes, I'm worried about your safety. I'm interested in where you're heading and just how well you do."

"And how would you know? Once I leave here, I'll be out of your hair and it won't matter…"

"It will matter, and I can find out. Gillian Hart of Denver, Colorado who writes for a small paper. Won't be hard to find you."

Gillian tried to stamp down her racing heart beat and calm the rush of blood through her head so she could think straight. Would he bother to look her up? She wouldn't be much surprised by anything this man might do at this point. *The* Hank Dennison had been looking after her, helping her every time she messed up, even after stalking him and seeing far more than she should have and…

And maybe they'd given him a bad rap. Maybe he wasn't such a bad guy. Or maybe he was an incredible actor.

One thing was for sure: she couldn't drive right now. Even if she could manage with her left foot, she couldn't overcome the dizziness setting back in well enough to drive safely down dirt roads and all the way back to Durango.

She did not want him to drive her back to the hotel, though. He'd done too much already. She'd been seen with him too much already. Needing time to think, she put it in park and turned off the engine.

"Want me to take you in the truck instead? I can get someone to come back with me to pick up the car."

Her head shook without her willing it to do so.

"Okay, so what do you want to do?"

"You're giving me the option now?"

"Yes. It's fully your decision."

What did she want? She didn't even know. She wanted to be home in bed, after a long shower, buried under her blanket until all of this just went away. And yet she didn't want all of it to go away. She wanted ... to start again, at the beginning when she'd met him and do it right.

Of course there were no do-overs in real life. And she didn't know what she wanted. He was right. She didn't.

The grayness swept back in. She needed time to fight it, to think. "I ... just want to sit here a minute. Is that okay? I know I'm still on your property, so if I move a few feet down the road and sit there..."

"You'd still be on my property. The whole area is mine once you turn off the county line road."

She stared up at him. "I've been trespassing a hell of a lot, then."

A grin skirted around his lips. "I'd say you have."

"It's not posted."

"Don't usually need to."

Gillian noticed for the first time the fine wrinkles around his eyes and the corners of his mouth, and the bits of gray at his temples mostly hidden within his dark blond hair. He wasn't close to sixty as she'd expected, but he wasn't too awfully young, either. His face was kind, too kind to be the man she thought she'd been sent to interview. "I'm sorry. Really. I'm..."

"Well, let me ask you something. Would you be sorry if you still thought I was just Henry?"

"Yes. More, actually. I liked Henry."

His head cocked the slightest little bit. "Didn't seem much like it."

"And vice versa. But then you..."

His strong rough hand returned to her face. Gently. "I'm still the same guy."

"No, you're not."

He drew it back and straightened. "Okay. Sit here as long as you want. I'm going to go lie over there in that hammock in the shade and regenerate some energy to deal with whatever you decide to do. Come let me know." He propped the crutches up beside her door and walked off looking not cocky, only self-assured, and maybe a little bit tired, as well.

It was a stupid thing to say. And it insulted him. But he wasn't the same, not to her. Hank Dennison had made it to the top where she could only dream of being, and although it was very unfair and she knew it was, Gillian couldn't help her envy. It was awfully hard to like someone you envied, even if it was your fault and not theirs. She could like Henry the guard or whatever because he didn't make her feel less than she wanted to feel because she had come as far as he had, as far as a guard or whatever.

Hank was different than Henry.

He was at least different in her mind and that's what mattered.

While she sat in the car with very little breeze coming through the open windows to break the heat, with sweat rolling down the side of her face and soaking, again, the back of her blouse, Gillian realized her family had to feel the same. When she made it big enough to move to the city and become a feature reporter, their only comment had been to be sure not to act high and mighty around them.

It was insulting as hell. And she'd just done the same. Except she was no one compared to Hank Dennison. It wasn't the same.

Was she really someone to Henry? Something inside her wanted to think she did actually matter to him. It made her feel more important. To matter to someone so self-reliant and so willing to help and ... and so kind ... made her feel bigger, more ... just more.

But he wasn't just Henry.

She really wanted him to be just Henry.

Not that it mattered. She was going home.

Except she didn't want to go home.

"Hell and damnation." She banged her palm against the steering wheel, cursed again at the pain it brought, and dropped her wet forehead against the hot, hard plastic. She didn't want to go home. Never before had she been out on a story and not want to go home.

She also didn't want to do the story. She did. But not the story Karenne wanted.

And Henry didn't want to be a story.

How could she now?

With a deep breath, Gillian knew she had to at least tell him she wouldn't and then she'd figure out how to leave him alone without too much more hassle on his part.

Her palms stung against the handles of the crutches. If he sent them with her, she would keep them. Forever, maybe. Just because.

She made her way slowly, noticing the strong scent of pines within the sweltering unmoving air, a smell she used to hate, to where he lay back on the hammock, head on his arms folded above his shoulders, eyes closed. "Henry?"

"Hank. Might as well start calling me that." His eyes stayed closed. His body held still.

"I thought you were sixty or so."

He opened one eye inquisitively. "Not quite."

"Far from it, I'd say. What are you, early forties? How'd you do so much so early in your life?"

"This for the story?" He'd closed his eye again.

"No. For curiosity."

"Didn't do your homework before you came?"

"No, actually. I didn't want to know more than I did already and I didn't much care. I didn't want this story."

"So you said."

"You don't believe me."

"Doesn't matter what I believe." He shooed a fly away and returned to his position, fully relaxed, looking not at all like a man who needed Valium. "I'm forty-nine."

Forty-nine? Gillian studied his face. Other than the very fine lines around his eyes, he didn't look like he could possibly be almost fifty. His cheeks were taut with strong low cheekbones. His brows and lashes were both still thick and full. Even his neck looked young, not draggy or wrinkled or... "Are you serious?"

He looked at her again. Calm. Not answering. Just looked at her.

"It's just... For someone in your line of work, I figured... Was it not as stressful as I'd think it could be at times?"

"At times?" His head shook with a fast expellation of air. "You should have done your homework before you came up here. So, Gillian, what are we doing next?"

"I don't..."

"Don't know yet? Then why did you hobble over?"

Sarcastic ass. He really was. "I..." Maybe she wouldn't tell him. Maybe she'd let him wonder. "I don't want to go home..."

"Empty handed? You're not, though, are you? You've seen all of this. Actually you've seen quite a fair bit. You're a writer, aren't you? You can't make a story and embellish what you've seen here?"

Her face grew hot and the heat traveled down her neck. She wouldn't tell him. If he wanted to be an ass, he could think what he wanted. "At all, actually. I was going to say I... You know what? Never mind. If you would be kind enough to drive me back to the hotel, I'll do what I can to repay your trouble and I won't bother you again."

"Your rental or my truck?"

"I don't care. Really, I just don't care anymore. Whatever works best for you. I need a long cool shower and clean clothes and I don't care how anymore."

He adeptly sat up and got off the hammock without falling on his face as she probably would have. Gillian wished he'd fallen on his face. She would feel just a little bit more on his level that way.

Petty. And she was above that. She really was. At least on good days she was. But right now she just wanted to shower and eat and ... and crawl under the covers in bed and stay there for about three weeks. She didn't even care which covers, the hotel or home. Anywhere she could hide was fine. Anywhere she could be left alone to nurse her wounds, physical and mental, until she felt she could face the world again.

"Is that a no?"

She looked up at him. He'd been talking but she had no idea what he said. "What?"

"Are you all right?"

"No."

He cocked his head to study her. Then he straightened. "Let's get you back to the hotel."

Gillian let him take over, which she never did, and slid into the passenger seat of the rental. Hank put her crutches in the seat behind her and walked around to take the driver's seat. Luckily, he didn't talk. He apparently sensed her need for quiet, a rare need, and let her look out at the scenery she hated.

She didn't really hate the scenery. She hated the thoughts of the past they stirred within her, thoughts she had nothing to do with back in Denver. She kept herself too busy, too distracted. She went to shows alone, in small bars for local bands, in galleries for special features. Even to movie theaters where she would pick one to watch spur-of-the-moment just to immerse herself in anyone else's life.

She was good at staying distracted.

But not out here.

The town, or settlement rather, of Carbon Junction came within view and went out again. Within minutes, they were in Durango where she breathed easier. At least it was a real city. Not Denver, but a city more or less.

Before she knew it, they were at the Strater.

She finally looked over at him. "I have to take the rental back since obviously I can't drive it. If you drop me off there, they can bring me to the hotel."

"I'll take care of it."

"But ... I have to sign the paperwork and..."

"I'll take care of it." He got out and came around to first grab her crutches, then to open her door and give her a careful hand.

"They have my card on file..."

"I know how rentals work, Gillian. Just get in and get your shower and feel better. Here." He handed her a card printed with his name and a phone number but nothing else. "Don't share this. It's not for your story. I have an answering service. When you get back to

Denver, let me know you're there safely so I don't have to look you up."

"What makes you think I'm going right back?"

With a light grin that didn't look much like a happy grin, or even a gloating grin, he offered to walk her just inside the hotel, to help with the steps and the door.

Gillian accepted, breathed deeply at the cool, fresh AC air and clean indoor scent, and thanked him again. "Really, I can call them and have them pick it up here and meet them to do the paperwork..."

Hank set a hand aside her face. "Just go take care of yourself. See your doctor when you get home to check that ankle and your hands. And to check that dizziness if it's unusual. If it's normal, you should fix that, too."

"Is this all a bribe to keep me from writing the story?"

He stared a moment, then drew closer, very close, holding her eyes. "I wish you wouldn't, but it's your call. No bribery. Only one person helping another in need. Some of us still do that."

Her skin burned where his palm touched it. Her eyes watered. She took a fast deep breath to control it. "It wouldn't be necessary, anyway. I've already decided not to write it. I'll probably get fired, but I don't care about that anymore, either. I'll ... go back to retail and let rude people who are spending money they don't have look down at me and snub me while I'm just trying to support myself while helping them buy stuff they can't afford. Like I have room to talk, right? But at least I'm not rude and ... and this doesn't matter to you." She shifted her hands and her weight to try for less pain in her palms and ankle. It didn't work.

"Anyway, I'm not writing about you. Don't worry. If Karenne wants the story, she'll have to do it herself, or send someone else. Which she might do, but I'll try to stop her."

"Thank you." His voice was soft and deep and entirely sincere.

"Least I can do." She tried to force herself to walk away from him, from those pretty deep blue eyes looking at her like ... like she was worth that look. "Do you want to come up? I'll order coffee and..."

"No." He lowered his hand and backed away.

"Are you sure? I owe you that, too, for your…"

"I can't have anyone see me go up to your room. This is as far as I go. People looking for a story are always lurking, less straightforward about it than you were."

Life returned around her and she realized people were close enough to see them, to pay attention. "That would get tiring."

"Part of why I'm not in town much. Anyway, have a good warm or lukewarm shower, don't make it cold, and sit and rest that ankle. Get room service and eat well. If you're not heading home in the morning, find somewhere here to get that looked at. Never mess around with your health, Gillian. It's too important." He stepped back farther, toward the door.

"Hank." She hobbled up close to him again. "I … um…" Hell. She didn't have a clue what to say. So she kissed him.

He pulled away, looked at her like she was crazy, and went out the door.

Hell. She'd messed up again. A friend nearby. He had *a friend* nearby. A *she*. Probably a girlfriend. But she only meant to … to say thank you. Nothing more.

"Who in the holy hell are you trying to kid, Gillian? You're enamored with Mr. CEO Hermit. What is *wrong* with you?" She noted some guy look over at her talking to herself, hoped he didn't hear what she said, and hobbled to the elevator.

Twelve

Soaking in the tub, which she never did at hotels, Gillian closed her eyes and wondered why on earth she would have kissed the man. Enamored. Fine. She'd been enamored plenty often. It didn't mean she went around kissing them.

He had nice lips, though. For an older man. Forty-nine. Seventeen years older than she was. Still, at thirty-two, she didn't feel much younger than he was old. And still again, he'd been nearly a legal adult when she was born. No, no, no. That wasn't good. But maybe it was. He would have ... he *did* have a maturity she didn't find enough in men her own age. At her age, they should be plenty mature. They'd been adults, more or less, for over ten years. It was often hard to tell.

And it didn't matter. She was stupid to even worry about how much older he was, just as she'd been stupid to kiss him. She'd never see him again. In which case, why did it matter that she'd kissed him? A little kiss was nothing compared to ... to ... all the time she'd spent annoying him. Poor guy. He'd be glad as hell when she was back home.

So would his female friend, Gillian guessed. A pang of jealousy crossed her heart and she pushed it away. It wasn't him she wanted. She wanted someone like him except not a hermit and not ... not a CEO who had suddenly shut everything down and put so many people out of work. She didn't want that.

No explanation. No remorse. He just shut it down. Since it wasn't a publicly traded company, there were no investors to lose their money. There was that. She read an article written by someone supporting him that said as much. It was his company to do with as he pleased and no one had the right to condemn him.

Except the thousands of workers suddenly out of jobs with little warning sure did. Why had he closed it instead of selling and saving those jobs? She'd done her homework well enough by following the story as it happened. His company was based in Denver. How would she not know the story? There had been offers to buy the place. He refused.

Gillian swirled her hands in the warm soapy water and tried to reconcile Henry with Hank. Tired. He'd mentioned being tired more than once, lacking energy, despite a well-toned body that said he should have plenty of masculine muscular energy.

And yet there was the Valium.

What was his story? Even if she didn't write it, she wanted to know.

Finding it impossible to relax with the thought swirling her head the way her hands swirled the soap in the warm water that had grown plenty cold, she got out, ran the shower long enough to rinse the bubbles from her body, and grabbed a towel.

Was that a knock on her door? Who on earth would be there? Drying briefly, only enough not to drip water all over the carpet, she wrapped the nice big hotel towel around her and hobbled over to look out the peep hole while trying to keep the towel from falling, except there wasn't a peep hole, so she left the chain hooked and opened it enough to peep around the edge.

"I was starting to think you weren't going to answer."

She stared at him. In nice pants and a tucked-in navy shirt, the sleeves rolled nearly to his elbows, he looked every part the role of businessman. Had he trimmed his hair? He was freshly shaved.

"And you're not dressed."

She glanced at herself and back at him. "Why are you here?"

"Have you eaten?"

"No. I'm not... I've been in the bath."

"So I see. How about meeting me downstairs? How long do you need?"

"Why?"

"They have a nice theater here in the hotel. Would you join me for dinner first and then a show? Next show isn't for an hour or more. Gives you time to get dressed. Say yes and I'll grab seats."

"But... I'm..."

He skimmed her bare shoulder and arm, down to her toes, then back to her face. "You're wearing more than I was yesterday."

She grew hot from head to the toes he found. Gillian had always hated how easily she blushed. A curse passed down from her mother. She hated it more now, in front of the always calm and cool Hank

Dennison who apparently had no problem eyeing her.

"Please. Have dinner with me, at least. I think I owe you for being so gruff earlier."

"You don't..."

"Let me think I do. Twenty minutes?"

"What?"

"Can you be ready in twenty minutes?"

"Um..."

"Twenty-five then. I'll be downstairs." He walked away.

Gillian stood with the door open wondering if she had gone to sleep and was dreaming until a middle-aged couple walked by and the man scoped her out. His wife pulled him away while giving her a dirty look.

Hank ignored the looks from a couple of locals he recognized while he reserved a table for dinner and pre-ordered their meals. He'd told her he wouldn't go to her room and then he had. Reckless. Someone would catch him doing so and spread it. Wouldn't matter to him, but it might to her. Of course she'd said everyone wanted their fifteen minutes and so maybe it would work in her favor. Maybe it would give her the limelight she wanted to get her career moving.

Maybe he'd just tell her to do the damned story and see what she'd end up writing. Of course then it would look like dinner was a bribe to convince her to make him look good. Even if she didn't make it sound like that, someone would.

Success wasn't all it was cracked up to be.

Sometimes it was. For instance, he was happy as hell to be able to put the rental car fee on his own card, and to tell the hotel to charge him for her room instead of the paper, which was fair, he supposed, since he talked their star writer out of her big story. He wouldn't notice the expense. And he was glad to be able to take her to a nice dinner and the theater in exchange for all she'd been through without worrying about how to pay for it. There was that benefit. And it was a nice benefit. No doubt about it.

He'd paid for it, though. Dearly.

Unwilling to let the thought spoil the night, he pondered the kiss while wandering the hotel waiting for her to come down. Nothing more than appreciation, he decided.

Hank found himself by the front door and walked up to the window looking over the street. A jolting thing to be inside what felt like an old-time parlor looking out on modern times. Kids walked past bobbing to whatever music they played from a "smart" phone, looking as though they wanted to be taken any way but seriously with the scruffy baggy clothes and big holes in their earlobes a pencil and pen set would fit through, not that they had any idea what a pencil and pen set were or how to use them with any real success.

His father would have put a fist to his head if he'd walked around that way, if he looked one iota as though he didn't mean to be productive and successful.

Hank chuckled at the thought, at the times he'd been called lazy and shiftless. His mother always defended him, always said he was going to be big time someday with his brains and his attitude. He wished she'd lived long enough to see she was right. Although, without trying to live up to her wishes after her death, he wasn't at all sure he would have bothered.

A good woman. His mother was a genuinely good woman and every day he hoped he was living up to her expectations. Even now. She would understand his retreat from the world.

A soft touch on his shoulder took him from his thoughts and he turned to … not the same woman who had been a pain in his ass the past two days. She was in a long thin flowing ivory skirt with a draping dark green blouse clinging to her breasts and floating down to the edge of her skirt in front, farther down in back.

"This okay?" She looked entirely and unnecessarily unsure of herself.

"Luscious."

She smiled. "Thank you very much. I'll take that as the best compliment I've had in a lot of years. It would look better without the sticks."

"I don't know." He tilted his head as though he had to think about it. "That's actually rather charming." As a distraction, he checked his watch. "You're early. We have fifteen minutes yet."

"You said twenty-five minutes. I'm only five minutes early."

"Yes well, I expected ten minutes late."

"I don't like to be late. And maybe you should be more careful about your gender assumptions."

"Nothing to do with gender. I showed up last minute and you're..." He nodded at her foot. "Not in your best form at the moment. I also thought you might have to take time to consider whether you would come down at all or tell me to go straight to ... well, you get the drift."

"Point taken. Guess I should watch my assumptions, also, huh? And yes, I did use some of the time thinking about telling you what you could do with yourself. About, oh, thirty seconds or so."

He couldn't help but smile. "Would you like to sit down? I'll find a couple of drinks while we wait." He nodded toward the circular cushioned bench beside the check-in desk, walked with her, set a hand on her elbow to help steady her as she lowered, and told her he'd be right back.

Gillian kept waiting for the question. Or the assumption. About the kiss. Through dinner he was sweet and charming, with only an occasional teasing barb, which she'd come to realize was a built-in personality quirk. She was coming to appreciate that quirk. It kept her on her toes, mentally, since she liked to be ready with a comeback to show she could keep up with him.

Their table in the little theatre within the hotel was close to the front and he gave her the best seat facing the stage.

Despite her common sense nagging at her, Gillian agreed to another martini. It had been a long week. A very long painful stressful week. And yet, now, sitting with Hank Dennison in the gorgeous Henry Strater Theatre waiting for the show to start, a live show, which she loved, she realized she had not one urge to be in bed under the covers unwilling to even move enough to adjust her pillow.

She wanted to be exactly where she was. The thought of it, since it had been such a long time since she'd felt that way, made her eyes water.

"What's wrong, Gillian?"

With a quick shake of the head, she took a too-big sip of her martini.

"Would you rather leave?"

"No." She gasped it out and then found her voice and repeated herself.

"You're unhappy. Say so if..."

"No. Quite the opposite. I'm ... actually not unhappy at the moment and it's odd. Odd enough to shake me up a bit. I'm sorry." She took another drink, smaller this time.

"It's odd for you to not be unhappy?" His gorgeous worried eyes held hers.

"I'm ... just finding myself, I guess. Looking for..." She sighed hard. "I guess I don't even know what I'm looking for. Hard to find it that way. Never mind me. I'm sorry. This is wonderful and I'm loving every minute of it. I'll just think of going home tomorrow and then I'll be back to normal. Don't worry. I'm fine."

He was silent a moment, watching her, then he shifted his chair closer and grasped her hand. "Don't go home tomorrow."

Gillian felt his heat, he was so close, or his closeness was making her own body heat up again. Which she didn't want. She absolutely did not... Did she? Yes. To be honest with herself, she did. But he...

"In case you're wondering, I am flirting. It's been quite some time since I tried, so I may not be doing it well and I'm not good at it."

"Oh, I think you're very good at it. I'm just not sure why you're bothering. I've been nothing but a mess, an uncoordinated, wimpy pain in your ass, which usually I'm not. Really. In my own life, I'm together and cool and ... well, often called cold, to tell you the truth, and I'm very coordinated. I'm rarely sick. I'm pretty sturdy. This... I'm just so thrown off, by myself..."

"And at home, you're rarely not unhappy."

She bit her lip to stop the sudden overwhelming emotions. Gillian usually hid them well. No one saw it. She could be sinking in a fast-moving whirlpool twenty feet under with no visible means of escape and no one saw it. This... She was too thrown in this place. She had to leave.

When she started to get up, he held her hand tighter and grasped her arm gently with his other hand, moving closer. "Don't leave."

"I can't..." She swallowed hard.

"We'll talk more later. Sit back and enjoy the show for now. Will you? Please?"

"No more talking?"

"No more talking."

She nodded and took another sip of her martini, then requested ice water instead. He ordered it for her immediately and released the grip on her arm, but he stayed close, her hand in his. The server glanced at their hands and at him and walked away.

The girl knew him. Hank's look said he realized she did. Still, he kept Gillian's hand and relaxed into his chair and said nothing.

His calm helped her relax. When the room darkened and she got absorbed into the show, she felt him move their arms to rest on his leg and she didn't object.

Thirteen

She felt like an idiot. Such a wonderful evening at the theatre with a charming, gracious man, and all Gillian could think about was that she'd lost too much control and wasn't able to talk to him.

She was a journalist. Talking to people, digging into who they were, was her trade, for pete's sake. And she was plenty curious about Hank Dennison. There was plenty to be curious about. She'd had him pegged in her mind before she arrived in the wilderness. Super smart. Super savvy. Super arrogant. And hard as those rocks he lived among.

Half right. Smart and savvy, the man was, indeed. Maybe he was arrogant, also, but not nearly as much as she'd guessed. No more than she was, or at least no more than she seemed to everyone else. Hard? Not a trace of hardness reflected off Hank that Gillian could see. Self-assured, yes. That wasn't the same as hard. It wasn't remotely the same as hard.

Henry aka Hank was no more hard than Gillian was cold.

A glance at the hotel alarm clock told her she should get out of bed and make arrangements to go home. She groaned at the thought of going home. Or of getting out of bed. Or of not going home. Maybe all of it. It was a just-stay-in-bed day.

But it wasn't her bed and she wasn't paying the bill so she had to do something other than stay in bed.

Another groan and she flopped over to her other side and stared at the wall. She could slip out of town real quick. Head to the airport while Karenne arranged her flight home. Sit and people watch until her flight time. Anything to stay the heck away from Mr. Billionaire ex-CEO Mountain Hermit.

She would do that. As soon as she could make herself get up.

"In case you're wondering, I am flirting."

Why? The gray sinking tumbling darkness swirled in around her as Gillian asked herself over and over why Hank Dennison would flirt with her, after the big mess he'd seen of her. Why?

Just crawl out of bed, Gillian, and go home. Just go. Get up.

Or not.

Maybe she just wouldn't.

"I'm sorry, Sir. She's not answering."

Hank thanked the desk clerk and paced around the Strater's reception area. She hadn't checked out. An hour left before check out time. So she was waiting until last minute or she didn't plan to leave yet. Or she was in the shower.

He stared out the window from old to new, from brown leather and carved wood to gray cement and phones stuck to everyone's ears or palms. Giving her what he figured was enough time to finish the shower and at least wrap in a towel, he asked the clerk to try again.

Still no answer.

So he went up. Against his better judgment.

He knocked softly at first, so as not to startle her, and then louder. Was she swearing? He chuckled as her annoyed voice came barely through the door.

The door opened. "I'll be out soon. I over..." She stopped when she saw him. Stared.

"Expected housekeeping?"

"Yes. I have to pack. It's late..."

"Don't pack. Come to breakfast with me." He let his gaze fall over her long T-shirt atop bare legs.

"I can't. I have to leave. And..." She backed up behind the door except for her face and the arm holding it. "I'm not dressed."

"I noticed. I'll wait downstairs."

"No."

"No? Should I wait here?"

"I can't... I'm leaving. I have to call Karenne and get a flight and I have like fifteen minutes to throw myself together before they charge for the extra night..."

"Gillian." He stepped closer. "I'll take care of the extra night. Let's have breakfast and then I'll take you to the airport after you've had time to eat and pack, if that's what you want. Or I'll take you tomorrow."

She started to speak, then stared, then started again. No words came. She was entirely too flustered.

"Don't have a panic attack or anything. All right? It's just breakfast. Coffee."

"I have to go."

"Why?"

"Work."

"It'll wait another day."

"Easy for you to say. Some of us have deadlines and time clocks, or the equivalent of that."

He waited for her to realize how it sounded.

"Sorry. I just mean... I have to get back to work."

"And I think you need time off. Don't even start to suggest I don't understand needing time off or that I don't know the signs of desperately needing time off. I do. I ignored them. That was a mistake. I want to help you not make that mistake."

"Why?"

A deep breath took over and he nodded. "Okay. Tell you what. If you come to breakfast with me, I'll tell you why. Deal?"

"Just let it go already." Gillian backed away farther.

Hank figured he could be wrong for trying to start what he couldn't finish, but he enjoyed her company, pain in the ass and all. It had been a long time since he'd honestly enjoyed anyone's company, other than Susan who ran the health store and reminded him of his mother. She was feisty and never failed to tell him exactly what she thought of his decisions. He liked that about her. Gillian seemed much the same, except younger. Too much younger, possibly, but as he only wanted her company for a while, until she gathered herself and decided what she wanted, he figured it was fine. He wouldn't lead her too far in.

She was the one who kissed him. He'd been trying to keep distance. She crossed that line and broke through. She didn't know what she was doing. Hank knew, also, that it was his image she liked, not him personally, but that was fine, as well. Companionship wouldn't hurt either of them. Companionship never did. It was the deeper stuff that brought the trouble. He didn't want deeper. Neither did she. At least he thought his assumption, in this case, was correct.

So, instead of honoring her request to leave her the hell alone as he normally would, he stepped into her doorway. "Ever go to a spa?"

She stared, silent.

"There's one just up the road. Great for unwinding. Interested?"

"I have to get back to work."

"Mineral springs. Huge pool. Facials. Massages. They even do a technique called energy therapy. I go now and then. Sure you're not interested?"

"Why?"

"Why what?"

"Energy therapy? Why do you need it? You keep talking about lack of energy, but look at you. Why..?"

"Come to breakfast, Gillian."

She fought with herself while she stood there gazing at him. Mineral springs. Spa. Yes, very tempting. Even more tempting was the thought of doing it with Henry ... Hank, since he would be nearly undressed again.

Energy therapy. Why?

"You're down to about seven minutes by now, anyway. Can you pack in that amount of time?"

"Probably." Not that she wanted to.

"Guess I'll keep stalling you longer, then, until it's too late to worry about checkout time."

"Why are you doing this?"

He slowly moved up to her without even trying to hide the fact that he was looking at her bare legs. His dark blue eyes rose to her plain hazelish-brownish-nondescript eyes. All of her was nondescript next to him. "Curiosity."

"About what?"

"You."

"But I'm not..." She backed up. "I'm not slightly interesting enough for you to be so curious."

"I beg to differ." He stepped forward again, ran fingers along her hairline while he studied her face, then backed away. "Only about five minutes now."

"I don't think I can make that. Not on crutches."

"Might as well come to breakfast, then."

Hell. Of course she gave in. Karenne would kill her for the extra day and no story. Or fire her. If she didn't quit first.

After the day of a hearty but healthy breakfast where she realized spinach could actually taste good when prepared right, followed by relaxing at Trimble Spa and Hot Springs where Hank suggested the mineral springs might help her ankle and where she spent too much time lazing in the sun watching him swim, Gillian thought quitting wouldn't be horrible. Running away with Hank Dennison, or rather, staying hidden here with Hank Dennison, wouldn't be so horrible, either.

Karenne called a couple of times. The first time she had quickly said she was with Hank and would have to call back later. The second time, her phone was locked away at the spa along with her clothes and she'd yet to return the call after finding the message. At least the "with Hank" comment would make it sound like she was working.

Back in his truck, they were both silent. Until her stomach growled and he offered dinner.

"You don't need to, and I still have to find a place for the night. Really, I should have argued harder about staying right there since I had to pay for the room anyway."

"Only a late checkout fee. The room has been booked for months. They couldn't just let you stay. And don't worry. I have it covered. Do you like Mexican food?"

"I like nearly any food. What do you mean?"

"Good. We'll run through Zia Taqueria and grab it to go. There are only a few places I eat other than at home. That's one of them. They grow much of their own produce in a big greenhouse and buy most of the rest locally. You can't get fresher."

She shrugged as an okay and questioned him more about her accommodations, but he didn't budge other than to say no, he wasn't taking her back to his place since she didn't seem at all enamored with it and he only had the one bed.

"I could take the red eye instead of waiting till morning. Solves two issues."

Hank had started to pull out but stopped and looked at her. "Is that what you want?" His gaze was almost like a pouting puppy dog.

She tried to say no and then tried to say yes and couldn't say anything. The bed comment got to her. Even if he was telling her he fully expected separate beds, separate rooms. Even separate buildings. Still, he'd mentioned it.

"Tell you what." He grasped her fingers gently. "We'll pick up dinner and go eat and if you still want a red eye, I'll take you to the airport. Deal?"

"I don't know, Dennison. I thought the deal was that if I went to breakfast with you, you'd tell me about your fatigue/energy issue and you still haven't done that. Should I risk believing this deal?"

He pulled his hand away and put the truck back in park. "Want to tell me again you're not doing the story?"

"Already said I wasn't."

"People say a lot of things."

"Yeah. They do."

He captured her eyes, pondering. Understanding. "Okay. I'm fighting a health issue that's fairly serious. It saps my energy at times, some days more than others. It's not contagious, so you don't need to worry. It's also why I try to eat healthy and avoid putting anything in my system that'll make it harder to fight. Good enough?"

Gillian felt a knot form in her stomach. *Fairly serious.* Trying to ask what it was, she found herself tongue-tied. Maybe she didn't want to know. She nodded, useless to do otherwise.

Fourteen

Hank ran into the office at the Apple Orchard Inn to grab keys to the Prairie Spy cottage. Gillian had been silent throughout the drive to the Inn, other than placing her to-go order. He kept expecting further questions about his illness, but they didn't come. He wasn't sure whether to be relieved or insulted.

She still didn't ask questions when he came out from the office, until he pulled up to the little cottage with a big covered front porch, complete with rocking chairs, overlooking the prairie and mountains.

He turned the truck off. "*This* is a cottage."

"It's a house."

"A matter of semantics, I suppose. Either way, it's yours for the next few nights, or as long as you decide to stay, up to a week. It's booked after that."

"I don't know what you're trying to accomplish, Dennison, but I told you I have to get back to work." She stared at the place with no noticeable expression.

"Don't call me by my last name, Gillian." He shifted to face her better. "It's Hank. Or Henry, if you'd rather. Even Smartass or Jackass, if you like, as many have. But don't call me Dennison as though this is a business arrangement."

"Isn't it?"

He sighed. "To what end?"

"I don't know. Guess I'm trying to figure that out."

"I enjoy your company, as I said. And I'm not in the business game anymore. I'm just a simple guy living day to day." Literally. Some days better than others.

But she didn't believe him. He could see all over her face that she didn't believe him. "Let's go sit on that amazing porch and eat while the food's warm."

"It's a beautiful place. Three times the size of my apartment. Trying to make it hard to go back to that, Dennison?" She finally looked at him. "Sorry. Habit. Keeps people at more of a distance."

"Which is why I asked you not to do so with me. I understand you better than you think." Instead of waiting for a response, he got

out and went around to help her down. When she had her crutches
positioned, he grabbed the food and led her to the cottage porch.

Dusk fell.

Gillian realized with a start that it had to be after nine p.m. for the
sun to be heading down. As much as she loved the warmth of
summer, she hated the long days that seemed to never end, to never
let her get enough dark time. She didn't sleep well in the summer. It
took her body too long to adjust to losing the energizing light. Short
winter days at least gave her an excuse to go to bed early.

She sighed. They were still sitting out on the porch. Or rather,
again sitting on the porch. She'd insisted on washing up before she ate
after the day in public waters. Of course he shook his head about that,
as well. Mineral waters, he said. Healthy.

Still, they were public. So she showered quickly and washed her
hair. Hank waited outside. For privacy, he said. Gillian figured that
much privacy was rather unnecessary at this point, but she didn't
argue.

"Still want to go catch a red eye?"

She looked over to see if he was serious or gloating. He looked as
though it was an honest question. "No." It came out without having
to consider it a while as she normally did. She didn't want to leave
tonight.

Maybe she didn't want to leave at all.

"Good. How about a little trip tomorrow? There's something I
want to show you." Hank looked far too relaxed on the rocking chair
on the cottage porch, asking her to stay home from work another day.

"Hank, I *have* to go back to work."

"You're not ready."

"Really?"

"Really." He stopped rocking and leaned forward. "Give me a
week. One whole week. You have vacation time, right?"

"Already used it."

"Okay, then take unpaid vacation."

"I can't. Don't you get it? I'm barely making ends meet. This is
already…"

He stood and took her hands to pull her to her feet. "Relax. I'll have you covered."

"Don't." Gillian yanked her hands away and nearly toppled when her ankle screamed about the weight she put on it. "Just don't. I'm not that kind of girl. I don't want your..."

"Oh, come on." Hank reached over to grab her crutches as he kept her from falling and settled them back under her arms. "That's not what I meant."

"Isn't it?"

"Gillian, get over the money thing, would you? Look at me as me, not as what I have. I'm not trying to buy you. I'm not trying to bribe you."

"What is it you're doing, then? You could be my father, you realize. I mean, you were old enough to be a father when I was born. That's..."

"So it's my age bothering you, not my money?"

"Both." She shook her head. "No. Neither. It's..." Holy hell. It was. Both. It was. But it was unfair, both ways, and she knew it. Still...

She had to go home. Back to work. To a job she didn't want, an apartment she didn't like, a city she didn't fit. Still, she had to go home because she'd chosen that. If she wanted something else, she'd have to change it herself.

Hobbling away from him, she got down the stairs and a good way out into the lawn, then gave in to her throbbing hands and raw underarms – how did people use wooden sticks to walk all the time? – and stopped to watch the ducks light onto the water or surrounding grass, settling for the night, she supposed. Maybe she would become a duck and simply wander around with a backpack of clothes and nothing more and go where she decided...

Gillian shook her head at herself. Wouldn't happen. She needed the creature comforts. Electricity. Running water. Air conditioning or heat. Radio. Her computer. Although she realized she hadn't actually opened her laptop since she'd arrived in Durango. Unusual. Her mail box was likely overwhelmed by now.

Maybe she'd just delete the whole thing without looking at them.

Karenne. Where was her phone? She never didn't know where

her phone was, either. But honestly, she didn't care.

"Hands sore?" He came up from behind and stopped almost at her side but more at her back.

"I have to go home."

"I know, Gillian. I'm not trying to get you to stay. No longer than a week. Just because I enjoy your company. And because... I can see how much you need a break. Or a change. Something. It worries me."

"Why do you care?"

Hank walked away from her, not far away, and stopped as he looked up at the tips of the mountains, mostly bare and reddish-purple. Most people looked up and saw barren desolation. He saw life. Different life. More intense life. Harder, but more meaningful. Closer to ... whatever came next.

He needed her to stay because she was full of life and afraid of it. Both. He wanted her not to be afraid of it since she had so much of it left, or should have. He wanted her to know him for who he was, to remember that. She was sent to him for some reason. She had to stay long enough.

"Hank?" She came up close beside him. One of the crutches touched his leg before she moved it. "How serious is your illness?"

His chest heaved, and he kept his eyes on the mountains. "Hard to tell. I take things day by day." When she was silent, he turned to her. "I'm not being evasive. It is serious, Gillian. They wanted me to fight it out in some hospital drugged up and heaving my guts out while being watched twenty-four hours a day. I didn't want that, so I came out here."

"But..."

"I watched my father and my younger brother fight it out in the hospital and it did them exactly no good except to make the end miserable for all of us. I won't do it. I have no one worth fighting like that for. And they say it can cure itself at times, with good food, with clean air, by cleaning out the toxins and adding stuff that strengthens the body. All in all, I think I'd rather chance that than the other."

"You have cancer."

"Yes." And he could finally say it without emotion, only as fact.

"But I'm currently stable, and I'm doing my best to stay that way."

Her eyes watered and the last thing he wanted was pity, so he turned and started walking again, farther from the cottage, toward the mountains. When he finally stopped and turned, she was sitting where he'd left her, on the grass, watching him.

With a sigh, he returned.

"I can't keep up." Her eyes were shiny but dry. Controlled. "And I feel like a baby for fussing about my hands when you're... But they're killing me... I mean... Sorry. Bad choice of words. I do that..."

Hank chuckled. "This is why I want you here. You make me laugh. I mean that in the best way possible." He sat next to her and grabbed a deep breath, staring at the mountains. "I closed the business for my health. The stress was killing me. Literally."

"Why didn't you sell it and keep those jobs open? And I'm asking only for myself. Off the record."

"Off the record." He wasn't sure he cared anymore about the record. He figured he might as well explain. "The only buyer interested in keeping it going wanted to unionize it and make it publicly traded."

"So?"

"So." He shook his head. People didn't get it. Would she if he tried? "So they would have shipped any of the jobs they could overseas and would have started manufacturing any part of them possible with cheap foreign parts in order to increase profit. They would have kept their eyes on the stock exchange rate more than on the quality, would have kept those workers who fit the statistics no matter how lazy they are or how badly they did their job instead of those best qualified. And it would still be in *my* name. It would be *my* reputation at stake and they wouldn't care what they did to it as long as profits increased. So I said hell no and I shut it down. Yes, I ruined my reputation anyway, but at least it's only anger at me and not fault with my products."

"They were your creation." Her voice was soft, questioning, but not really a question. "All of those cool things that help people ... keep moving. The glove-like foot wraps that are easy to wear, for arch support, arthritis glove-socks for toes that support without cutting off circulation, the knee things...”

"Yes. All mine.”

"How... I mean...”

"My mother had crippling arthritis. They gave her drugs that didn't help much and caused other issues. All she wanted was some extra support so she could stay on her feet, as you're supposed to, to keep the muscles and tendons mobile so they don't stiffen, and everything she tried was bulky or hurt more or...” He shrugged. “I figured there had to be something better. When I couldn't find anything better, I created it. From the floor up. All of it. I funded it myself. Worked up from nothing. Eighty, ninety hours a week. Whatever it took. Which meant over five years of no income beyond enough for a cheap apartment and cheap food.

"My guess is that's part of my problem now. I destroyed my body pushing so hard to get there and then trying to keep it up there. I held out as long as I could waiting for the right buyer who would keep it going the way it was established, but my body gave out. I had to stop. And now many of those who benefitted from the jobs I provided, who did their forty hours and went home to their families and well-rounded meals and nice houses...”

"Now they're calling you a villain. Why didn't you argue? Why not explain like you just did to me?”

"Because one person at your side might listen, but groups of people don't. If I said that publicly, I'd be villainized for being anti-union, which isn't exactly true, and for degrading the typical American worker, as though there is such a thing. There are good workers and not good workers. Some I can trust; some I can't. But I can't say that. It would backfire.”

"There has to be a way...”

"Good luck finding it. And you do realize they all had unemployment benefits to help them during their transition to new jobs, right? They had it because I paid it in for every one of them. So I was helping to pay their bills for some time after they weren't working for me any longer. They don't think about that. They think of it as government money, and of course there is no such thing. It's taxpayer money and business owner money. The government has no money of its own. It all comes from someone else's sweat and blood. Still, *I'm* the villain. No matter what I provided, it was never enough. The more benefits I added, the more they wanted, including dog and cat insurance, for hell's sake." Hank stood. He couldn't sit. It always set his boiling point too high to think about it, which didn't help him at all. He had to calm himself.

He listened to the crickets nearby and the frogs croaking in the ponds, with an occasional quack from a duck settling for the night. It didn't matter anymore. This was his life now. He was happy in it. Carving sculptures that no one would see until ... later. When he wouldn't have to hear what they thought.

"I'm sorry." Gillian came up beside him, brushing his arm. "For the stupid things I've said. And for ... well, all of it."

"Thank you. Accepted. And you should know I paid myself the same as I paid my upper management, except I worked nearly twice their hours and I invested most of it. If they'd done the same, they'd all have what I have. Everything above that, I put back into the company and expanded to create more jobs."

"I didn't realize. Really, people should know..."

"They wouldn't listen."

"That's why you never married? All those hours..."

"Right. I had a few relationships, but it didn't work well. I was too driven. I don't blame them. I blame myself." He grasped a quick deep breath and turned to her. "That's why I care that you need a break. Because I know the dangers of not allowing yourself time to unwind, to recover, to have play time, socializing time. I don't want that to happen to you. I don't want you to make yourself sick pushing too hard, stressing too much..."

"It could, anyway. It happens to little kids, no rhyme or reason..."

"Yes. But stress is a killer. It is. And I think you have too much going for you to throw it out the window for a job that doesn't even make you happy."

"Does anyone's? Honestly."

"Yes." He looked back out over the pond. "Mine did. Probably still would if I hadn't pushed too hard, if I'd relied more on others, and my biggest mistake is that I didn't, that I figured I could keep doing it myself. But, Gillian, a career should make you happy, or at least content. Working only for a paycheck in a job you hate is no way to live."

"Not earning a paycheck isn't, either."

He grinned. "Okay. But there has to be a happy medium."

"Good luck finding one." She rolled her eyes.

"Well, at this point, I don't have to worry with that. You should find one, though. I know they're out there. I've seen it." He touched her arm. "Take what you love and do something with it that gets you where you want to be. If you can't find something, create it. That's the beauty of the system: it's all there waiting for you to make your mark, to do something new, to help it flourish enough it spreads and gives others new life, as well. You can do that. I truly believe you can. Just don't try to do it all yourself like I did. I was too proud to accept help when it was offered. Be proud, but not too proud."

She didn't answer. Instead she gazed up at the mountains, at the flock of birds flying over.

Hank figured he better not push any further for the night. "So. Now that that's out of the way, how about staying the rest of the week? And don't say yes out of pity or guilt or whatever. Say yes because you need the break and being in my company isn't all that heinous anymore." He grinned, teasing.

"It never was."

"Is that so? Could have fooled me."

"It was my own company I wasn't enjoying. I just took it out on you. Sorry again."

"Let's go out for ice cream." Hank didn't wait for an answer. He guided her slowly back to the cabin, waited until she got a sweater from inside, and helped her to the truck.

Fifteen

Gillian rolled over on the soft mattress and fresh-linens-scented pillow toward the window where a nice clean breeze drifted through the screen, cringed at sudden nausea, and pushed herself to the pretty little bathroom, cursing at the pain in her ankle but having no time to grab the crutches. She got to the toilet barely in time for her stomach contents to come shooting out.

She'd eaten too much the night before. It took too long for her system to stop expelling and then to stop dry heaving. So much for *garden fresh*. It had to be the Mexican food. Or the three scoops of ice cream and then a rum and water on top of the Mexican food. Could be she just overdid the good stuff Hank offered. Too much good stuff was still too much.

He'd actually offered coffee after the ice cream, but the coffee shop was closed and so they stopped at a bar and grill for coffee but Gillian ordered rum instead of coffee, afraid coffee would keep her up too late.

Big mistake.

He'd stayed to talk for the longest time, late into the night, so she might just as well have had coffee.

She'd offered to let him pull out the sleeper sofa since it was in the cottage hotel he was paying for instead of making him go all the way back to his cabin. Also a mistake. His expression said she shouldn't have asked. Even if he didn't agree to stay. He'd left abruptly.

"*Why* do you keep *doing* these things?"

After sloshing handfuls of cold bathroom sink water into her mouth to rinse it, Gillian made her way back to the bed and started to sit on the side of it, but slid down to the floor, pulled her knees up, and dropped her head on top of them, her arms around her head. *Just go home. Gillian, just go home. Get up and go.*

Not now. She would give it a few minutes. Let her stomach settle. Go shower. Or not. What did it matter? She'd likely get stuck beside some big sweaty guy on the plane, anyway. No one would smell her stench over his. And she had no one to impress, no one to care if she went home, to her empty apartment.

She'd shower before going back to work where someone might care.

Work.

Her whole body shuddered at the thought.

But it was what she chose. What else did she know how to do? What else did she want to do?

Travel. Not that she could do that without a job.

Write fiction. Not that she could do that without a paying job.

Walk along the stream. The cold mountain stream. In bare feet. This time without twisting her ankle. With Hank at her side.

She picked her head up. "Stop it, Gillian. He backed away from you when you kissed him. Stupidly. And again when you asked him to stay. You shouldn't have done it..."

So many things she shouldn't have done. Like come out here in the first place. She'd known better. She should have fought harder. But what else could she have done?

Maybe she would just sit right there and let the darkness take her. Granted, that was harder with the fresh breeze and the birds singing... If she had rocks and the energy, she'd go out on that big porch and shoo them away so she didn't have to hear their stupid happy chirping.

Maybe she should go out on the porch. The fresh air could help her nausea and her mood, she supposed. A short walk in bare feet... Right. On crutches. With her hands still sore. Very relaxing, that would be.

Maybe a bath with the salts and lavender oil Hank left her. For unwinding, he said. Like it would help. The man didn't at all understand depression. Or her. Or that she could hardly make herself get up out of bed some days because her body was far too heavy and she had no interest in doing anything whatsoever. And she didn't know why. Or what to do about it.

Maybe she'd just curl up in a ball and stay right there until they came and locked her away somewhere so she at least wouldn't be a pain in anyone's ass who wasn't being paid to take care of her.

~ ~

Hank knocked harder. Maybe she actually took his advice and was soaking in the tub. Maybe she wasn't up yet. Checking the watch he almost never wore these days, he decided to plant himself on the rocking chair and wait.

The air was crisper this morning than it had been the past couple of weeks: a sign fall was about to move in. The reward for getting through summer's dog days. Hank loved fall. This first day of the year when he could feel its promise was his favorite day of the year. He no longer celebrated holidays other than a general acknowledgment in his mind of those that mattered. He didn't decorate. Nature did his decorating. His winter squash would need to be pulled before the first frost and stored in the cellar, the side without the ice. Leaves would start to turn suddenly, and soon, he guessed. He would miss having fresh tomatoes, cucumbers, herbs... Maybe his next project would be a greenhouse, a small one.

Would it matter long enough to be worth the effort?

Why not? Many of his carvings wouldn't last long enough for anyone to see them. He did it for himself. Even a couple of years of fresh produce during the winter would be worth it. And maybe more than a couple of years. *Keep a positive outlook.* He heard his friends say it. Heard their voices. Remembered their offer to help in any way they could.

From Denver. They were purposely stuck in their city life. Hank figured he had every bit as much reason to worry about them as vice versa.

And Gillian, who didn't belong in Denver. But could he convince her before she let it destroy her? She was stubborn. Independent. Willful. It wouldn't be easy. Of course, that was the type of woman who could make it without all of the modern conveniences. She would. If she'd try.

He didn't hear any noise from the cottage yet, but he knocked again. "Gillian?" Did she actually sleep this late? In her city apartment where she woke to walls and buildings and traffic, he could understand. Out here in the beauty of the mixed mountains and plains, the blue-winged teals flapping and feeding and swimming along the edge of the pond, tiny lark buntings flitting about the feeders close enough to the cottage to watch them, not close enough for the birds to be bothered by a couple sitting on the porch ... why waste time locked inside just to sleep late?

He watched what looked like a red-tailed hawk floating along the side of the pond, likely searching for breakfast. Hank loved hawks. Something about them spoke to him. Birds of prey, yes, but only enough to survive. No malicious intent. Only nature doing what it did. Taking only as much as it needed and no more. No regret about doing what it needed in order to survive.

Hank sighed, checked his watch again, and knocked harder. "Come on, Gillian. Rise and shine." He paused as he heard himself repeat what he'd heard every morning he was forced to get up for school. On weekends, he was up early, often outside long before anyone else was up. His mother, his saintly mother, told him every weekend morning he needed to, please, wait until she was up before pushing a chair to the door and unlocking the chain to get out so she could at least look out and check on him. It did no good. He liked to be outside first thing in the morning. Except on school days where he knew he'd be confined all day.

And then he'd confined himself. With work.

He shook his head and decided to try her door. Maybe the rattle of it would jolt her awake.

It wasn't locked. He cracked it just enough. "Gillian?" There was no answer, but he heard noise of stuff moving around. "Hey, safe to come in?" Still not getting an answer frightened him, particularly with the door unlocked, so he stepped inside.

She was packing.

"You could have at least answered my knock." He moved closer.

When she saw him, she jumped and pulled tiny earphones out of her ears. "Damn! You could have knocked. About gave me a heart attack."

"I did. Five or six times. Music that loud will ruin your hearing."

"How'd you get in?" She played with the little square thing clipped to her shirt.

"Door was unlocked."

"Couldn't have... Oh. Guess I forgot last night. After I went back out…" She shook her head as though she'd alarmed herself and continued stuffing clothes into the now-bedraggled suitcase with scuffed wheels that he'd carried for her.

"Leaving today?" Hank held his ground.

"Have to get back to work. I told you that."

He nodded. To himself. "I hoped you'd do one last thing with me first."

"Hank, really, I have to go before I get fired." She tossed a bit of deep red lace and black satin into her bag, quickly, trying to hide it.

"Planned to have company while you were here?"

"What?"

He nodded toward the lingerie.

"No." She threw something on top of it and brushed her fingers through her hair, pushing it behind her ear to try to hide the pink creeping into her cheeks.

Hank knew he should leave it alone, but he couldn't help himself. "You wear that for yourself?"

"I… It's none of your business. If you don't mind…"

Rubbing a hand over his jaw, he had to keep from laughing. She was too delightful when she blushed. "Gillian." He moved up to her and set a hand alongside her face. "One more day. I'll call your editor and make it all right, if you want. There's something I want you to see."

She shook her head and pulled away. Her eyes were different. Avoidant. Without even that spark they usually had. Her whole mannerism was withdrawn. It scared him. He could not let her leave that way.

At this point, there was likely only one thing that would change her mind. "I'll let you do the story."

She turned back, silent, questioning.

"Stay the rest of the week and I'll give you my blessing to write whatever you like. I'll even pose for a photo at the cabin, if you want. Let the world see it. If you'll stay four more days."

Her gaze fell to her suitcase and silence fell over the room. It was possible she didn't want to deal with his illness, and he didn't blame her. Neither did he. It scared people. He knew it did because he'd reacted the same. Avoidance. As though that would make it go away.

It didn't, of course.

Well, eventually it did. When the fight ended. At least it did for the fighter. Not for everyone else. It never went away for them. He was sure she didn't need that, either. "You don't have to keep in touch. After the story. Just go home and write it and move on to the next one. Nothing more. Simple."

She raised her eyes, stared a moment, then limped out to the porch. To the rocking chair. Where he stood and watched her. Oblivious to the beautiful nature available as a gift to her senses, she studied the porch floor, the wood planks. They were nice, too. Wood was beautiful; he'd always thought so. But her staring was avoidance, not appreciation.

"Okay. Grab a sweater and come with me."

She didn't acknowledge him, didn't move as much as a finger, so he grasped her hands and pulled her up from the chair. "Where are your crutches?"

"Inside. It's not as bad today." She pulled her hands from his light grasp.

"Good, but I wouldn't push too fast or you'll make it worse again. Can I look at it?"

"It's fine, and I have to pack. Thank you. For everything." She extended a hand. For a handshake.

"Are you kidding?"

"I have to go back to work."

If she thought he was letting her walk away, fly home, with only a handshake, she was seriously misguided. He took her outstretched hand, raised it, and placed a kiss on her palm where it was still healing from the protruding rock.

"Don't do that." Her voice was soft, her eyes moist.

"Gillian, obviously I'm not asking for long-term ... anything. Long-term for me could be a year or two and that wouldn't be fair, so I only..."

She yanked away and went out into the yard.

Hank let a deep breath course through his body and followed to stand behind her. Setting his hands on her hips, he waited to see if she'd pull away again. When she didn't, he kissed her shoulder, her bare shoulder beneath a barely-there tank top. Her body tensed.

It meant something to her. His touch.

Clenching his eyes, Hank swallowed hard. Damned woman. She had to leave, to go back to work. She shouldn't have stayed so long as it was. But not to Denver. She didn't belong there. And not when she was so overwhelmed by whatever was pulling at her, tugging her down. He couldn't stand the thought, especially when she'd as much as admitted to not having anyone to depend on back in Denver. Too risky. She had to at least realize she could count on him, connect with him if needed. Maybe she would write. If she wasn't worried that he would call on her for help.

He slid his hands up and around her stomach, hugging her from behind. Gently. So she knew she could pull away easily if she decided to do so. "Don't be afraid, Gillian. I'm not. It's all right. I've made my peace with it. And I'm sorry I've pulled you in, but you don't need to be concerned about getting too pulled in. I don't have a lot of friends, but I do have good friends I'll count on when I need help. I won't ask it of you. I do get lonely out here, at the cabin, at times, so I'm only asking for your friendship, just for the week if that's all you can do, with no commitment. I don't want you to feel at all obligated…"

She turned, met his eyes, and kissed him. Hard. With her arms wrapping around his shoulders. Not a passionate kiss. Not a friendly kiss. A why-the-hell-didn't-you-back-away-when-you-could-have kiss. A warning. A rebellion.

"Damned woman." He said it out loud, barely, not sure if he meant to say it out loud.

"Probably you're right." Her expression had turned rebellious, as well. "I probably am. Because right now, I'm half hoping whatever you have is contagious and you'll give it to me and I can just stay here and spend my last days with you." She kissed him again, slightly softer, with her fingers tracing down his shoulders, down his arms, and around his waist, hooking around his back.

Hank felt his stomach pull in, felt the beginning longing of wanting to have her. "Gill." He moved back to grasp her hands, to hold them, tightly this time. "It's not. Contagious. And if it was, I sure as hell wouldn't be this close to you."

"I don't think I'd care."

"Why?" When her head shook again, he released one hand to raise her chin. But her lips were shut tight, her eyes back to avoidant.

She couldn't leave. Something too important was going on inside her. Too menacing.

"You're coming with me today. Get a sweater. I'll wait here. But I'm not taking no for an answer."

Sixteen

Gillian scanned the place. She hadn't bothered to ask where they were going or why she needed a sweater in July when it had been so ridiculously hot. A train depot. Specifically, the Durango Silverton Narrow Gauge Railroad. And museum. So it said.

"Do you like trains?"

She shrugged. "Never been on one. Why? Plan to send me home this way instead? I like to fly. And I'm sure it's faster."

"This one wouldn't get you home at all, only up to Silverton and then back here. It's for fun. Sight-seeing. You understand what the word *fun* means, yes?"

She didn't bother to answer. Or question. Even when he said they were taking a bus. At a train station. Because they would have had to be there before eight a.m. to take the train there and back and he wasn't sure she'd want that much train journey.

Gillian used her crutches because it would look ridiculous to carry them instead, but she did put a touch of weight on her foot, enough to take pressure off her hands.

The bus wasn't a run-of-the-mill city bus. It was a huge shiny white thing with big windows, and since he let her choose their seats, she went all the way to the back. She always had. Whenever possible. She hated having people behind her when she couldn't see what they were doing, what they might be throwing that would land in her hair or startle her. Not that adults on this bus heading to a probably ridiculously expensive train ride, just to ride on a train, would be childish enough to throw anything. Still, some things lingered.

He didn't question her choice. She slid over by the window, stuck her walking sticks as out of the way as possible, and looked out. Not at him.

He'd let her kiss him. She couldn't claim he returned it, really, but he allowed it. Even if she shouldn't have done it.

It was a dare. A you-should-have-let-me-just-go-home statement. He'd accepted the dare and hadn't backed down. A worthy opponent. Except she wasn't up to the fight. Any fight.

At least her stomach had settled. She supposed she wouldn't

throw up all over him. Just in case, she had a couple of plastic grocery bags tucked inside her handbag.

Glad he allowed her the quiet she wanted while looking out at rocks – rocks and trees and narrow road and mountains and steep drop-offs and water, repeated ad nauseam until she was nearly nauseated again – she was glad when the bus finally pulled into a gravel parking area and kicked them out. With time before their scheduled train departure, Hank took her for a casual lunch at the Brown Bear Café and suggested she might want more than a salad since it was a somewhat long ride back.

With a quick excuse of eating too much the night before, Gillian used very little of the Italian dressing she'd requested and ate slowly and carefully while he talked about the ghost towns in the area and the mine tour and that he appreciated Silverton being still a rough small west town rather than transformed into a tourist trap. He was trying to get her to talk and she knew he was, but it was all she could do to simply function. He hadn't asked if she wanted to come, hadn't asked if she liked trains before he got her there. It wasn't her fault if she wasn't acting appreciative enough. At least she refrained from telling him she'd rather be home in bed.

When he helped her manage getting up into the train, Gillian did look around at the thing. She had to admit the presidential car with Pullman seats and only two other couples sharing their space was nice. Gorgeous, really. Even if the burgundy floral velveteen, or maybe real velvet, on the seats clashed with the blue square overly patterned carpet. Maybe it didn't quite clash, but it was too much pattern. Too much color. Even the ceiling was patterned. Just too much. She would have been happier if he'd taken her onto one of the regular train cars like regular people, or even on the one that was all windows with an open top.

Or she was trying to find reasons not to enjoy the trip. If she allowed herself to be fully honest, the farther they got into the journey, the more she loved the train and its scenery. If she hadn't gotten tired and chilled, Gillian would have stayed out on the observation deck the whole time. That would have defeated whatever purpose Hank had in reserving the presidential car, though, she supposed.

He hadn't talked much, other than to play tour guide and point out spots along the way through the San Juan mountains. Her favorite was the view of the Animus River. She hadn't thought much about it while driving next to it or over it, but from the train far above looking down, it was majestic.

By the time they got back to Durango, she felt guilty for not talking more, for not showing her appreciation. It was stuck inside. Deep inside. She didn't want to talk. She didn't even want to be appreciative. She wanted to be left alone.

And yet she didn't.

He watched her. Closely. Trying to figure out what her problem was, she supposed, as Corey, the ex, always said. *"What's your freaking problem, Gill? Can't you just shake it off and have a good freaking time once in a while?"*

Just shake it off. She'd asked him if he didn't think she would if she could. He'd said he figured she enjoyed wallowing in being unhappy, like it was some kind of *freaking* obsession.

Idiot.

She wished he would have just said what he meant. The word was fucking, not freaking. *Freak* was something entirely different. And he said it entirely too often. She'd thrown a thesaurus at him once. Told him to expand his vocabulary. He hadn't talked to her for two weeks.

Almost two weeks. Then he got lonely, or bored, or something, and insisted on makeup sex she didn't want or need.

The end of the end.

On the way from the Durango train depot back to Carbon Junction, another Zac Brown Band song came on Hank's truck radio and she shoved the thing off.

"Thought you liked them." He didn't argue, just glanced over and kept driving. Back to the inn that was more spacious than her full time place. Or at least that direction.

"Depends on the day."

He chuckled. "Depends on the day? You like music some days and not others?"

"Yes. Especially that happy bouncy click your heels together stuff.

It's okay sometimes. Not other times." Maybe Corey had been right. Maybe she was obsessed with being unhappy. But she didn't think she was. She just couldn't simply snap out of it. It had to run its course.

Like the river. Sometimes it was smooth and sometimes it bumped and crashed over rocks. It couldn't change that; it had to just keep moving along and take whatever came.

"Okay."

She heard a question in Hank's *okay*, but she kept her gaze out the window.

"Did you actually enjoy the train or did you say so to be polite?"

Gillian glanced over at him. "I'm never that polite." Her smirk irritated her. "I mean that I say what I mean. If I hadn't, I would have said so."

"Okay."

"Don't say that again. I may throw a thesaurus at you and then you'll..."

He laughed. "Throw a thesaurus?"

"Wouldn't be the first time. Yes, I mean that literally, but he had it coming."

Hank rubbed his jaw. "You dislike the word *okay* enough to throw a book at someone over it? It's a perfectly good word."

"It's not one word in particular. I don't like constant repetition. It pisses me off."

"Okay."

She threw a glare, but he was smirking again, not looking at her. Effing man. So arrogant. So sure of himself. And she didn't mean *effing*. She meant...

No. She couldn't even think that word about him. In any form. *Not safe, Gillian. Don't go there.*

At least it was a more appropriate word exchange than *freaking*. Effing didn't mean anything else. It was an abbreviation. Perfectly correct.

"Where do you want to eat?"

She startled at his voice, the calmness of it. The friendliness. After she'd been so snippy. Even so, the assumption that she'd want to have dinner with him again annoyed her. "I don't."

He stopped at a light. "You don't know or you don't care?"

"I don't want to eat." She shouldn't have said it that way. But that's what she meant.

Hank put the truck in park and turned to face her. "You barely ate lunch. Or the soft pretzels I got because you barely ate lunch. What's up, Gillian?"

"Nothing's up. I have days I don't eat. Not a big deal."

"That's bad for your system."

"Of course it isn't. People fast all the time. It's cleansing."

"New age hogwash."

"Really? Coming from the man with lavender essential oils? Or does that belong to a girlfriend? Is she out of town for the week? Is that why you're giving me a week to stay? Keeping you from being alone?"

He stared for some time, until the truck behind them honked. Reluctantly, he put it back in drive and remained silent until he turned into a restaurant parking lot. Some hometown no-name restaurant, plain, rectangular, white-painted wood that needed a new coat or two, not even effing shutters to decorate it. She never ate at a place that looked so uncared-for. It felt too much like a sign of what she'd find inside.

Without bothering to ask if it was okay, he pulled into a space in front, turned off the engine, and came around to open her door, handing her the crutches.

"I'm not hungry."

"Fine. Don't eat. I'm starving and I have no wish to upset my system more than I already have. Are you coming in or waiting in the truck?"

He expected her to refuse, to have to talk her into it, but she sighed and accepted his help down. Hank would rather she'd argued, held her ground, since he knew it was more normal for her.

Pushing his luck, or pushing her for a better reaction, he set a hand on her back, which was tricky around the crutches, while he opened the door. Surprisingly, she didn't pull away from him.

"Well hello, Aaron." A burly woman nearly ran them over.

Hank cringed. "Good evening, Mrs..?" He remembered but preferred to let her think he didn't.

"Oh, you're such an awful tease." She looked at Gillian with one of the fakest smiles he'd ever seen, and he'd seen plenty. "Careful about believing anything this one says, dear. He's an awfully good actor. I'm Lila Belle Lithgow Thomas. Call me Belle for short. And what, pray tell, happened to you?" She eyed the homemade crutches.

"Only a twisted ankle." Hank jumped in. "If you'll excuse us..."

"Well of course I won't, not until you introduce me to your *friend*. You've forgotten every bit of polite society rules, Aaron Forrester, living out there by yourself, like I said you would. About time you had a woman at your side. How long has it been?"

He felt Gillian's look and rubbed his fingers along her back. He supposed that answered her *girlfriend* question. "Mrs. Thomas, allow me to introduce Nona Yolanda Dietrich Benning. She's a long-time acquaintance in town for only a short time, so if you'll excuse us now, we have catching up to do."

Gillian didn't skip a beat. "Call me Ms. Benning for short. It was nice to meet you."

Hank had to force himself not to laugh as he steered her around the woman and in through the screen door.

"Nona Yolanda?"

"An acronym of sorts. I've used it before, when I got tired of being asked who I was with and how serious it was every time I set foot in public with a woman."

"And you were out with a lot of different women?"

He paused as the girl walking past told them to seat themselves, and guided Gillian back to a corner table.

"Okay. That wasn't my business. I apologize for the insinuation." She settled in her chair and eyed him across the table. "So what does it stand for?"

"None o' your damn business."

"Really? You used it on me. I think I could know..."

"Nona Yolanda Dietrich Bennett. None o' Your Damn Business." He accented each first letter.

She smiled, the first he'd seen all day.

"And I'm not the way she made me sound."

"Sure you are. I've learned that already. Half of what you say you mean as a joke. And unlike Belle of the ball, I'm smart enough to know which is which, when you're joking and when you're not. At least most of the time. I didn't at first…"

"Didn't take you long."

"Was it a test?"

"Not at all. Just a habit. Not a good one. Gets me in trouble."

"I just bet it does." She leaned forward a smidge. "You should at least be careful to do it to those smart enough to get it."

He shrugged. "Maybe I'm not concerned about those who aren't. And yes, that makes me a snob. You might as well know that."

"I have news for you, Mr. Dennison, or Aaron Forrester, or Henry, or whatever you're currently calling yourself: I already darn well knew that. Doesn't bother me. There are far worse things."

A sigh of relief rushed through his body and dissolved the tension that swept in at the sight of the obnoxious busy-body. Mrs. Thomas knew exactly who he was and she constantly tried to out him, even if she did use his assumed name publicly. It was very likely she drew most of the reporters who had come to find him. One of the upper crust of Durango society, at least financially, the woman hated that he'd spurned society, that he spurned her way of life. Except he didn't. He couldn't care one iota less how she chose to flaunt her money. Not wanting to do so himself was not a dig at her, but she had it in mind that it was. As Gillian said, not smart enough to get it.

So be it. He was smart enough to get around her.

And, apparently, so was Gillian. She would make a good partner for him, from what he'd seen so far. Of course a couple of days could be deceiving. And a partner wasn't what he was looking for.

Or it was. Since things had changed.

Seventeen

Hank watched her face while she checked her phone and closed it without answering. "Someone you don't want to talk to?"

"Not at the moment."

Maybe he shouldn't have brought her to Eno after dinner. She was finally starting to come out of her mood, had a light glint in her eyes, and he didn't want to take her back and drop her off yet. But now, as she surveyed the crowd through the local acoustic band, tables full of people laughing, and couples hanging on each other with drinks in hand, she was sinking back into herself.

"Rather have a martini than coffee?"

She looked at him as though trying to figure out if he was making a point. "No. I'm good with this."

"They have several nice wines, also. Do you drink wine?"

"At times. Not much. Why are you offering?"

"I wouldn't want the coffee to keep you up all night."

"Doesn't matter." She took a good swallow of the almond and vanilla coffee to which she'd added plenty of sugar.

If he ordered wine himself rather than the herbal chai, she might have agreed, he supposed. But it was the last thing he needed while trying to straighten his system back out. "Gillian." He leaned forward over the small, square table. "Tell me you'll consider changing jobs and doing something that makes you happier. Maybe even ... a different city, or somewhere smaller. I'll help you relocate if you need..."

"I'm fine where I am." She drew back against her chair.

"Fine. You're fine where you are? Do you hear yourself? Is *fine* really good enough?"

"Not everyone can make the choices you did. Not everyone is capable..."

"The hell they aren't capable. What they aren't is willing."

"Easy for you to say. Not everyone has your smarts. Not everyone has the same capability..."

"Most would have more capability if they'd work at it instead of playing victim. You should know. You have plenty of smarts."

"Not like you. Not even close. So don't compare..."

"You have every bit as much ability as I have. And I know you have the determination in there somewhere. What you need is the willingness to sacrifice a bit of comfort now in order to have more comfort later. A choice. You make it or you don't."

"A choice. That's it? Just make a choice?" She raised her chin. "I'm smart enough. Yes. But some people get help and some people get pushed back..."

"*Everyone* gets pushed back and *everyone* gets help. When you get pushed back, you figure out how to get up and work around it. When you get help, you need to recognize it and make it work to your advantage and be grateful, not condescending. That's a choice."

"You think I'm being condescending by refusing your offer of help?"

"You are being condescending and you have been since the minute I met you."

"Is that so? Then why are we here tonight?"

"You tell me."

Her chest rose and fell and she turned away, sipping her coffee as she went back to studying the crowd, mainly a young college crowd. Noisy. Cheerful. Hank enjoyed it and he didn't. So much potential in those young energetic faces. So much would be wasted.

"I'm leaving. If you'd rather, I'll call a cab." Gillian stood, grasping for her crutches.

Hank stood beside her and gripped her elbow. "Why have you stayed so long when you kept saying you couldn't?"

"Because I... You asked. And I can see why you were good in business since it's awfully damned hard to say no to you."

"You wanted to say no?"

"No. Yes." She met his eyes. "This is wrong, Hank. I shouldn't have stayed. I've mixed work with pleasure and I know better than to get involved with..."

"With your story subject. Have you decided again to do the story? Is that why you're being so evasive all of a sudden? I told you I'd give you my blessing..."

"If I stay the whole week. A bribe."

He nodded with a deep breath. "Fine. I'll give it to you anyway. Want to go somewhere quieter so I can answer whatever questions you still have? Then you can stay or leave. Your call. I don't want you to feel forced to hang around with me."

Her eyes glistened as she bit her lip, and she pulled away, heading toward the door.

Hell. Hank sighed and motioned to the server he wanted the bill, gave her a good tip, and was stopped by a young woman in a low cut white tank top and nearly painted-on jeans asking him to dance.

"Thank you, no. Excuse me."

A scent of green olives and alcohol drifted from her lips as she leaned closer. "I know who you are. They're talking about you over at that table." She nodded toward a group of middle-aged men who turned away at his glance. "Want to come sit with us? My friends and I find your story fascinating..."

"You have no idea what my story is."

"Sure we do. Everyone does. We think it's cool that you'd walk away from everything to live by yourself, but we figure you get lonely out there wherever you hide. Sure you don't want to come talk with us since your friend left?"

"You realize you're young enough to be my daughter." And not the way Gillian meant it, if he'd started far too early.

The girl giggled and pulled at a strand of hair. "Do you have daughters my age? I bet they love having a daddy like you. I would..."

Hank pulled away before he had to hear more, just in time to see Gillian talking to a man closer to her age, a bit younger, he supposed. She was near the door, edging that direction.

He watched. Waiting. She said she could protect herself. He didn't want to act like she couldn't. Still, the girl was on crutches and it put her at even more disadvantage than the obvious height and strength difference.

Ambling closer, just in case, he saw her pull away and look over at him. Instead of continuing toward the door, she shifted his direction. He took it as a hint and stepped up his pace to meet her, to tell the guy to back off, hoping not to have to do more than that.

Gillian stopped in front of him, raised a hand to his face, and kissed him. Harder than the first two times, and longer.

Hank figured she might be using him to tell the guy she wasn't alone. So be it. If she wanted to play that game, he could play it better. Moving in, he circled her waist with one arm and wrapped the other around her shoulder, holding her head in as he deepened the kiss, feeling only a slight resistance and then no resistance. Her body leaned into his, a hand touched his side, the other the back of his shoulder. He heard the music, the clinking of glasses, laughter, and hoots and hollers, for the kiss, he figured.

People knew who he was. And he couldn't care one iota less if they did.

It wasn't a kiss to tell someone to get lost. It wasn't a vengeful kiss. He'd received those. He knew them for what they were. This was different.

This was real.

Her eyes remained closed when the kiss ended, her head tilted down enough he had to tilt his own to see her face. Not a ploy. Not for an article. Her expression said otherwise. Real.

"Gillian." He whispered beside her ear.

Her arms slipped up around his shoulders, and her mouth touched the side of his face as she spoke. "I didn't mean to be condescending."

"I know. That's why I'm here. Why are you?"

Raising her head, she sighed as she gazed at him. "I don't know. I shouldn't be. But I'm not unhappy when I'm with you, except when I keep telling myself I have to go. I do have to go. For so many reasons."

"Let's walk a bit. Are you up to it?"

She looked down to find the crutches that fell when she released them and a young man handed them to her. Hank thanked him and helped her reposition the things, although he wanted to just leave them and sweep her into his arms and take her back to the inn...

And he couldn't. He had too little strength left. It couldn't lead anywhere.

She looked too tired to walk so they decided to go for a drive instead.

Hank steered out to the edge of Durango, up a hill to a lookout spot where the view of the sparkling city lights would make a nice backdrop to sit and talk, and turned off the engine.

"No." Gillian tensed and pulled away from him.

"What's wrong?"

"Not here. Go back ... to the city. Anywhere else."

He didn't ask why. Starting the engine again, he headed down the hill and sensed her relaxing. "Where should we go?"

"Your place?"

"Gillian..."

"Just to talk. No more. Right?"

"Of course."

She eyed him. He could feel the piercing stare even through the dark. "Henry..."

"Hank."

"No. Just... when I look at you, I see Henry, not Hank. Is that condescending? I don't mean it to be. I just need a Henry right now and that's what I choose to see. Can we leave it at that?"

He was silent a moment as he paused at the crossroads. Left to town or right to his place?

"I'm being a pain in your ass again, aren't I?"

He felt himself nod. "Yes."

"You can take me to the inn. I should go back anyway, call my editor, let her know I'm still alive since I haven't bothered, and..."

"What exactly is a Henry, Gillian?" He kept both hands on the wheel while the truck idled.

"Fair question, I guess. Hard to answer."

"Try."

She nodded. "An equal, on my level, as strong, as stubborn, capable and independent, but ... still reliant on ... on..."

"Others. For his living."

"Yes. As Hank, you're too different and..."

"Hank is who I am."

"Is it?" She shifted closer and took his hand from the wheel. "How much do you need others? In order to survive."

"I don't."

She nodded, biting her lip.

"And you think Henry does?"

"Yes."

"So you want me to be Henry because…"

"I need to matter."

After a minute or two of silence, he released her hand, put the truck into gear, and drove back into Durango, to her cottage at the Inn. Neither of them spoke and he was glad she didn't. She sat still when he'd parked, when he'd turned off the engine, until he opened her door and reached a hand to help her out.

She walked beside him to the door without a word. He opened it, told her good night, and shoved a hand against the door when she started to close it. "Gillian." He stood directly in front of her. "What you need is to figure out what you honestly want. No one can make you feel like you matter until *you* feel like you do. As I said, your job isn't right for you. Find what is. Here."

Moving past her into the cottage, he found a note pad and scribbled fairly legibly. "This is the friend I mentioned who lives down the road. I won't be back in the morning. Sleep in. Take a walk around the pond. Unwind. But call her if you need to reach me before I get here. And for the record, she's more than old enough to be my mother and often acts like she is."

He touched the soft pale skin of her warm cheek. "I want you to be not unhappy, Gillian. You have to do that. It's not in my power. Or anyone else's, either. Remember that. *You* have to do it."

When he left, Gillian felt the huge pit open up inside, the blackness, the gaping hole and its surrounding numbness that made her not give a shit. About anything.

You have to do it. Just like saying *get over it.* Just as bad as effing Corey. *Don't burden me with your problems, Gill. I have my own. Take care of your own issues and just act happy.*

Talk about wasted days. Not only wasted, but exhausting and painful. She shouldn't have come. She should have told Karenne to shove her story and taken the fallout. And she should at least tell her editor she was alive and well, maybe not so well but well enough, but she didn't give a shit about that, either.

Parking on the hillside overlooking the city brought Corey back too far, the makeup sex she hadn't wanted that he pushed her into. In his truck. Despite her saying no. Not their first time or anywhere close, he kept reminding her. Telling her she could enjoy shit if she'd let herself, to let herself enjoy it...

She didn't bother to shower or even brush her teeth. She stripped out of her clothes, left them at the bedside, and slipped under the covers. Not even the luxurious feel of the bedding mattered tonight. Nothing mattered to her tonight, except sleep.

Hank unlocked the door to his townhouse, dropped the keys on the entrance table, and paced.

He didn't want to drive all the way out to the cabin tonight. He wanted to stay close. Why, he didn't know. She could very well take off at any time. First thing in the morning, he'd call Gia in Denver and have her find Gillian's address and number and ... and what?

Damned pain in the ass. He was better off...

But he hadn't quite been truthful. He didn't need people anymore, and maybe he never really had. But need and want were different. He wouldn't tell her he needed her to stay because he didn't. He could function fine on his own. At least for now. Wanting her to stay was entirely different.

Trying to decide his next move, Hank lowered onto one of the few pieces of furniture he'd shipped from his Denver condo, an old chair passed down through his family, and dropped his head in his hands, elbows on his knees. He needed rest. But he'd never sleep tonight.

I need to matter.

She couldn't tell she mattered to him? Why in the hell else would he work so hard to get her to stay as long as possible? She was out of her mind.

Eighteen

Gillian lowered onto the seat beside the tiny double-paned scratched plastic window, latched her seat belt, and felt a tear trickle down her cheek when the plane's engine whirred into motion. Swiping it off fast before anyone saw it, she gritted her teeth and held her stomach.

Two days in a row, she'd had to jump out of bed and rush to the toilet. Afraid of what it might mean, she'd packed quickly while calling Karenne to tell her to book a flight as early as possible. She'd had to nearly run to get to the gate. Her editor apparently didn't allow for transportation time to the airport in the equation of *as early as possible*.

She hadn't called Hank's friend to tell him she was leaving. She didn't leave a phone number or address. She did try to put the cottage bill on her own credit card instead of his, but the woman wouldn't take it. Hank's word was stronger than Gillian's. There was no use fighting it.

Tracing her finger in the fog mark her breath made on the window, she drew a cabin. Hank's cabin. With the fantasy creatures carved in the trees. Why fantasy creatures? She wished he'd answered only that one question. For her own curiosity. She wasn't doing a story on him. She couldn't possibly do a story on Hank Dennison now. She couldn't invade his privacy more than she had, and she damned sure couldn't let herself dwell on him enough to do a story.

She would miss him. Gillian missed him already. But he didn't need to deal with her issues on top of what he was already fighting, and he definitely didn't need to deal with the newest mess she'd probably gotten herself into. She did it. She would deal with it.

But she would miss him.

Hank sat in his truck outside the Apple Orchard Inn and went over last night's conversation in his mind. She'd left without a word. He wasn't surprised. He was, however ... what? Unsure how to describe his feelings about the whole thing, he decided to go on to the cabin and get to work, get himself back on track. Purge out the restaurant food and the turmoil of the past few days. Get back to focusing on his own life.

She had to make her own choices.

He had to make his.

Allowing a long, deep breath, he turned the engine over, peered out the window toward the cottage he'd hoped would help bring her respite, enough to see what she was missing, and with a shake of his head, turned his wheels toward home.

Except he stopped at Susan's store to use the phone. With a quick call to Gia, Hank asked her to find an address and phone number for Gillian Hart. He had to answer the minimal questions of how he was feeling while she had him on the phone, and she asked three times what was wrong and who, exactly, Gillian was to him. He couldn't answer.

"Please, just find her info for me and send it along. Will you?"

"You know I will. Should I contact her? Anything else you need me to do?"

"Don't contact her, but do you mind if I give her your phone number in case she needs anything? She's on her own out there. I'm not sure she actually will, since she's independent as holy hell, but I'd feel better if she could."

"Of course. And she sounds like someone else I know."

"Can't even argue. Thank you, Gia. I have to run. Tell Curtis hello."

"Hank, are you sure you're okay?" Her voice echoed concern. "Do you need us to come?"

"No. I'm doing fine."

"You promised me you'd say so if you need us."

"And I will. Right now, I only need you to do this for me. Please."

"Of course. Take care, you."

With a thank you to Gia and another to Susan, he tried to leave, but she insisted he stay for lunch, for her special homemade noodle soup in which she used zucchini for noodles and filled it with sweet potatoes, cabbage, flaxseed, carrots, and assorted herbs. She pressed for information about this girl who had him rattled, and Hank gave her the basics.

"Sounds like that girl has some issues. You sure you need to get yourself involved in all that?"

"That was absolutely my first thought, that I don't need this. I came out here to unwind, de-stress, and I've been telling myself I shouldn't get involved. But, if the last thing I get to do on this earth is to help Gillian Hart come into what she could be, I think I'll be far happier when it comes time to let go. She needs someone, Susan. Besides, who knows how many she'll pass it along to if she gets help, or if she doesn't? I think she could make a difference, more than she realizes."

"After all the times you cursed the media, the *damned reporters*, so you've said how often? It's one of them you want to help?"

"Well." He finished the last of his iced green tea with raspberry infusion, using actual homegrown raspberries, and sat back against the chair. "Maybe I had one last thing to learn."

"Don't talk that way. You've got a lot o' life ahead of you. I know it. Don't argue. More tea?"

"Guess I'll hope you're right. And these days, I have more reason to hope you're right. Thanks, have to get going. I want to get started on building a greenhouse."

Nineteen

"Come on, Gilly. Enough is enough. You've been home for three weeks and you've hardly said two words about what happened out there." Karenne raised the large paper cup marked as chai latte sweet no whip, with her name boldly written across the top along with a smiley face, from the young male barista she always flirted with, Gillian supposed, and sipped noisily with her too-red lips barely touching the black plastic lid.

"Doesn't matter." She sipped her own barely sweetened and lightly scorched Folgers with a touch of creamer from the mug she kept at work and thought about the Durango Coffee Company. Hank said he'd have to take her, to introduce her to their organic French roast. He only drank organic coffee these days, as much as possible. He'd thrown out his own rule about that, and about restaurant food, often the few days she was there. She hoped it wouldn't hurt him.

She thought of him too often and usually let herself revel in the memories of walking with him, just talking. But she had to put herself back into work. "Where are we on the trash strike story?"

"It's covered." Karenne set her cup down and stood, a sign of annoyance. "I want you on the local food story. Go out and talk to people at farm markets. Get their take, their reasoning. See how much they actually know about where food comes from, how it's processed, if they think organic is sustainable, if they really know much about the GMOs they protest..."

"Why?"

Setting a hand against her hip, Karenne gave her that look, as though Gillian was not allowed to ask questions, like she was back in the school days of *listen, don't speak.*

With a swallow of her coffee she wished was organic French roast, she tried a different track. "Fine. I mean, number one, why are you moving me from the strike story, and number two, why are you doing it at the end of farm market season?" Did her editor know more about what Hank was doing now than she admitted? The sudden correlation struck Gillian as odd. She wanted to ask, but she didn't want to feed her editor any tips, which Karenne had been pushing hard to get.

"Number one, you apparently don't want the big stories, since you blew the one I sent you on, and number two..." She brushed the salon-do hair beside her face and shrugged like it didn't matter. "Because I'm your editor and I assign stories as I see fit."

Gritting her pride from inside, without letting it show, Gillian refused to let it get to her. "That story should have been done at the beginning of market season, when I first suggested it, not now while the season's ending. Who cares now?"

"You know what? I'm not asking. As I said, you blew the one I sent you on, the one I really wanted..."

"And you sent someone else to do it after you told me you wanted it only for my own good. Obviously not true. But I told you I'd repay the plane ticket and hotel expenses..."

"There's nothing to repay." Karenne returned to her soft leather chair and held the hem of her tight above-the-knee skirt while she adjusted her crossed legs to keep it from riding too high. "And Kevin can't get near the guy. He's not talking. To anyone. The jerk actually pulled a shotgun on him."

Gillian tried hard not to laugh, then set a hand on her stomach and fought the sudden nausea. "Then leave him alone."

"Sick again?"

"Look, just leave him alone, okay? I'll do the food story, or any other pissant thing you want to put me on. I don't care. Just leave him alone." She had to get up, out of the office. Fast. Third time today. That's what she got for eating. She couldn't keep anything down.

Her editor followed this time and stood with a hand on her hip staring when Gillian came back out of the stall. "You need to see a doctor. You may have something nasty you brought back from out there."

She cleaned her mouth out, then washed her hands and her face. She didn't bother with makeup anymore unless she was going out for an interview. "I did see one. I'm not contagious, as I said. Please, would you just do me that one favor?"

"Which one is that, Gilly? How many have you asked for since you got back?"

"The only one that matters. Leave him alone." Her eyes watered and she turned away to try to hide it.

Karenne moved in. "What aren't you telling me? If the man wasn't like sixtyish and rather unattractive, from what I've heard, I'd think..."

"He's not sixtyish. He's forty-nine. And he looks ten years younger than that. He's very attractive. Very sexy, really, if you must know..."

"Sexy? Hank Dennison?" Her jaw dropped for a second. "You *slept* with him."

"No."

"Tell me the truth."

"I am telling you the truth." Her stomach growled as though she could do anything about it.

"No? Then who did you sleep with? Because my guess is you're pregnant."

"You guessed right, but it's none of your business and it was not Hank Dennison, or anyone else having anything to do with the story I didn't write and ... and what do you mean there is nothing to pay back?"

"Your bill was paid. All of it: hotel, food, and car rental. We even got reimbursement for the plane ticket. So tell me again you're not carrying Hank Dennison's kid and that's why you're covering for him."

Paid. He paid it all? Her head shook; her eyes watered. Damn hormones. No wonder she'd been so emotional when she went out there. The dizziness. The emotions. Fatigue.

At least the ankle was good by now. Just a sprain. She'd done well to stay off of it, her doctor said.

He paid her expenses. After she'd been so bitchy. After she'd left without telling him. He even sent his effing address and friend's phone number, not only the one in Carbon Junction, just down the road from him, but one in Denver. Someone he said she could trust if she needed help.

Damned man just couldn't leave well enough alone.

"So what do you plan to do, Gilly?" Karenne handed her a paper towel to dab her eyes.

"About what?"

"Are you serious? The kid you're carrying. What are you going to do? Are you at least in contact with the father?"

"No, and I won't be. What do you think I'll do? I'll have him on my own. So I'll do your food story, but don't send me on anything risky. No paragliding or whatever in the hell else comes to your mind."

"You're sure about this?"

"I'm not sure about anything anymore. But this happened, so it happened. I'll deal with it like I deal with everything: one hour at a time."

"There's always adoption, you know. You might give that baby to someone better equipped to handle a kid, since you're not apparently interested in the father, anyway. In the meantime, try saltines or oyster crackers. Worked for me. This should pass soon." She walked out.

"Thanks for the congratulations." With sarcasm dripping from her voice, Gillian knew Karenne hadn't heard her. She didn't want her to hear. She wouldn't give her the satisfaction of knowing her insult had cut too deep.

With the excuse of scouting out the food story, Gillian left the office, got safely to her car, and lay her forehead on the steering wheel to regroup. Someone better equipped? Did she mean financially or mentally? Hard to tell. Either way... Someone better equipped to be his mother than his own mother? Gillian was self-supportive, barely, but she was. She was thirty-two. She was, she thought, reasonably stable, other than the depression, and maybe that's what Karenne meant. But women did it through harder struggles. She would never hurt her child. Would it affect him too much? She couldn't even keep a boyfriend around. Should she do this?

Apparently God or nature thought she could do this. It wasn't like she'd been trying to. She was trying not to and it happened anyway. She could do this. One hour at a time. Like everything else. Isn't that what everyone did, whether or not they admitted it?

Determination kicking in, Gillian shoved Metallica in the CD player and focused on James Hetfield's voice talking about planet earth dying. She started to think maybe the songwriter needed to visit Hank's cabin and look around at the gorgeous living breathing nature, and then pushed herself away from the thought. She couldn't let herself think of him and his cabin until she stabilized herself.

It wasn't a big deal. Women had kids all the time and often on their own. So could she. Her only issue was her low-paying job, but she could fix that, too. Her email kept bringing offers of copywriter training. She'd started looking up job opportunities for freelancers to write copy for ads and found plenty. Not something she would particularly enjoy doing, but she could do it. She was good at selling, at convincing people she was right. It's why she was so good at her job, why she got the stories where it was hard to get people to talk. She could convince them when others couldn't. How much harder could copywriting be?

A long, loud honk behind her made her jump and she noticed the light was green. For all of two seconds, she imagined. People had no patience. They were all about themselves. Sure, asshole, make a pregnant sick depressed single woman jump a mile in her seat because you can't wait two damned seconds after the light turns.

She eased out slower than she normally would just because he pissed her off, and because she didn't feel good, and turned off onto a less used road. It would take her longer to get home that way, but she wanted less traffic.

Honestly, she wanted to be left the hell alone. Like that would happen in Denver.

In the woods in the mountains outside Carbon Junction, it would.

Stop it, Gillian. It doesn't matter anymore. You're carrying some other asshole's kid. You can't go...

And he was an asshole. That was the hell of it. She didn't even like the kid's father. Stupid decision to start dating him. Too many martinis. And now...

Because she didn't have enough issues already.

Pulling into a parking space on the fairly quiet street, Gillian made sure her doors were locked, shoved the CD off when the Justice song came on because she couldn't deal with that, too, dropped her head on the steering wheel, and allowed herself to cry. Or rather she couldn't stop it.

What had she done? It was all her own doing. At least she recognized it was her own doing, her own choices, that got her where she was. She didn't even *like* sex with Corey. That was the kick of the whole thing. She had never enjoyed it much after the first guy, the only one she'd really wanted, the one she was happy with until he decided he couldn't deal with her depressive episodes and walked away during one of her "cold" spells, as he called it. He'd tried to come back once. Gillian told him to get lost; if he couldn't deal with her in good and bad, she didn't want him. It was the right thing to do. Karenne agreed she couldn't let him come and go. Still, it had taken a lot out of her willingness to really try again.

Talking with Hank had been nice, though. She didn't care if he didn't want more than long talks, walking together, an occasional nice dinner, and maybe theatre every now and then. Or a concert, if he would go to something besides a country act. She might even agree to do that with him.

And yet he'd dumped her when she said she needed to matter. He took her back to the hotel and dumped her off, like all the rest. Because she didn't matter. What good was she doing anyone? Even her job had become no more than a paycheck. A *food story*. Why did it matter? People were going to eat what they wanted no matter what she said. And why shouldn't they? Why should her opinion matter to anyone in the world? What made her think she had a right to ... to tell anyone else what they should think?

She didn't.

Hank was right.

She'd become a journalist to inform, to get the facts out there to people so they could decide, and instead... She wasn't a journalist. She was an opinion columnist. Like almost everything she read recently.

Sniffing hard to control herself, Gillian reached into her center column for tissues, found an empty package, cursed, and leaned over to grab fast food napkins out of her glove compartment.

"Ohhwww..." Pressing a napkin to her face to stop the nasal drip, she set the other hand against a pain in her stomach. "Don't do this." She found herself breathing too fast and forced it to slow. "Please. Be okay. Don't do this." She looked down at her hand over her stomach, where the baby she hadn't let herself think much about made its presence known. Strongly.

She had to take care of herself better. She had to calm down ... for the sake of this child, this innocent little life depending on her...

Gillian's hands shook. Her tears started again. She most definitely mattered. At least to this little one, she did. Everything she did now mattered.

Giving in to the release, she turned off the engine and reached, more carefully this time, for more napkins.

"Okay, little one. It's you and me in this together, right? We'll teach each other how to do this?" A warmth built up from within and she found herself smiling at nothing. Not at nothing. At this little life she created, even unintentionally and rather unwillingly. And she did want it. Deeply. She couldn't remember the last time she wanted anything half as much.

"I'll do my best for you, sweet baby." Gillian lightly massaged her stomach as her tears dried, as her breathing calmed. "Starting right now. And maybe try to be a little bit easy on me, okay? Can you do that?" If the child was even a little bit easy on her, it would probably be the first easy thing in her life. That would be a very nice switch.

Unwilling to go home to the empty apartment quite yet, she surveyed the street and found a little diner. That would work. It was out of the way enough it shouldn't be too crowded, but she wouldn't be alone.

Gillian checked her face, ignored her red eyes, and shoved a hand through her hair. Good enough. She grabbed her red leather briefcase, a splurge but not as much as it looked since it was on a seventy-five percent clearance when she bought it after looking at it for months, and held her head up as she made her way to the diner.

The greasy hamburger smell that hit her when she opened the door was truly ... luscious. Okay, but it was. Still, she had to start eating better and so she ordered a chef salad with dressing on the side and an iced tea with no sugar. Maybe she should do water instead for no caffeine, but she was a caffeine addict and cutting down too fast would only give her headaches she didn't need. She would cut down slowly.

And she would get back on her treadmill, which she hadn't touched since she got back from Durango. First, her ankle needed time to heal and then she just didn't care.

"Are you okay?"

Gillian assured the gray-haired sweet-faced waitress she was fine now and thanked her for the tea. Pulling her notepad out of the briefcase along with her favorite pen, she started a letter that had to be written. For herself if nothing else.

How to start it, though? Out on the sidewalk, a middle-aged couple held hands as they ambled by, talking, in agreement about something or other, so it appeared by their expressions and nods. A beautiful sight.

Gillian sighed. She wanted that.

Turning back to the blank notepad, she stopped over-thinking and jumped in:

Dearest Henry,

I had to write to apologize for my abrupt departure. As I was flying out, I thought of the coffee shop we were supposed to visit and ... and of your eyes. You have beautiful eyes, you know. I suppose someone has told you as much plenty often, but I'm writing this without my editing cap on and just letting it flow while I can make myself do it, so you'll have to get whatever you get...

Twenty

... My salad is sitting here getting warm, so I suppose I should eat and get home and on my new path. You were right, of course. I was on the wrong path, but if I haven't quite found my way by now, at least I'm headed that direction, I believe. Thank you for being right and willing to say so. I am forever grateful for the very little time I had with you as both Henry and Hank and I wish you all the very best with a very full heart.

Be well. Stay warm up there in that cottage, sorry, cabin, this winter. I'll be thinking of the beauty of your view, the silence of the soft snow as it falls around you, and of those magnificent carvings you wished I hadn't seen. Maybe I understand them now.

Things have a way of changing as new life appears, and before long, I'll be thinking of you having to give up bathing in your gorgeous mountain stream. In the meantime, do be careful of your footing. The rocks are slippery.

All my best.

Love, Nona Yolanda

Hank rubbed his scruffy chin as he sat outside the post office and looked at the envelope again. It had her address along with the fake name he'd given her. Protecting his identity or her own?

He'd finally shaken off that pushy guy who'd been sent to do his story. Obviously, Gillian had been good to her word and refused to do it. She didn't say if she was still working there at all or if she'd been fired for refusing. She'd said damn little.

But she'd written. And she seemed ... not unhappy. Maybe she met someone...

The thought of it put a pit in his stomach and he had to stop thinking of it, of her with someone else.

Gillian with someone else wasn't right.

Love... She'd started with Dearest and ended with Love. Purposely. She was a writer. She chose her words to be the way she meant them, not off-hand and carelessly as many did. Dearest and Love.

Dearest Love.

He couldn't keep sitting there in the ten minute parking spot where he could not make himself pull out from until he'd torn open the envelope and read her words, so he put the truck into drive. But he didn't want to head back to the townhouse where he'd been staying much of the time since she left. He'd spent a few nights at the cabin determined to get himself back on track, but he couldn't make himself work. Mainly, he sat on the front porch and sulked. When that weighed too heavily on him, he returned to the townhouse, did some research while he was there, did a lot of reading at night, and wandered the sidewalks or trails during the day when he couldn't force himself back out to the cabin to start winter preparation. Offers of companionship came along while he dined by himself or sat out along the river with a book in hand, but he'd shaken them off, also.

Companionship wasn't what they wanted. Not the kind he wanted.

Pulling onto a side street with open parking spots, Hank nearly jumped out of the truck and stuffed the letter in his jacket pocket. Unsure where he was headed, he walked and thought of her, of her letter. New path. Thank you. It didn't sound like she was angry with him, as he'd expected, for his abrupt drop-off.

She was only thirty-two. Too young to be tied up with him, especially given the circumstances, but she wouldn't be tied up for long, he expected. She was active and healthy, or at least healthy-ish, and she could easily start again, easily attract someone else later...

Stop. You can't think that way.

He paused in his tracks and took a long deep breath of fresh mountain air ... not as fresh as at his cabin. His cottage. He chuckled and started to walk again.

Finding himself in front of the coffee company, he took another deep breath and went in. While waiting for his coffee, he wandered and found a notepad set. He bought it along with his coffee and at second thought, added a pound of organic French roast whole coffee beans, and a coffee grinder.

He sat close to the window and opened the notepad.

Dearest Nona,
In lieu of having coffee together this morning, I'm making the best of it and

sitting at Durango Coffee Company — excuse the non-masculinity of this letterhead as it was the most masculine they had to offer — sipping on the most luscious organic French roast I've ever found and looking out over the mountains where the Aspens and Oaks are already beginning to boast their yellows and reds, reminding me of you. Your red aggression and your yellow cheerfulness echo through my thoughts...

What a sap I am. My apologies.

If tourists plan to be here during the best of Aspen Gold season, they will have to make earlier plans than usual, with the early chill in the air. It will soon be a magnificent time to sit on my cabin porch and soak in the changing nature. You are right, of course. Everything changes with time. Perhaps it's worth a revisit...

Hank stopped and rubbed his chin. Why the hell not? Probably wouldn't get an answer, anyway. Her letter sounded like a final tie-up. She might not even bother to read his ramblings.

There was no one else he wanted to talk to, so he kept going.

Considering what he'd written, Hank accepted a refill of his coffee and watched people walking around in jackets or bare-sleeved. Most times he would have been bare-sleeved, as well, even in the chilly mountain air of early September. He grew cold more easily than he used to. Age, he supposed. Or at least he hoped it was only age. Of course he also had less fat cushion than he used to have. He was almost ashamed of the way he'd let himself go through those years of constant work and frivolous relationships. Fueled mainly on fast food or high calorie sugar-filled restaurant meals, it was inevitable he'd gain weight.

Living in the cabin cured that faster than he expected. On top of being invaded by cancer cells.

He wouldn't think of it. Positive thoughts. He'd trained himself to be positive, to be calm, to let go of things that didn't matter enough to risk his health.

Still, he thought of her constantly.

It was time to get back to work, more than simply cutting wood to add to the firewood pile and adding to his canned goods and bottled mountain water supplies. At least he'd heard from her. He would have heard sooner if he'd bothered to check his mail. The letter had been sitting there for nearly two weeks. Now that he knew she was doing well, he could go on with things, start taking better care of himself again.

First, he stopped back at the post office and threw the letter, the coffee, and the grinder into a box, with some packing help from the sweet lady who worked there and always had a big smile. He addressed it to G. Hart. No first name, but at least her real name. For her privacy, he listed his PO Box address without his name. The sweet lady looked at him curiously for that but said nothing.

Time to get back to the cabin and resume life.

Halfway back, thoughts of her slammed in too hard: thoughts of the life he wanted and had a glimpse of when she was there being a pain in his ass, which felt far too much like his last chance at it. Hank had to pull over as the past several years jammed together with what he nearly might have had. The illness. The despair. Anger. Recovery. Through it all, he'd kept his cool, more or less, after the fit of anger passed. And he rebuilt his life. Again. Away from the long years and long hours of building up. He'd just walked away.

Not that he had a lot of choice. He had no strength to run it. Too many days he couldn't even get out of bed, his body was so weakened by the chemo he'd agreed to start, for a short time, until he walked away from that, too. It was his. His business. His legacy. He didn't want it destroyed or transformed. So he shut it down.

And he was the bad guy.

Every damned reporter who showed up threatened to make what he'd kept secret public with their constant digging as to why he'd done what he'd done. It wasn't their business. He'd built it with his own hands, his own work, seventy to ninety hours a week between three different jobs and living on next to nothing while he saved everything to build up his own investment where he'd risked every penny and then some on that business. He'd provided thousands of jobs throughout the years, well-paying jobs with decent benefits. He hadn't turned on his employees. They'd turned on him by voting for higher and higher business taxes and asking for more and more benefits until his thriving business threatened to fall to red tape and greed, worrying his gut non-stop for months until it became a physical illness. And they called him greedy.

He laughed in between the frustration, the tears. So many damned years of working so hard, of helping so many, and he was the bad guy. He'd nearly stayed in bed and let the cancer do what it wanted.

But his mountains called to him, the ones he could barely see at a distance from his office windows when he could make it in to his office. So he'd walked away.

For what?

She wanted to matter? He laughed again, frustrated laughter. No one mattered. No one didn't matter. Everyone just was. He'd accepted that by now and it was fine with him. What mattered was spending his days in peace and letting the world go on past without him. He'd gotten used to that idea, as well. He had nothing left to leave behind other than whatever carving work survived for however long, and he was good with that.

Well, the money, of course. He shrugged and wiped his face with his flannel shirt tail. Some of it was marked for things he supported. He had no heir, no family to speak of, no one who had stood by him through the worst of his illness other than Gia and Curtis. In Denver. And they were doing fine on their own, always reaching out to others in need. And Susan, who was already listed in his will. He wanted to support her work to try to help others get back to nature...

Calmed by the sudden thought, Hank cleaned himself up, turned the truck around, popped Zac Brown in the CD player, and went to find a phone.

Twenty-one

Gillian wrote while she walked. On her treadmill, slowly. Her third freelance job was on her laptop. Three accepted job requests in her first week made her wonder why she hadn't done it before. Trying to get into the heads of people purchasing whatever each company was trying to sell was her niche. She was good at it.

"Don't worry, little tiny one. Mommy is going to take care of you just fine."

The term *Mommy* made her stop walking. She hadn't called herself that before, but every day she felt more like one. She didn't even mind the morning sickness much anymore, and it was better since she'd learned so much while writing the local foods and farm market story for Karenne. She was eating better. She felt better.

She felt ... not unhappy. Of course, some of that could be from the oils Hank had Susan send her. Uplifting and soothing oils: lemon, orange, Ylang Ylang, bergamot, sandalwood, plus lavender, which made her chuckle when she saw it. She switched them out in her diffuser that was sent with it depending on her mood. The man apparently didn't intend to simply let things go between them. He was definitely some kind of Don Quixote on a rescue mission of sorts, and it was working, since some of what kept her mood raised was his continued correspondence.

Much of it, though, was the little life inside.

Smoothing a hand over her rounding stomach, she went back to work. Gillian thought best on her feet. Combining exercise and work was perfect for this job. The fresh air she got while walking around farmers markets for the story didn't hurt, either, even if it wasn't as fresh as Hank's mountain air.

She thought of him often, especially at night when she tried to sleep. Maybe after little one came, she'd go visit, check on him, show off what she was doing and let him know all was well.

Mostly well. Evenings got lonely. When she paused to enjoy the turning leaves, she got lonely, but she smiled through it while remembering his comment about her red aggression and yellow cheerfulness. She didn't think she'd been all that cheerful while she was there. Her thoughts had been too full of *I don't want to do this*. Except when it turned to *I don't want to go home*. Dinner and theatre and ambling the sidewalks of Durango with pleasant conversation. Mostly pleasant.

Mostly she wanted to visit to show him who she really was. Optimistic. Steady. Determined. Dependable. She was. Even through her long-term depression and shorter term depressive episodes, she managed to tell herself it would pass again and things would be okay. At least deep in the back of her mind, she could tell herself as much. It was enough to get her through.

At a knock on her door, she frowned, slowed, and got off carefully. She did everything carefully these days in order to protect sweet baby.

Leaving the chain in place, she peeked around the corner to find an elegant lady a bit older than herself wearing what looked like a Versace jumpsuit.

"Gillian Hart?" The friendly face also had a friendly voice.

"Who's looking for her?"

"I'm Gia Forrester Franklin, Hank's friend. He said he mentioned me in a letter."

Hank's friend. Gillian froze as she stared at the woman.

"I'm sorry to just drop in, but he rather insisted and I never have the heart to turn him down. I won't ask to come in since I wouldn't appreciate a stranger doing that to me, but I have a bit of shopping to do in the area and thought I'd treat myself afterward with a smoothie at ink! Coffee. I don't do coffee, but I love their smoothies and the view... Anyway, I'd love if you'd join me. Will an hour work for you?"

She talked fast and Gillian had to let the mental dust settle before everything sank in. She said the first thing that came to her tongue. "How is Hank?"

The woman grinned. "Worried about you, which is why I'm here. You must have done something to that man to make him go to such trouble. He doesn't usually, you know."

"You're ... a friend, as in ... girlfriend, or ex?" It was rude, but she had to know.

Gia laughed. "Oh, heavens no. My husband worked for him. We came all the way from Indiana to work for him and ... well, we liked it here, so we stayed after he closed shop. My family isn't happy about it, but when you get to a place you feel is really home, you have to stay there, you know?"

Gillian shrugged.

"You haven't found that yet? Well, keep looking. It matters. Anyway I'm rambling and you're..." She cast her eyes down at what Gillian was wearing, a skinny tank top and thin stretchy capris, her normal treadmill clothes. "You're expecting."

She looked down at herself. She did show, but not a lot and...

"So, you and Hank are ... well, more than he admitted?"

"No. It's not his. We haven't..." Heat flooded her cheeks and spread to her ears. "Um, come in, but never mind the disaster. I'm working two jobs and..." She didn't bother to finish the sentence while she undid the chain and let Hank's friend inside, apologizing for the clutter.

"No, don't worry." Gia took her hand. "So you have someone already? Does he know?"

"No. I mean, I don't. This..." She set a hand over her child. "This was very unintentional, a... I can't say mistake because I couldn't admit later that I ever called it one, but it was accidental. I'm very much single."

"Okay. Again, does he know?"

"No." Her eyes moistened. "I didn't know yet when I was there. You said he's okay?"

"He's... He just moved back to the cabin a couple of weeks ago or so. He hadn't been able to be there much since you left." Gia set a hand to her mouth. "I said too much. Sorry. I'm a talker. My husband says so all the time..."

"Where has he been?"

"His townhouse. He goes there when he needs to rest."

Gillian walked away, trying to let everything settle. *Needs to rest.* She turned back. "He's not okay, then? Is he..?"

"He's a fighter. Always was. And a good-looking one for his age, too. If I wasn't so married and so in love with my dear husband, I'd be tempted, actually. He's... Please, come with me today. Are you busy?"

"I'm working."

The woman looked around at the laptop and treadmill. "Well, how about a break? We'll go shopping and have a smoothie or whatever you want and talk more. Please. It'll make him feel better."

Gillian managed to get it out of the very talkative woman that the mountain air was part of his recovery, or at least endurance, so he insisted. It seemed a hard place to recover, with so much work just for everyday survival. But then she'd heard of people increasing their workouts for illness recovery, so maybe it did. Modern life wasn't physically hard, at least not for many. Her treadmill was proof of that. She wouldn't need it out there in the mountains. There was wood to chop, and water ... well, he did have a well and a generator so maybe that wasn't a big deal. He didn't have a microwave or air conditioning. He grew a lot of his own food.

It would either make you stronger or kill you, as the saying went. Maybe he'd gone to take his chances.

A shudder went all the way through her core as she opened her door after three hours and more of shopping and eating and chatting and wandering along the river in the park, sitting now and then to regain energy.

Gia was fun, she had to admit. Gillian wouldn't mind spending time with her now and then...

But she had to see him. Gillian had to go check on Hank in person. She had to explain everything and not through a letter. She could still fly. It was early yet. She'd read all the dos and don'ts of pregnancy. Flying was still okay.

Before she ran through the shower and went back to work, Gillian got on her laptop and looked up flights to Durango. A cheap redeye was fine. On Monday she'd call Karenne and say she was working on a story and wouldn't be in the office for a few days.

She only needed a few days. A couple of days to see him and explain and have coffee if he still wanted to do that, then a redeye back and a day to recover.

She should wait, though. She'd go after the baby came and take him to introduce to Hank. It would give her time to quit thinking of him constantly first.

Deciding to go last minute was only fueled by Gia talking about him, and that wasn't a good enough reason. Gillian had to give herself time to think more about it. Impulsivity got her into too much trouble. It was time to slow down and make herself reason things out rather than jumping.

Twenty-two

With a warm coffee cup in her hand, Gillian looked out over South Platt River at the trees nearly in their peak season while Gia talked about the flat land of her Indiana hometown and her family, mainly about her favorite cousin Eli and his newest child, the third so far, and how the family was taking bets about whether his wife would give in for a fourth. A friendly happy wager, the way it sounded. He'd "captured" his wife on the east coast while working there, a Jersey girl, no less, and convinced her to move to his farm town. They had plans to visit Ireland, but children kept coming along.

Gillian considered saying they should have learned how to prevent that, but she had no room to talk. And it sounded like those little ones were the delight of the family, at least to his cousin who didn't get to see them in person very often but took full advantage of video messaging and sent them Colorado gifts.

"So, enough about my family." Gia smoothed her fingers, boasting well-manicured rust-colored fingernails, along her pixie-like haircut that was longer at the front and sides than most pixie cuts, to move a strand of hair behind her ear. "You haven't said anything about yours."

"Nothing to say, really. I'm the black sheep. Haven't talked to any of them in ages and I couldn't care less."

The hand waved through the air, dismissing the thought, or her family. Gia was highly expressive with her hands. Showing them off, maybe, with the pretty, long fingers that matched her tall, thin figure. She was taller than Gillian by a couple of inches, as a guess. And stronger-boned, but not close to stocky. Her face, though, was daintily triangular with small features. A beautiful, vivacious woman. Gillian could easily see her with Hank, to be honest. "You know..." Gia often interrupted her own sentences with a swallow of her smoothie. "Usually the black sheep is the most interesting for one reason or another. I imagine you would be, more than the rest."

A snicker escaped before Gillian could stop it. "Yeah. Interesting. The only one not married by the time I was twenty-two and producing kids by the time I was twenty-three. The only one not in a real job, so they say, as in working with their hands, mostly in the earth, some with cars or in construction. But all real jobs that *matter*." She stopped at her own words. She'd heard it often. *You're not doing anything that matters, Gee. Time you grew up, isn't it?* "The only one in the family who doesn't matter because I left instead of joining the family business or at least staying there in the middle of nowhere with no opportunity. I'm too uppity now, they say. Maybe they're right."

"Oh, Gillian." Gia took her hand and squeezed it. "What a bunch of maroons they are."

She raised her eyebrows. "Maroons?"

"It's from that cartoon with the rooster."

"I'm very unfamiliar with cartoons."

"Really?" Gia glanced at her stomach. "Bet that'll change before long. Anyway, it's a family saying by now. Morons, of course. I have family in construction. That's what Eli does, and his father. I respect it. But they respect those of us with different leanings just as well. Eli's wife is a writer with a penchant for taking in stray animals right and left, which drives Eli crazy, but he still respects her for it. She can be a flighty little Jersey Girl at times, but also sweet as heck and she makes him so happy it's hard to believe. Have I told you yet that I just adore her to no end? Maybe it's why I grabbed onto you so fast. You're not flighty and you're more social, but there's still something similar.

"Anyway, the world needs all kinds, and families should respect that, and each other, regardless of different paths. Mine didn't like that I left, but they never once made me feel like I'm wrong for being here where I think I belong. They're just glad to see me when we can get there, and they're glad I'm happy."

Gillian got up to pace while she sipped her coffee. It was different than the coffee Hank sent her, but still wonderful. She couldn't say one was better than the other. Of course the water they'd use in their shop would be different than Denver water and that could matter.

"Hank isn't close to the small amount of family he has left, either. Different reasons."

"Please..."

"Okay, I know I agreed not to talk about him, but you're thinking about him. I know you are. How about I ask him to come visit me and you can drop by, just to chat, you know. It's hard to get him out here and it's been two years since he has, but he might..."

"No. Let him be." Gillian ran a hand over her child and kept walking. She enjoyed her now weekly walk-and-talks with Hank's friend, but she considered Gia her own friend by now and wanted to keep it that way. They didn't need to interact with Hank, as well. They could keep their friendships separate, if Gia wouldn't talk about him.

"I think he'd be okay with it, Gillian. I really think he would."

"With what?"

Gia glanced at the hand over her stomach. "He's not judgmental..."

"Don't. Okay? I barely know him. We ... five days isn't enough to..."

"It can be."

She felt her head shake. It was only attraction. Curiosity. Whatever.

"My Curtis proposed on our third date. We'd seen each other exactly three times. It was a set up. We've been married for three and a half years and we couldn't be happier. Five days can be enough."

Three and a half years. Gillian had dated guys nearly that long without knowing them well, before it crashed. She hoped Gia's marriage wouldn't, but three and a half years didn't reassure her at all.

As they headed back toward their cars, Gillian considered the difference in the view along the Platte and the view along the Animus. There wasn't much comparison, really. The park areas along Denver's river consisted of some grass patches breaking the river from the busy streets and high rises that interfered with being able to see the mountains. Young people sat in the grass or stood along the rocks beside the river, mostly with their heads buried in their phones. The older crowd sat at round umbrella tables on patios overlooking the grassy areas talking or playing on tablets. One young kid was fishing with a man who was probably his father. They wouldn't eat anything they caught out of the river, Gillian didn't suppose, or at least she hoped they wouldn't.

The trees were scattered and short, more decorative than

anything. A couple of little pines were half brown and she had to wonder if they were deciduous pines or diseased pines. The former, she hoped.

She sighed at the difference between her view and Hank's, more than only physically. They were too different. Too...

So what if they were? She missed him.

Twenty-three

"I need to go to part time. Thirty-two hours instead of forty."

Karenne looked over thick red reading glasses at Gillian from her desk where she was going over the paper's layout, her least favorite part of the job. "Are you sick? You look good."

"No, I feel fine. I just need more time for ... other things."

Setting the pencil down, Karenne got up and came around to her. "So, your little copywriting gig is doing well, then?"

"How did you know about that?"

"You know you should have told the paper you had a second job."

"It's just an at-home thing. It hasn't interfered."

"But it is now."

"No."

"Then why do you want to drop hours?"

"Something else I'm doing."

"And that would be?"

She almost said Nona Yolanda Dietrich Benning, but managed to hold it back. "My business." Gillian could see her editor didn't like her response, or maybe her friend didn't like that she didn't know. But they hadn't talked much other than about necessary work stuff ever since Gillian didn't get the Hank Dennison story. If she wanted to be that way about it, fine.

"Maybe you don't need this job anymore." Karenne turned on her heel and walked away, back to her desk. Shutting her out.

Didn't need the job? Gillian didn't want out completely. She wanted to keep a foot in the door. But she would absolutely not beg. "Are you firing me?"

"No. If I fire you, we'd have to pay unemployment. I don't have room on my staff right now for a part timer. Your choice."

Heat welled through her body as she stared at the woman who'd called her a friend. So much for that. It was an excuse...

"Actually." She looked up again. "I can drop you to twenty hours if you want that."

Twenty? "No. I'd lose my insurance."

"It's not worth it to us to pay insurance for part time, so that's the offer. Twenty or forty."

"Karenne..."

"We're struggling already, Gilly. The paper's in trouble. I shouldn't be telling you, but with the mandated wage hike and mandated insurance costs, we're probably going to have to drop insurance for everyone except management, anyway."

"You can't..."

"If we go under the required number of employees, we can. "

"People are getting fired? How can they do that?"

"It's either a few people or everyone, myself included, and I don't want to start job hunting again. They're trying to balance the business between a rock and a hard place and they'll do what they have to do to keep it running. Sorry, but that's how the world works, and it's time you opened your eyes."

If she didn't have her little one to think of, Gillian would take herself off their payroll immediately and let someone else stay. But what would she do? For now, she'd have to ride it out and try to pick up more freelance jobs and work up to where ... where she could afford self-employed insurance. She could do that with fewer hours at the paper, but it would take time. If not for her little one, she'd lose a couple more hours of sleep each night, but the exception to feeling good so far was the fatigue. She was sleeping more often, even napping on weekends, which she never had before.

The dark hole of feeling stuck started to creep in, but Gillian knew it for what it was and pushed it aside. She didn't have extra energy for that. Not now. She had to think.

"Well?"

She raised weary eyes to her editor. "I'll let you know tomorrow. Either way, I'll at least give you two weeks as I'm supposed to." With that, she turned and left the office.

She could give up her Sunday walk and talks with Gia, she supposed, but she would rather not. They refreshed her after the week's long hours of two jobs and her project. Maybe she'd have to give up on her project until she was more financially stable.

The thought hurt her whole being. No. She'd have to work around it. Somehow.

~ ~

Hank had to dig nearly to the back of the paper to find her article. A nothing story. Well written, though. Straight facts. No sensationalism. The effect of her copywriting job, he assumed.

Gia kept him filled in, although he'd told her not to repeat any private conversation. If Gillian wanted him to know anything personal, it was up to her to tell him.

At this point, he figured that wouldn't happen. He'd heard nothing from her since her letter thanking him for the coffee. Two months ago. He'd written three times, twice with gifts, once simply to check in. She only answered the first one.

Sitting cross-legged in his mini pop-up tent with a small fire at his feet for a touch of warmth, he sipped his coffee and gazed out at the sharp peaks of the Grenadier Range softened by partial snow cover. The tall narrow pines below still boasted at least part of their dark green, but the smaller trees around them had fully yellowed with October's cold. Those in higher elevations were full yellow fading into brown by now.

The snow would reach him soon. Every winter since he'd moved into the Animus Mountains, he'd stayed in the cabin. At times, he'd been snowed in for days at a time, but he'd planned for it and although somewhat stifling, he got a lot of work done.

Hank wasn't sure he wanted to stay there this winter. The fatigue that came after Gillian left was trying to move in on him again. It worried him, but he tried not to let it encompass his thoughts.

With a large deep breath of chilly mountain air, he also half considered moving back to the suburbs of Denver. He shuddered at the thought. She would maybe agree to see him now and then if he did, for a quick lunch or coffee date, but the thought of the traffic, crowds, city water and smog... No. He'd had enough of that.

Maybe later. When he couldn't care for himself well enough. He wouldn't mind being close to Gia and Curtis. For the support. At that point, though, he wouldn't necessarily want Gillian to visit. He didn't want that Hank, a sick and dwindling man, in her memory. He'd far rather she remember him bathing naked in the mountain stream.

Twenty-four

Gillian pushed herself out of her chair when Sally said Karenne needed to see her. The story she was working on, about someone suing someone for something so ludicrous it shouldn't even make the news, was not going well. It was too hard to keep her personal opinion out of the way.

And maybe she shouldn't. Ever since she'd insisted on straight facts without lending an opinion, her stories had slipped farther back in the paper where probably no one read them. At least she'd regained her professional integrity. And she was, so far, still getting a paycheck. Having decided to stay full time until she was better set financially, she did whatever story was assigned without argument and did her best professional job with it.

It was only background these days. Survival. As was the copywriting, although she had plenty of jobs at her disposal. Her work reviews were good. Gillian didn't quite call herself "in demand," but there was always another job waiting when she finished one. Mentally, if not time-wise, her own project was taking front and center in her life. It was purging and healing and made her tired but gratified. It had top preference, after only her little one.

Every day she felt new changes in her body and instead of groaning about the minor pains and inconveniences and her roundness that was quite obvious by now unless she wore loose, heavy clothes, which she rarely did, she welcomed the whole experience as much as she welcomed the coming little angel who would change her world, who had already changed her world. Movies now made her cry, and instead of fighting it, Gillian let it out. Not that she took much time for movies anymore. She wanted that time to work. Or to walk. Much of her copyrighting time was spent walking for inspiration, but outside, not in her apartment. She walked and pondered and noticed birds and butterflies, thinking often about the bird houses outside the Inn he'd put her up in, beside the lake. And about the way he liked hawks. The way he looked at experiences nearly like children did.

Whenever she was out walking and saw babies and other little ones, Gillian stopped to watch them, paying attention to how the parents treated them and how the children reacted. She smiled at their laughter and at their excitement about every little thing most adults ignored, the way even a bright fluffy white dandelion looked like an adventure when they puffed on it and sent the seeds flying. Most adults only saw a nuisance weed. She hadn't thought much about them one way or another until a little girl stomped and threw a fit when she wasn't allowed to pick one and blow on it due to her mother's fear of it staining her clothes.

Let the clothes stain, Gillian figured. The girl would soon enough grow out of it, anyway.

She looked forward to seeing everything through her baby's eyes in new ways she would never imagine on her own. The way Hank did. He noticed everything and was enamored by nature the way children were. Watching children reminded her of Hank. But then, nearly everything reminded her of Hank. Gillian only hoped Baby could stay more like him, and that her child wouldn't pick up whatever genetic garbage led to depression.

The thought made her sigh as she knocked on her editor's open door.

"You have to go back to Durango." Karenne stared as though Gillian had plotted against her in some way. "He wants you. Now. Before winter sets in."

Wants her? He *wanted* her? "Um..."

"Gillian, hello. Hank Dennison. You know, the guy who was supposed to be our big story. He wants you to come do it."

"Uh, do what?" Before winter? Why..."

"The *story*, Gillian. Did you sleep at all last night?"

The story. Before winter. "Not much. I was uncomfortable." She rubbed her stomach. *The story.* Hank's story. "Wait, are you sure? Or are you just pushing me to do what I said I wouldn't in order to help the paper?"

"Here." Karenne shoved a piece of paper at her. The same note paper he'd used for her letters, the *not masculine enough* note paper with flowery vines along the side.

She skimmed the very business-like neatly handwritten note. He would give the paper full permission to run the story and answer any question for it, but only on two conditions: only Gillian could come talk to him, and they would not change one word of what she wrote.

Her head shook, and her hand.

"Please do this for us. It could mean saving jobs, Gilly." Karenne's voice was soft, as it had been when they were still friends.

Jobs. Help the paper. Before winter. He wasn't well. He wouldn't be doing this unless he wasn't well. Her heart thumped. Hank wasn't well. She had to go to him. It wouldn't wait.

"Gilly? Will you?"

With a sniff to hide her sudden emotional surge, she nodded. "Yes. But not for that reason." She looked up at her editor with moisture making the hopeful face blurry. "I'll do it. Because he asked. Because ... I think his story should be heard. But Karenne, if I do this, and if you change one word after we both trust you, I will not only walk away, but I'll sue. Or I'll help him sue. I mean it. And I'm keeping this note that show his conditions."

Her editor studied her for some time and then glanced at her slightly protruding stomach. "Sure it's not his? I'll understand if you lied before to cover, but I'd like to know, before I send you back out there..."

"It's not. But I ... really wish it was." She hadn't let herself say it before or even think it, not really, not as a fully cognizant thought. She had to bite her lip to stay in control.

"You're sure you're okay to do this? With the way you feel, as emotional as you are these days, and with as hard and crafty as Hank Dennison is..."

"He is *not* hard, not more than he has to be. He's ... luscious, actually. Laugh if you want, but he is. And yes, I want to do this if he wants it. More than you can imagine. How soon do I leave?"

Twenty-five

Her gut twisted just a touch as the plane lowered its landing gear; it twisted far more when they hit the runway and the intercom said *Welcome to Durango*. Karenne had arranged a driver since she worried about how Gillian would feel when she got there. A good thing. She was nervous as all hell about seeing him again. And she was slightly nauseated from the pressure change. Or from the stress. Something.

At least it was cold enough for a long bulky sweater over lined leggings so her roundness wasn't obvious. She never tried to hide it back in Denver, but for now, she'd rather talk to him without his knowing. Keep things easy and casual.

Except for her nerves and racing heart.

Gillian let everyone else go ahead of her. Once she stepped off the plane it would be more real. Karenne had put her in the Strater again, although Gillian said she'd stay somewhere less expensive since they were floundering. Her editor set a hand on her shoulder and said this story could change that and if it didn't, it wouldn't matter.

Talk about pressure.

Maybe that's what her nerves were about.

"Right, Gillian. It's about the paper you're nearly ready to walk out on. Get a grip and at least admit it to yourself."

When some guy turned to look at her, she decided she maybe shouldn't talk to herself in public. She'd have to save it for ... for the mountains with Hank. He already knew she was a bit off. It wouldn't surprise him further than she already had.

The man was full of surprises himself. She still wondered why he changed his mind and why he wanted her to do it after she'd been such a pain in his...

"Baggage claim is that way." A friendly airport worker pointed. He must have thought she was unsure where she was going, never mind there was only one way to go from there and even a child could find their way back to baggage claim in the little one floor airport.

"Thanks." She wasn't unsure where she was going, only why. And then what? She considered asking the helpful guy that, as well, to see how much help he could actually be.

Don't be bitchy, Gillian. It's not his fault you're in this fix.

She managed to keep that thought inside her head while making her way to baggage claim where her driver was to meet her, with a very necessary stop at the restroom first.

Hank paced back and forth in the hallway between the restaurant and gift shop. He shouldn't have come an hour early, especially since her plane was fifteen minutes late due to a wind delay. He'd taken space at a table at the restaurant as long as was practical while indulging in a meat and cheese plate along with tomato soup. Then he wandered around the gift shop and considered buying her a Durango sweatshirt, but decided it would be too gauche, or too pointed. He hoped her editor had stayed true to her word and hadn't let her know he was picking her up.

When a group of people headed into the hallway from the terminal area, past security, Hank forced himself to stay still and wait, although his feet kept trying to move forward. No use rushing her. Especially when he was so unsure how he'd react to his offer to her paper. Could be she was resentful of the intrusion, of him forcing their hand, of knowing she was unlikely to refuse when they needed the story. It could very well be a curt, brief visit, professional and no more.

When the last traveler dribbled through the gate, his gut clenched. Maybe she'd decided not to come. It had to be her flight. Only one arrived at a time. He'd seen the board that said they'd landed nearly fifteen minutes ago. It had to be.

Relax, Dennison. Maybe she stopped for coffee on the other side. Maybe she was starving and grabbed a sandwich from the first place she found, which was on the other side of security. She wouldn't make the driver she expected wait, would she? He'd done it, though. There had been times when he got off a plane, he had to hit the men's room first and then grab anything decent to eat, with as skimpy as flight meals were. He'd even done it to Gia and Curtis. Now, he was ashamed of doing so. Waiting on someone else when there was nothing you could do but wait was a horrendous feeling. Of course, his friends wouldn't have been half as anxious to see him as he was to see her. Nervous. Unsure.

He rubbed his chin while he moved slowly toward the security exit.

Finally, a woman in a stylish long blue and green plaid coat caught his eye. Gillian. His heart raced. *Idiot. Knock it off. She's here for a story, for her career. Nothing more. And she was probably pushed into coming by her struggling little paper.*

Her hair was slightly longer than before and she brushed a strand from her face while she pulled a rolling bag behind her. A different bag, not beat up, but no bigger. She didn't plan to stay long. Unless the other was at baggage claim.

Hank took a few steps closer. She wasn't paying attention to who was around. She was tired. The fatigue showed even from a distance.

He swallowed hard when she came out of the narrow security hall and into where he could go up to her, but he held back. Something was different about her. Maybe it was the long coat and long, thick sweater. Or her light brown hair that was less manicured, more natural. He thought she might have gained some weight, as well. Her face looked healthier, had more color, but natural color instead of painted-on color. She looked more like someone suited to his mountain cabin, less to the big city.

Or his imagination was getting the best of him.

She looked around finally, right at him, then away. Then she looked directly at him and stopped.

Hank headed slowly toward her, keeping his cool, or at least trying to look like he was keeping his cool.

She broke into a smile.

His body relaxed. "Need a lift?"

"And how do you mean that?"

The question took him aback, for only a second or two. Instead of answering right away, he teased with a scan of her luscious body, too covered as it was. "You look good."

"Well, at least I'm not hobbling."

"Throw those old sticks away?"

"Nope. I keep them in a corner of my room."

"Plan to twist an ankle again?"

"No, but then I didn't plan to do it last time, either. You just never know what might happen." She studied him in return. "You've lost weight. Are you okay?"

His stomach turned. "I've been a bit down lately, but yes, otherwise I'm hanging in fine."

"Down..?"

"Mentally."

"But you're okay? I mean…"

At the emotion in her eyes, he couldn't resist touching her face. "Only out of sorts."

"Same here."

"Have you been? You look more … I'm not sure how to say it. Less unhappy?"

With a light grin beneath moisture-sparkling eyes, Gillian caught him in a soft hug, not a close hug; her hand was still on the handle of her bag. "You were right. And you are right. I'm doing much better." She pulled back. "This is just … a normal down in the dumps thing, only because … well, we should talk. Not here. Do you think we could maybe go have coffee or something? No work. This is a flying day. I don't have to work today."

"I would love to go have coffee. Or something. Honestly, I wasn't sure you'd come, or at least not without some force by your editor. I hope you're not upset that I arranged it without your okay."

"Oh, Hank. I've been trying to come back to see you for the longest time. I just … wasn't sure I should."

A deep sigh heaved through his body. "Yes, we definitely have to talk. Let's get your bag. Do you have another one?"

"No, only this."

He glanced down at it. "You don't plan to stay long?"

"They're giving me four days, including flying days, to get what I need and said I can write it back at the office."

Four days? "We'll see." He figured they'd damned well give her whatever time she needed to get the story they wanted.

She felt distance, even with the sweet greeting.

Gillian would like to have cleaned up a bit and changed clothes, but she didn't argue when he drove straight to Durango Coffee Company. She couldn't argue. Her head was too full of thoughts of Hank, of how he'd lost weight. And her heart kept telling her she was where she belonged, so she was fighting with her head that insisted she go back to Denver and not get closer to him.

While he ordered coffee, she wandered the shop full of packed shelves of colorful mugs and plastic glasses with lids and cards and fun kitchen gadgets. At one time, she would have had a hard time passing up all of the cute things she would insist her little apartment needed. These days, there were few things she couldn't bypass fairly easily. She couldn't, though, just wander past the glass jars of candies. Her sweet tooth forced her to grab a bag to fill. She'd been good. She deserved it. Still being half good, she bought dark chocolate rather than milk chocolate and counted it as a win.

Hank smiled and added her candy to the order, although she tried to pay for it herself, and led her to a table next to the window. She tried to distract herself by studying other shoppers, some in warm clothes, others still in summer gear trying to look tough, she supposed. Hank wore a light jacket and jeans like a regular person. Somehow she had trouble seeing him there in the coffee shop, chatting like ... like normal folks. And he looked uncomfortable, until he caught her eyes and relaxed.

The thought of it melted her heart right into a sloshy puddle of goo. What was it about the man? The wavy dark blond hair? The deep blue eyes? No. She wasn't nearly shallow enough to be captivated by only his appearance, even with as much of him as she'd seen.

She pulled her coat off her arms and let it drop over the back of the chair while he neatly pulled his jacket off and hung it properly across the chair shoulders. They were so different. Too different. Weren't they?

The question kicked in her penchant of giving anyone she met the third degree. "So why the change of heart about the story?"

His chest rose and fell and he took a careful sip of coffee. "Thought we weren't working today."

"That's not exactly work. I'm not about to start throwing questions at you. But I am curious..."

"Let's just say I'm glad you're here."

Gillian wasn't content with letting it go at that, but she was too flattered to argue. What was wrong with her? Arguing was her thing. She was good at it no matter what the situation. She wasn't distracted easily.

But, just sitting there with him was nice, too. She'd wanted to just sit with him so often over the past three months. She supposed she should enjoy it while she could. Before she had to work.

"Gia says you're doing well these days." He eyed her over his coffee.

"Yeah? Just how much has she said?"

"Only that. Nothing personal. I'm glad the two of you met up. I've felt better knowing someone was there for you if you needed."

Grabbing a chocolate from the plastic bag and offering them, she shrugged when he refused. "I enjoy her company, but really, I'm good on my own, too. What about you? I've asked about your health every Sunday when we meet. She wouldn't say anything except you were doing okay, said I should ask you myself if I want to know more."

He chuckled. "That's Gia. I suppose you heard all about her family back in Indiana."

"Yes. But you're changing the subject."

"I am."

"Why?"

"Can that wait?"

She studied his face, his cheeks that had lost color, his hair that had lost some sheen. "I'm not sure. Can it?"

He reached out for her hand and squeezed her fingers gently. "I didn't bring you back here to worry about me."

"Why did you? You were so against the story. You've hidden from everyone else, even pulled the shotgun on Kevin when he came to try. So what's going on here, Hank?"

"It wasn't loaded, and all I did was take it to the porch when he pulled into my drive. I didn't point it at him. I imagine he made it sound like I did, though."

"I ... don't know, actually. I didn't ask him. I told Karenne to leave you alone, and she has since then, as far as I know. Not that she wouldn't do it behind my back."

"No one else has been out to my place. If they're around town, I can't say. I will admit I'm locking my doors these days, just in case."

"I'm glad, and I understand why you want privacy. So again, why did you change your mind?"

His gaze on the table between them, he was silent a while, until she thought maybe he wouldn't answer. Then he looked up, directly meeting her eyes. "I wanted you to come back. I'm not sure about much of anything else right now other than that I wanted you to come back. I guess I needed to know..." He leaned in across the table and lowered his voice. "I need to figure out why I keep thinking about you, if it was only a fluke that your company meant so much to me while you were here, if it was only my lack of company in general..."

"I annoyed the hell out of you."

He grinned. "Yes and no. Most of it was my own ... oddities, should I say?"

"Yes, you are a little odd."

He raised his cup in a salute. "Who but the odd are worth a newspaper story?"

"Good point." She met his cup with the tip of hers.

"I've been reading your work since you left. It's good work, Gillian. Honest. Straight. There are a lot of fluff pieces in the paper. I see why they're struggling. It seems to be trying very hard not to offend anyone and that doesn't work for a paper, not for very long. I even went back and skimmed earlier copies. It used to have some grit, but it lost it about a year ago. What happened since then?"

"We changed editors."

"They should try again."

"I guess I won't tell Karenne that."

"Or you should."

"I can't. She's my friend, kind of, or we were. I'm not so sure anymore."

Hank rubbed his thumb along the top of her hand. "Well, I'd say not too much, she isn't. You deserve better stories."

"Oh. I used to have, until ... until I refused to do yours and then started being more careful about reporting just the facts and not the sensational bits, which of course are what people actually want. So she gives me the stories that aren't really stories, so it doesn't matter…" She stopped with a sigh. She had almost convinced herself it was fine, but it wasn't.

"If you do my story, I want you to use it as a stepping stone. Get yourself up and out of there to the bigger leagues before she destroys the paper, and your career with it."

"Didn't you say I was on the wrong path? Now you're saying to stay on it and take it even farther?"

"You straightened your path. It's not the same as it was."

Straightened her path? Gillian nearly laughed out loud. She'd complicated it all to hell is what she'd done. Reclaiming her hand, she popped another chocolate in her mouth and thought she might have to get a bunch more to take home with her.

"That was meant as a compliment."

She nodded through savoring the luscious candy.

"You know…" Hank hesitated while he watched people walk past on the sidewalk. "Destroying a business by worrying too much about what people think and not enough about what needs to be done isn't exactly good for the community."

"Neither is slandering your neighbors."

"It's only slander if it's untrue. It also has to take away their earning potential to be considered slander, which people either don't know or ignore when they toss that word around."

"Yes. I know. Still…" She washed the chocolate from her mouth with the equally luscious coffee. "Last time I was here, you jumped on me about what I do: expose those who need to be exposed. Or at least what I used to do. Why are you changing your mind?"

"I've been reading your stories, the earlier stories, before the fluff. I jumped to some conclusions last time I shouldn't have. But as I said, it's only slander if it's untrue, and half truth is as bad as untrue. That helps no one. I'm not against journalism. I'm against false stories, false accusations that ruin people, one-sided stories, and sensationalism only to sell papers. That's not what the free press is meant to be about. You've been leaning that direction in the past year.

Maybe it did sell. Maybe people did read it. But at what cost?"

"And now that I'm writing *straight*, no one reads my stories, so what is the point?"

"I read them."

"Only because..." She grabbed a fast deep breath. "Can we walk, maybe? I've gotten into the habit of walking and it clears my head, relaxes me..."

"Am I making you tense?"

"No. I'm making me tense. I... I'm usually very together and level-headed and in-charge, but whenever I get around you, all of that blows right out the window and I don't know why and I don't like it, except..."

"Except?"

"Except I like talking to you. I like being here with you. And I don't understand that, either. You're not my type at all. You're... Hell, you're nearly fifty and I'm notoriously drawn to younger men, barely younger. I'm not a cougar or anything, but a year or two..."

"How has that worked out for you so far?" He watched her over his cup as he took a good swallow.

"Obviously not well since I'm thirty-two and single. Still..."

"Maybe it's time to change that part of your path, too." He got up. "But no, I wouldn't mind walking."

"I should go check into my room and..."

"Can that wait?" He glanced at her feet. She was wearing the same blue Keds as the first time she'd come. "Those are okay for walking on sidewalks, I would assume."

"They are, as that's generally where I walk."

With a teasing nod, he offered a hand to help her up, pushed in her chair, helped with her coat, and held the door.

The wind was chilly and she pulled her jacket farther around her front. They passed an art store and Gillian thought about suggesting they wander in, but she preferred to shop alone so she wasn't influenced by whoever she was with. She notoriously let others influence her. Some time ago, she'd made a pact with herself not to accept help from salespeople, as well-meaning as they were, because she too often ended up with what she didn't want that way. Not trusting her own fashion instincts made it too easy to give in to someone else's. She loved her blue Keds, the ones that apparently amused Hank, because she'd shopped alone, put her eyes on them, and made a beeline, then forced herself not to ask the sales lady how they looked. They were one of the few things she owned that truly suited her.

As they walked along Durango's main street without talking, she sipped at her warm strong rich coffee and hardly missed the sugar. She'd gotten herself mostly away from sugar over the past couple of months since writing the article on farm markets and talking to the woman who studied health and nutrition. Refined sugar was toxic to the system, she'd said. Gillian wasn't honestly too worried about her own, but her sweet baby didn't need it if it was that bad.

She also nearly insisted on going into Maria's Bookshop, a beautiful glass-fronted shop showing off its treasures, not only the shelves full of books, but gorgeous red brick walls featuring artwork of some kind that she couldn't see well from the sidewalk. Gillian could spend hours there, but that would make it hard to talk with Hank, so she put it on her list of things to go back to do while alone, either a morning before they met up to work or an evening after he got tired of her questions.

Out of habit, she made mental notes of city details she might want to use. The grandiose red stone buildings in an older style with modern touches, arches and columns centrally featured. The smaller shops all in a row in different heights and colors. The spattering of short trees among the buildings, all in a neatly planned row along the sidewalk. The casual dress of those window shopping or jumping in and out of shops. And of course the massive bare mountains towering over and sheltering the city.

Durango felt different to her now that she could walk without her palms and underarms aching from the Hank-made crutches. Strolling along with her coffee, keeping up with Hank just fine, was much nicer.

When they got to the end of the main part of the city, he led her down to a walking trail beside the river and headed back the direction they'd come. "Still okay?"

She nearly jumped at his voice, and the question. "Yes. Why?"

"Your ankle healed well, then?"

Relief surged through her system. The ankle. Not the baby. He didn't know. "Yes. Thank you, and thanks to you. My doctor congratulated me for having the sense to stay off it."

With a nod, he kept walking, slower now, his focus mainly on the river. He'd finished his coffee a while back and dropped the cup into a trash can, so his hand, the one next to her, was free.

Gillian considered grasping it but didn't quite dare. Instead she, somewhat accidentally, moved closer to him while avoiding an insect of some kind crossing the sidewalk and let her hand rub his. A silly teenage-like prank, she told herself. But it worked.

He took her hand, entwining their fingers. "Let's sit a while." He led her off the sidewalk, toward the smooth slow-moving river, to the grass just above the jagged rocks, beside a white light pole. The poles lined the path and Gillian thought it might be nice to walk along the river after dark with only the path lights guiding them. Not alone. Even with her pistol secure in her handbag, she wouldn't wander out there alone at night. No sense asking for trouble.

Twenty-six

"Are you sick?" Gillian couldn't keep herself from asking. It would explain the story, why he suddenly wanted her to do it instead of simply giving in to her. And she had to know. "I mean, are you still stable, or..?"

Hank raised her fingers to his lips for a kiss. "As far as I know."

She turned toward him. "As far as you know? Don't you ... get checked regularly or something?"

"Should. So they say. But no. Like I said, if it happens, it happens. I'm doing what I can to prevent it, but if it does, it does. I can't spend whatever time I have left worrying about it. I came out here to recover. To get healthier. Stronger. Less stressed. And ... if it didn't work, I wanted to..." He looked out over the river, up at the mountains. "I want to spend my last days, whenever they are, out here in nature, not in an office or a crowded city. And definitely not in a hospital bed staring at white walls with well-meaning strangers buzzing around."

"But... You could afford a nice, private room rather than a shared plain white room, right? Wouldn't that... I mean... You should give yourself any help you can. You're so young, still."

"A well-decorated sick room would still be a sick room. Too depressing to think about. Mental status matters when you're fighting ... anything. This..." He motioned toward the river and mountains. "Being around so much real life makes me more willing to fight than I would be if I was stuck inside some hospital suite getting injections and heaving my guts out from the chemicals. I understand the point. I understand doing whatever doctors think might work. But it's not for me."

She forced a deep breath and held herself back. It was his business. She had no right to interfere. Still...

"Gillian." He set a hand alongside her face to pull her eyes to his. "I asked you to come back because I hated how we left things. I hated that you told me you needed to matter and I dropped you off at your hotel and told you to do it yourself. I'm sorry about that. I couldn't, at that time..."

"No. Don't be. I had no right to act like you owed me anything. You don't, of course, and I know you don't. Yes, I was upset at first, because you were right and I knew it. It wasn't your issue to fix. It was mine. And I didn't know how, or think I could. But I've... Well, things changed on their own, more or less. Some on their own. Some of my doing. Okay, all of my own doing, but some planned and some not. But I don't need you to make me matter. Okay? I don't. It was unfair to lay that on you after only five days of ... of being a huge pain in your ass trying to do a story you didn't want. I'm sorry. And I'm glad you wanted to see me again. I hate how we left things, too."

His eyes glistened. "You do matter."

"I know." She gave him a soft grin. "More than you realize."

He tilted his head. "You mean you know it more than I realize or you matter more than I realize? Because I'm not sure that's possible."

"Neither, really. But thank you." Gillian couldn't help herself. She met his lips, readying herself to brush it off, to explain...

But the soft kiss quickly became heated and intense, on both sides. Her arms slid up around his shoulders and her body melded into his as much as possible while sitting side by side on the grass. In public.

She pulled back at the thought. Somewhat. He cradled her against his side and kissed her head and they sat that way some time watching the river flow along in front of them, with an occasional yellowed or reddened leaf floating along the currents.

He was still stable, as far as he knew. Maybe it was her business enough by now to ask more. It would sure as heck affect her. He'd asked her to come back. She had the right to ask. "So, I know we said we weren't working today, but ... how did I never see reference to you being ill?"

"I kept it quiet, with plenty of personal favors and some payoffs. I didn't want it spread everywhere."

"But at least people would understand..."

"Would they? I doubt it. And I don't want sympathy. I don't want it to cause arguments between 'he deserves it' camps and 'show respect for the dying' camps. People are at each others' throats enough, for bigger reasons, and smaller. I don't want to be part of that."

The idea caught her off-guard. She never would have thought of such a thing. But he was right. She'd read enough comments on news stories and elsewhere to know how much pettiness there was, how nasty people got when they figured they were anonymous and couldn't see who they were talking to. It was truly horrid at times. She'd stopped reading comments. Too often, it spun her right into a depression.

That needed to be part of the story. This story ... was far bigger than Hank himself, bigger than a company that closed. This... This was a story worth writing, one that needed to be written.

"I see fire in your eyes."

"You just put it there." She traced a finger alongside his face, studying the few wrinkles around his eyes, the strands of gray intermingling with his short dark blond hair. Looking closer, Gillian could see there were more than she'd noticed. They were well concealed within the natural color. But there was a good amount of it.

Forty-nine. The man was forty-nine years old and momentarily stable, fighting cancer invading his body. Talk about uncertainties. She had enough of those of her own. Still...

"Can I ask how I put fire in your eyes and what you're thinking?"

"No. Not yet." When he started to say more, she ran her finger across his lips. "You are truly luscious, Hank Dennison."

He laughed and kissed the side of her head. "Come on. I have my appetite back today and I plan to take full advantage of it."

They walked slowly, her hand on his arm, along the quietly surging river, then across the river into Schneider Park where they paused to watch a few kids at a skate park doing tricks of all kinds on their boards, crossed again at 9th Street and headed back to Main.

"How far does this path go?"

"About five miles total, some through the city. If we keep going that direction, it leaves the traffic noise behind and you hear the river better. It ends up on a bluff. We can go if you want."

"Maybe another day."

He looked relieved and she reclaimed his hand.

When they got back into the midst of the city, he guided her to the inside of the sidewalk and moved her hand to the crook of his arm. Being careful still. It looked more friendly and mannerly than holding hands. Less like a relationship. A few people did look at him curiously, but no one stopped him and said anything.

Her feet were sore by the time they reached his truck. When she walked with Gia, she'd worn walking shoes instead, but she hadn't planned for the long trek along the river. "Guess I should find my hotel and..." Gillian forced herself to continue. "Get cleaned up. Let you get on with whatever else you need to do. Can we meet tomorrow? I'll buy breakfast wherever you want."

"That is why you're here, isn't it? For work? To meet with me?" He played with her hair.

The man was actually playing with her hair. "Oh. Yes, I..."

"You're getting flustered again. Why?"

"I don't ... particularly want to let you go off on your own the rest of the night. I mean I... That didn't come out right." She sighed. "Are you up to putting up with me through dinner, also?"

A grin flitted around his lips before he pressed them against hers and pinned her against his truck with his upper body. As a gentleman would, he stayed slightly to her side and the only part of her body he pressed into, other than her mouth, was her shoulder.

He released her long before she was ready to be released. "How about at my place? I'll cook for you."

"Oh, but then you'd have to drive all the way back here and..."

"I mean at my townhouse. It's nearby, on the outskirts of town. It's set up for you."

"Townhouse?" Gia had mentioned it, but Gillian had forgotten. It was hard for her to see him anywhere but at his cabin.

"For when the winter is too harsh for the cabin, mainly. Or when I'm not up to that much effort and want a week or two that I can take a real shower without starting up the pump."

She looked away at the thought of him, the well-built sturdy-looking mountain man, not being up to ... anything. It was the last thing she wanted to think about with the way he was looking at her.

He pulled her face back to his with both hands. "Don't."

"I'm sorry. I..."

He kissed her again. A quick kiss. "I'm okay, Gill. And I look less tired than you do. So, is it a yes? About dinner at my place. And staying there instead of a hotel. Either?"

"Yes. Both."

"Good. Because the art festival is in a couple of days and it might be hard to get a good room. I took a chance that you'd accept my offer and told your editor not to bother with a hotel. I can imagine what she thought."

"I don't care what she thought. But she said she booked the Strater."

"A cover story."

"Ah, she's good at it. At covering, that is. More than I ever realized before, I'm starting to think. Art festival?"

"A fundraiser for the Durango Arts Center, full of fine and performing artists, a hundred or thereabout. People come from everywhere for it. Interested in going?"

"Yes. Of course."

"Good. Already had it planned." He lowered his hands to her hips, his body still preventing her from moving away if she'd wanted to, although she knew he would let her, if she wanted to.

She didn't particularly want to move away and didn't try. "Are you showing your work?"

He looked confused for a moment, then chuckled. "My tree carvings? No. I don't show my work. Didn't in school, either, come to think of it. Drove my teachers crazy."

It took Gillian a few seconds to realize he meant showing his work for math problems. She'd never understood why anyone wouldn't, how they'd figure it out without writing it out. She wasn't at all surprised Hank wouldn't have needed to, though. "Of course you did. You have that effect on people."

"Driving them crazy?"

"Yes." She circled his ear with her finger, along the gray strands. Silver, actually. In the sunlight, what there was left of it, they were silver, not grey. "And your work is worth showing, Hank. You should."

He moved his mouth close to her ear. "Let's go get you out of this bulky coat and off your feet."

She was startled a moment. It felt like the second hint that he knew what he shouldn't. Had Gia told him about the baby? She wouldn't have. Maybe he could see it better than she realized. Or maybe he was only being a gentleman. With his body moving away enough to run his fingers down the front edges of her bulky coat, he gave the impression he was not at all trying to be a gentleman.

If she was right, he would have to know. Tonight. Or he'd find out by himself.

Hank was nervous as he unlocked his door and showed her inside the house. It was ridiculous to be nervous. He wasn't staying longer than for dinner and then long enough after dinner to not eat and run. "It's nothing fancy, but it's clean. I just had a company come refresh the linens and clear out the dust, with natural cleaners, nothing toxic."

"It's beautiful." She looked around at the greens and browns, part modern part traditional eclectic style. "Bamboo floors?"

"Yes. And countertops. I tried to keep it very natural. No carpets. I hope you won't mind, but..."

"Carpets have chemicals."

"Right." He ran a hand down her back. "No fake fragrances, either. So if you'd rather go to a hotel, I'll call around..."

"No. This is nice." She set a hand on his chest. "It's really nice. Much nicer than a hotel. Thank you for trusting me to stay here."

"Thank you, Gillian." He whispered beside her ear. "For coming back. For taking the risk. Considering everything." He backed up. "Let me take your coat."

Keeping himself distracted, he hung their jackets in the front closet, grabbed her bag, and showed her upstairs to her room. She looked impressed, especially with the guest room having its own attached bath. He didn't bother to say it was for his own convenience. When he had company, which wasn't often, he didn't want to share a bathroom. Too personal. Even his office at his company had his own private facilities. Disguised to look only like a regular door, it had been his idea and he'd insisted.

"By the way, the car out front is for your use."

She looked back from where she was admiring the pull down luggage bench. Built on slides, it raised to become a simple desk or folded in to be out of the way entirely. His own design.

"You've gone to a lot of trouble. This…" She picked up a basket full of natural, organic body care items. "Is it a hint or only a guest room gift? You do this for everyone?"

"Not to the same extent. Take your time cleaning up. Go ahead and shower if you'd like. Everything's in there for you. I'm going to start dinner."

Before he got out the door, she grasped his fingers and kissed his face. "Something tells me you're going to become a very old mountain hermit."

"You know, I'm not at all sure I'd want to do that on my own."

"No. You probably shouldn't do it on your own."

He stroked her short hair down to her nape. "Is that an offer?"

"It's a little soon for that, I think. But I'll be down shortly. We'll talk."

Talk. Yes. They very much needed to talk if the woman was even somewhat starting to think long term with him. There was too much she still had to know.

Twenty-seven

Gillian couldn't help glancing into his room on her way downstairs since the door was open. A masculine room. Stripes in dark red and gray adorned the comforter that topped solid gray sheets, and matching abstract art decorated the walls. It looked more like the Hank Dennison she expected, to include each bedroom having its own bath. Why the man would live out in the woods when he had this, and could have much more than this, she didn't understand. For weekend trips, sure. Otherwise it just seemed masochistic.

Maybe he was. After all, he'd asked for her to come back.

Gillian hesitated at the thought. Maybe he was. In actuality. Maybe she'd just agreed to stay in a lunatic's house and ... and she wasn't sure he was more of one than she was.

More than that, she wasn't sure she cared.

Except for her baby.

"Like this one better?" His voice behind her made her jump.

"Oh. I was..."

"Snooping?"

"Yeah. I do that, obviously. It's a pretty modern look compared to your cabin."

"Not my idea. I had it done. I left it up to the designer who figured she knew my style. I didn't have the heart to tell her she was wrong, but it's functional."

Gillian nodded as though she understood, but she didn't really. Have someone else just come in and do what she wanted with your place without input, even?

"You like it or you don't?" He came closer.

"I barely saw it, just from here. I didn't snoop that far. Yet."

"Let me show you, then." He grasped her hand.

"Oh. No, it's okay. I..."

"You're curious. Let's quench that curiosity."

She pulled back when he started to move.

"You're nervous? Have I frightened you?"

"No. Yes. Maybe."

"I'm not staying here with you, Gill. I'll head back to the cabin after dinner. The place is yours." He raised her hand to kiss her fingers. "Although I'm not sure why you'd worry now when you were alone in the mountains with me, and I was naked part of that time."

"Thank you for the reminder." Her face warmed.

He chuckled and hugged her softly, over the bulky sweater she'd put on to help conceal her new shape. "Just trying to help you unwind. If you'd feel better, I'll call Susan over to have dinner with us."

"Susan?"

"From the health store. My friend down the road. It'll take her a little time to get here, but she will if you'd rather."

"The one old enough to be your mother?"

"And who's even more fiery than you are, and better protected. One of the few women I've ever known who can use a shotgun without it throwing them to the floor or dislocating their shoulder. She'd be glad to come chaperone just for the chance to meet you."

The woman sounded like someone plenty interesting enough to meet, but Gillian didn't, at all, want a chaperone. "Another time. Meeting her, I mean." She backed away enough to let him show her around.

Everything was perfect. Everything matched. No dust on the dresser. A single book, non-fiction she guessed, since it said something about America and Other Irish, on the nightstand with a well-placed reading light fixed to the wall above it. The throw rug beside the bed looked brand new. Twisted rags, like her mom used to make from their worn clothing, except smaller strands, neater, all red, black, and gray to match the bedding. Bamboo flooring again. His bathroom had a dressing room leading into it and it was spacious and open. Even the shower had clear glass doors. The one in her room was filtered glass for more privacy.

"Nice place for a mountain hermit."

"It works. Are you hungry?"

"Starving. But I'm curious. This looks far bigger on the inside than on the outside. How'd you manage that?"

"I combined the two townhouses into one. It only still looks like two from the outside to throw people off. I like my space."

"You are a very unique man, Hank Dennison."

"Well, how about you don't put that in the article? About the house, that is. Or maybe how to find it."

She'd nearly forgotten she was there to work. "Of course." Her heart sank a few inches. He apparently didn't forget she was there for work.

"Did you test your mattress?"

"What?" In the hallway, she stopped and stared at him.

"Your mattress. It's good quality. But let me know if it's not right for you."

"What are you going to do if it's not? Bring in a different one?"

He met her eyes. "Yes."

Gillian's stomach flipped. "Really? Or are you being funny?"

"I want you to be comfortable here."

"It's only four days. I've gone far longer than that without sleeping well, if I don't."

"Right. Well. I might as well tell you right now." He slid fingers through the hair she'd blown dry and styled. "I'm not giving you my whole story in four days. My guess is they'll allow whatever time you need to get it, whether it's a week or a month or … whatever it takes."

"So who gets to determine how long it'll take?" She felt herself drawing closer.

"I figure it'll take at least a week, closer to two. Of course, you can always take whatever you get in four days and go home. It's totally up to you." He kissed her forehead. "Let's eat. I'm starving."

"So am I. You smell good." When his eyebrows rose, she laughed at herself. "That came out really, really wrong. Two different things. Unrelated." Her face was suddenly hot.

"Sandalwood and clary sage."

"What?"

With a soft grin, he gently moved her face close to his shoulder, caressing the back of her neck as he did. "Essential oils. I hoped you'd like it better than the tea tree scent."

"I do. It's nice. Still not guaranteeing I won't bite, though."

"So maybe not too unrelated?" With a teasing smile, he took her hand.

With her gut tight from his flirting, which he was actually very good at, as it turned out, Gillian walked beside him down the stairs toward the kitchen that emanated a truly incredible aroma. He planned for her to be there for a month if she agreed? Maybe she would. She could do her freelance work from anywhere with internet connection.

Did he have? She hadn't seen a computer or any other electronic device. But then everything was spit and polished, surfaces clear, no clutter. If he had them, they would be put away, she supposed.

She hadn't tried the mattress, but she imagined it was fine. *Good quality*. Probably an understatement. The light gray and dark green comforter, chosen, she supposed, to be unisex in case of either female or male guests, was more her style than his and it looked plenty comfortable, but she hadn't let herself try it. She was too tired and figured it would be too hard to get up and moving again. It looked ... luscious. She smiled to herself at the thought. Everything about the man was entirely too luscious, too hard to resist.

It might take at least a month to get the full story.

The table was set. The large skillet sat atop the oven, uncovered and cooling. Nearly half an hour. He'd half expected her to come down in ten minutes in old sweats with her hair wet and wrapped. Something about the fact that she took so long to shower, or to get ready to come down to him dressed warm but nice in a long dark green sweater over tan leggings that modestly hinted of bare legs, her hair clean and styled, her face lightly done, lifted his spirits higher than they were already.

She hadn't argued about staying longer. She was unsure, though. Nervous.

Understandable. So was he. Nervous, anyway. Not unsure. He was more sure with her than he'd ever been with a woman. Not a good sign, possibly. His cockiness too often made him too confident, far more than he should be.

"That smells wonderful." She peeked into the pan. "How did you do that so fast?"

"I had the vegetables cut and ready before I left for the airport, and the meat marinating. Just had to throw it together. How does it look?"

Her eyes sparkled. "Absolutely irresistible. And the food, too."

It took him a second to understand, since it was so unexpected. But then, he was getting used to expecting the unexpected from her. "You're good at this flirting thing, aren't you?"

"I don't usually try. Am I doing okay?"

He slid a hand behind her head and gave her a quick, soft kiss. "Not bad for a pain in the ass who wears city shoes to climb a mountain path. Have a seat. I'll bring it over."

"I could get used to this." Her cheeks reddened. "I don't mean I expect this. I just..."

He kissed her again. "Stop being so nervous. No pressure here, Gill. Okay?"

"But there's ... something I have to tell you. Before I keep flirting."

Hank ran fingers alongside her face. A beautiful woman, with classic features, a strong nose instead of small and pert, a square face that made her look strong. Her hairstyle was cutesy and modern, as was the way she'd dressed a few weeks before when it was warmer. But otherwise, she was more real than cutesy and he appreciated that. Even her eyes and the slight bagginess beneath them, the barely there dark green liner along the lashes meant, he supposed, to hide what she would consider a flaw, screamed real and earthy.

Not a woman he would let go easily, whatever she had to say. There was only one thing he could think of... "You haven't hooked up with someone else? Another younger man instead of this decrepit one?"

"Hardly decrepit." She ran her hands along his chest, the firm, sturdy chest she constantly pictured the way she'd seen it while he was bathing in the stream – naked and haloed by the bright hot sun – and her eyes drifted down his frame. Holy hell, was he adorable in the kitchen, in his deep blue and red plaid shirt over a matching deep blue tee, both tucked into perfectly fit jeans, neat and proper, getting ready to serve her such an incredible meal he'd not only made, but planned ahead. "No. I'm very much..." She couldn't quite say single as though it equaled free since she was now a two instead of a one. "I'm not hooked up with some man. I won't be doing that again."

He caught her eyes. "You won't ... what?"

"Hook up. Just casually. And now I sound like I've made a habit of that. I haven't. Not that I've been particular enough..."

"Neither was I back in the day. I won't hold that against you."

"Most of us have had unparticular moments, right? But I won't again hook up with someone I know is just temporary. I can't anymore. There's too much at stake. So things have to change, and they have." Her eyes watered. She cursed herself mentally and tried to stop it.

Hank rubbed his thumb along her face. "What's wrong, Gill?"

"No. Nothing's wrong."

"I can see something's on your mind."

"Yes, but I didn't plan to... I figured, a couple of days, after we had time to ... well, think about ... whatever else..."

"About us."

"Yes. About us. If there is such a thing. If..."

"If you can handle my illness? Or my age?"

"No. It's not that. It was, but it's not. Because I can. I won't pretend it doesn't scare me, but it won't keep me away. I want you to know that."

"I'm glad." He smoothed his thumbs under her eyes, wiping moisture. "Since you're so unsure of things, let me tell you this now. I am interested in an *us*. I understand you have to be cautious. I understand it's not fair to ask it of you, considering my health issues. I'm willing to work this however you need and I won't ask you to stay longer than you can, but I'd like you to stay as long as you'd like."

"I'm having a baby." Gillian heard herself just say it. She'd meant to wait, at least until after dinner, but it came out. She wanted him to know. At the surprise on his face, the shock, or ... whatever it was, she pulled away and turned so she wouldn't have to see his expression. "So, really, I'm the one complicating things. And you're more than welcome to say screw the story, just go home. I'll understand. I just ...

couldn't tell you in a letter. I needed to tell you in person. Actually, I'd planned to wait until after Baby came and just bring him and..."

His silence mingled with the scent of dinner brought on nausea, from the stress of it, from telling him that way, from not wanting to see his expression and yet wanting to know. He could easily turn the visit into only business. He could cancel the story. Maybe just as well...

Gentle hands touched her shoulders from behind. His body closed in as he slid his hands down her arms to her waist, to her hips, and up beneath her sweater. She caught her breath when he raised them to her abdomen, over the swell, connecting with her bare skin.

"How far are you?" His voice was as gentle as his hands.

"Four months. I didn't know last time I was here. By the time I headed home, I suspected. I'm sorry. I didn't mislead you purposely. I didn't know."

"And the father?"

"Just an ass I don't ever want to see again. He doesn't know and he won't care as long as I leave him alone about it, which is what I want, anyway. So I'm on my own, but I'm okay with that. My copywriting is going well. I'm supporting myself fine. It's fine." Her voice shook. "It is."

He kissed the side of her head and pulled his hands out from under her sweater so he could move around in front of her. "You're okay with becoming a mother?"

"Yes." Tears fell. Happy tears. Yes, she was more than okay with it. "And I'm not *becoming* one. I am one. I'm eating better. I'm being careful. I'm making plans. I've even bought a few basic baby things, although Karenne says I shouldn't until closer to time, that it's too soon, but I just felt like I needed to. No, I *wanted* to, so I did, and I still, when I see baby things, I'm drawn to them. Maybe I shouldn't be so excited, given the circumstances, as she's said more than once, but..."

"Ignore her. That woman does not know as much as she believes she does." He took her hands. "Congratulations, Gillian. You'll be a good mom."

"You think so?"

"Absolutely. I think this little one will be very fortunate to have you as a guide." He squeezed her fingers.

"Thank you. You and Gia are the only ones who think so. That's a little disconcerting, with as long as I've known Karenne and ... and a few others, not friends really but those I hang out with when I need to. They all think I'm ... that I should consider adoption."

"Are you considering it?"

"Absolutely not. I may not turn out to be a perfect mom, and I'm sure I won't, but I'll do my best and I'll put Baby first and..."

"Which is all anyone can do. You'll be fine. They're wrong."

"Thank you." It came out as a whisper, the only way she could answer and stay in control of herself.

"Sit down, Gill." He held her chair and then took the wine glasses off the table to return to the small rack under the counter. "I have a nice Pinot Noir open I planned to offer since I just used it in the beef and it's a nice complement. From Oregon. A good year." He shrugged and pulled out a container of orange juice. "But maybe we'll do this instead. Considering."

"You can go ahead with your wine." Gillian fumbled with her napkin. "And water's good with me. I've been better about drinking it, although I hate the taste of our city water and I don't like bottled water much, either."

"Try this, then." He poured what looked like water from a clear pitcher into a plain clear glass. "Ice?"

"No. Thank you." She accepted and sipped it. Mountain water. It was impossible not to recognize. "You bring this in from the cabin?"

"I do." He also poured a small glass of orange juice to set beside her plate. "Vitamin C is supposed to counter the radiation from flying."

"Oh. I didn't get scanned this time other than the normal walk through. They tried. Somehow I always get pulled for that arms up X-ray thing, but I said I was pregnant, even showed them the little baby bump I have already, and they sent me through the other, so..."

"I'm glad. Drink it anyway."

"I generally only drink orange juice when it's mixed with peppermint schnapps."

"A luxury you'll have to forego for a while. Just humor me, Gillian. Please."

She gave in and watched him serve the Beef Bourguignon with plenty of vegetables. He was comfortable in the kitchen, not the picture she'd seen of Hank Dennison in her mind, before she knew him. Very little of what she'd expected was true. Gillian made a mental note to remember that in the future when she was sent on stories, to leave the presumptions behind.

Hank set their plates on the table, sat across from her, and raised his glass of mountain water. She met his with hers in a small clink.

"What did we just toast to, can I ask?"

"To good company." He winked with a light grin.

Dinner got far too quiet after she complimented him on the wonderful meal, so she looked around his place. It was all open, with no separating walls between the living area and the kitchen and dining areas. The bamboo softened the cold simple sparseness of the townhouse with its shiny black appliances and black leather furniture with dark brown and soft green accents. She had to admit that although she was glad for the modern conveniences of normal plumbing and such, Gillian preferred the look of his cabin and all of its natural wood. The house didn't fit him.

And it was too quiet.

"Looking for something in particular?"

"Um, no. Yes. Do you have a stereo in here somewhere?"

"Of course." He got up. "Have a particular request or just the radio?" Hank pulled one side of a small canvas with a painting of dark trees away from the wall between the dining area and living room. Behind it was a control panel that lit up at the touch of his finger.

"Okay, that's cool."

He grinned. "Come let me show you how it works."

"Oh, no, I don't want to mess it up."

"You won't. Come here, Gillian. You may want it while I'm not here with you."

She sighed at the thought of him going back to the cabin and leaving her there alone. Alone was okay. She was used to alone. But she only had a short time to be with him, and... Maybe. Maybe she'd just stay. Since he'd offered. Of course, that was before he knew about the baby.

He threw a questioning look as she took his side. "What were you just thinking?"

"Why?"

"Your expression changed. Your face is very revealing, you realize."

"Yeah. No matter how I've tried to change that. Makes me a really bad liar."

He brushed fingers through her hair alongside her face. "Then don't try. What were you just thinking?"

"I don't want to say right now."

With a slight pause, he nodded. "Okay. That's fair. So what music do you want?"

"You probably don't have it in that thing."

"Unlikely. Try me."

"Metallica."

He pulled back, questioning. "Are you serious? That's what you listen to?"

"I listen to a lot of stuff, but that's my go-to when ... when I need to just ... escape."

"You need to escape now? If you don't want to be here, say so."

Her head shook of its own accord and she wrapped her arms around him, allowing her head to rest on his shoulder. "I do want to be here. It was your comment. That I'd want it when you weren't here with me and my stupid head took that too far and ... back to Denver, without you. I'm sorry. I'm being ridiculous. I'm not clingy, Hank. Never have been. Truly. Why do I do this around you?"

He held her in close, a hand against the side of her face, the other on the small of her back. His head leaned down against hers. "Stay more than four days, Gill."

"Okay."

"Yes? Just like that?"

"Yes. How long do you mean?"

He kissed her forehead. "Until you want to leave, not until you think you have to leave."

"You might get tired of me long before then."

"Not likely. How about this for incentive? The place is yours for as long as you want it. It's fully equipped. I'll show you where everything is before I leave tonight. There's a computer at your disposal. It should have any program you need. If not, let me know and I'll add it. The phone has long distance included so you can do without your cell while you're here..."

"And you? How much do you plan to be at my disposal? Since I'm getting this flirting thing down, and all. I do realize I've thrown you with little one, here." She ran a hand over her child. "You weren't expecting a package deal, and you should be honest with however you feel about it."

He rubbed a hand over his jaw. "How about we finish dinner and then we'll talk more. And we'll try some Metallica later. For now..." Giving her a quick run through on how to work the stereo, he held a talk button and asked for Gabriel Fauré.

"Who is that?"

"My go-to. Listen."

Gillian nearly rolled her eyes at the start of a classical piece but was soon overwhelmed by the way the sound came from everywhere, like a concert hall. "Wow. How is it doing that?" She looked around for speakers.

"They're throughout the house, mostly out of sight. You can turn any of them off and on. I'll show you."

"And you have more than classical programmed in that thing? I don't really listen to classical."

"Don't know what you're missing, Gill."

"I could say the same about Metallica."

He chuckled. "That's fair. I'll try yours if you'll try mine for a while, at least through dinner. And yes, you'll find anything you can think of in there."

~ ~

Hank studied her throughout the evening, without bothering to hide that he was. Pregnant. The damned woman was pregnant? The whole time? How did you not know you were? He'd heard of women not knowing, some for an amazing amount of time which he figured was only hype, but he wasn't sure how they didn't realize such a drastic thing as having another human inside your body. He'd known about the intrusion in his own body almost immediately. He'd ignored it, told himself he was wrong, for too long, but he knew.

His aunt always told him he had extra sensory body wisdom, which of course was not an actual thing, but she insisted he did. He got it, she said, from his uncle, a rock star she'd dated for a short time before he was a rock star, who had the same thing and that his sacrifice wasn't really as much of one as they said since he was sick anyway. So she said, although that was never made public if it was true. Never mind his aunt's fling's genes would not affect his own. Of course he was also not Hank's uncle.

His uncle said she made it up about the guy because she had a ridiculous crush on him and wanted him to be part of her life, but he was ten years younger than his aunt and had never lived in the west while she'd never been away from the western part of the country. He'd always shaken his head in resignation. There was no jealousy; Hank knew the man always held a certain amount of pity for his wife for never being quite satisfied. With anything. The man had tried. Hank knew how hard he'd tried. His father talked about it often, how much a shame it was.

With every relationship, the first thing Hank looked for was that inability to find joy and satisfaction. Once he thought he saw a touch of that, he ended it. Fast. No looking back.

Maybe that was a flaw of his own.

But Gillian, even through what he expected was clinical depression or bouts of it, from what he'd seen and what she'd said, still found joy in small things. He'd caught her noticing and enjoying flowers along the path when they walked, and grinning at young children playing, even fingering the grass as they sat and talked beside the river. Her use of the word *luscious* was maybe his biggest hint that she *wanted* to find pleasure in things, and easily could.

And he wanted her in his life. He wanted her pleasure-seeking, her smile, her uncertainty through her independence that he found charming. He wanted her soft small hands against his chest and around his neck.

But he wasn't sure he should try to hook her to the kind of life he was forced to live, the constant uncertainty of his illness, the need to avoid so many things she was used to having, the possible ... early departure from her.

If it was only her, Hank knew she was strong enough to deal with it and move along. But she was pregnant, having a child that would need... Well, he supposed most of what children needed was care, security, and love, and he would get that readily from his mother. Still, a child should have a parent who would likely stick around for a good number of years. Maybe he could. He wasn't sure *maybe* was good enough.

On the other hand, maybe a touch of extra help even short term wouldn't hurt anything.

"My turn to ask what you're thinking about." Gillian set a hand alongside his head from where she sat next to him on the couch. When had she moved in so close?

"Time to switch to Metallica?" Not that he wanted to, particularly, but something more upbeat wouldn't hurt.

"That's not what you were thinking." She slid it down to his neck.

"No, but probably what I should be thinking."

She pulled back. "I've thrown you."

"Why do you say that?"

"You've been quieter in the past hour than you have since we met."

"You're saying I talk too much?"

"You know that's not what I'm saying."

Hank allowed himself a heavy sigh. "All right. Yes. You've thrown me somewhat, but..."

She nearly jumped up off the couch. "I'm not asking anything of you. I don't expect you to..."

"Gill." Hank grasped her hand and stood beside her. "I know. Are you up to going out tomorrow, taking a nice long walk? There's something I want you to see."

"Something I'll want to see?"

He grinned at her caution, the wariness mixed with excitement in her eyes. "I think you'll enjoy it."

"Okay. But we'll have to have this conversation, Hank. You know we will."

He nodded lightly. "Not tonight. Should I change the music?"

"No. This is nice. Do you dance at all?"

"Formally, yes. Casually, no."

"What does that mean?"

He took her right hand, set his own on her waist, and waited to see if she understood. Gillian, as he hoped, settled her left hand behind his shoulder and moved in.

"I don't know how to do more than this." She followed him in a basic motion, the one all couples used when they hadn't been taught to dance. "Except in clubs. Casually, I suppose you mean. Just moving to the beat."

"And that's what I don't do."

"I could teach you."

He grinned again. Definitely a pleasure seeker, this woman. "Deal, if you mean privately, and if you'll let me reciprocate."

"Deal. And I don't care where."

She didn't want to let him leave, even if it was closing in on midnight and he had a bit of a drive ahead of him. She supposed, though, that it wouldn't look good if anyone noticed. "Would they?"

"Would who, what?" He spoke next to her ear as he held her in a good night embrace.

"Oh. I didn't mean to say that out loud."

He chuckled and met her eyes. "Okay, but would they what?"

"I shouldn't say what I was thinking."

"Of course you should." He stroked two fingers along the side of her face, up around her ear, down to her neck.

Her chest expanded. Her heart raced. "I..."

"Would who what, Gill?" His fingers slid under her chin.

"Would anyone notice if you stayed? I mean, instead of driving back so late. It would be easier..."

"Not tonight." Raising his hand back to the side of her head, he ducked enough to meet her eyes nearly on her level. "Too tempting. And we need to talk more first. No, I doubt anyone would notice, but that's not my concern anymore. I have bigger concerns." He set a light kiss on her lips and opened the door. "Set the alarm system when I leave and remember to turn it off if you open the door. I'll see you tomorrow. Ten too early?"

"No. That's good."

"Wear walking shoes. Better than the blue ones. You have some with you?"

"Yes. I planned to keep up with you this time." She smiled and grasped the front of his shirt to pull him back in for a better kiss before he left. If he was going to be turned off by her coming child, she wasn't going to make it easy for him.

Twenty-eight

Hank asked again if Gillian was sure she was up to a two hour or more walk. She assured him she was fine and looked forward to exploring Hovenweep, the National Monument that spread from Colorado into Utah. The idea of seeing the Puebloan structures lit a spark in her eyes. Another good sign, as far as he was concerned.

Hoisting the backpack over his shoulders, he gave her a small thermos with a strap long enough to throw over her shoulder and led her first to the welcome center so she could find information, although he could tell her most anything about it she wanted to know, with as often as he'd been there.

He handed her a camera as they started on their journey. "It has a huge memory card. Take as many photos as you wish."

"You don't want to do it yourself?"

"I've done it plenty often. And that's yours. Thought it might be helpful for your work, too. This way." He purposely didn't give her time to respond so he didn't have to see her expression if she again thought he was trying to buy her in some way. The woman had to know he was smart enough to realize she wasn't the type to be bought with petty stuff, or at all. She had to be won, to be earned.

He looked forward to the challenge.

He was also smart enough to know that just because she'd made it clear she enjoyed being with him didn't mean she would want to *stay* with him. Hank learned long ago never to count on his eggs before they turned into full grown chickens. Hatching wasn't enough.

~ ~

Gillian could hardly contain her joy while not only peering at the amazing buildings made of stone and dirt that had stood for close to a thousand years, minus a couple hundred, but being able to touch them, to let her fingers absorb their strength, to let their strong earthiness pull uncertainty from her much weaker system. And being able to take photos from all angles, as many as she wanted, was a nice bonus to a perfect day.

Travel journalism. Who did that? She remembered something about it, but her mind was so full of so many things...

Gia mentioned it. Her cousin's wife. The shy one. Not shy. Gia said Delaney hated to be called shy. Anyway, she was a successful photo journalist these days and even managed to travel on her own now and then when her husband couldn't pull away from his work to go with her.

Who needed a traveling companion, anyway? It was nice to make your own schedule, to eat where you wanted, when you wanted, to sleep unbothered and get up when you wanted, to read or work on the plane without someone jabbering at you and interrupting. Gillian knew how to act snobby enough fellow travelers wouldn't bother her. She'd made an art of it. She liked to be left alone. In general, she preferred to travel alone.

She could get used to Hank traveling at her side, though.

And she'd have to get used to traveling with a baby, also. That might make it harder to read or work on the plane, she supposed. She'd seen and heard enough of them wailing during flights.

Hank touched the small of her back. "Are you all right?"

Gillian nodded and tried to push the thought aside. How would she be a good mom when she liked so much to be alone? *Later, Gilly. Don't think about it now.*

He must have confused her sudden emotional downturn for a physical one, since he led her to a path where a picnic table stood partly covered by a shelter. "How about lunch before we continue?"

The man had a whole meal for two in his backpack. Cured ham. Without chemical preservatives, he said. A white cheese block sliced and protected in a small insulated bag along with a good amount of fresh snap peas. Apples. For extra water and energy. Homemade trail mix.

The man was a regular Boy Scout. He laughed when she said as much.

"Experience. As I said, I've been here often. It's one of my favorite places to get away."

Gillian thought he'd already gotten away, but she didn't say as much.

Hank began to wonder if it had been a good idea to bring her out to the desert monument. He wasn't sure if something about it bothered her mentally or if it was hard on her physically, considering her condition. Not that he knew much about pregnant women and what they should or shouldn't do.

He'd tried asking if they should leave, several times, until she got annoyed and said if he hadn't wanted her to come, he shouldn't have asked. He'd tried to explain he was only worried about her physical condition and she assured him if there was any risk, if she was too tired, she would sure as heck let him know, and she would absolutely not be babied.

She ran her hand along Cutthroat Castle while he told her about the kivas, ceremonial structures. The group of building remains had likely been what they would call a town. A kiva was generally built into the earth and was said to connect the two worlds, above and below. The castle was built on a boulder instead, possibly a defense station. He couldn't do more than guess when she asked who they were defending themselves against. Other tribes, he assumed.

He told her the Puebloans ate sagebrush, either for the iron in it or to rid themselves of parasites, and they used the ready supply of quartz for tools and defense, that the villages were all based around springs and seeps, as every community had done through the ages and why when you flew over the land, you could still see how big cities based themselves around a large body of water, with smaller and more sporadic communities around smaller rivers and streams. Often you saw the trees thriving around streams more than the streams themselves, from 30,000 feet above the ground.

He was talking just to talk since she wasn't. Not that he minded silence in general, but something had her unnerved and that unnerved him, as well. So he talked. If it annoyed her, she didn't say.

A loud ring made her jump and she grimaced while pulling her cell from her back pocket.

"Yeah?" She threw him an apologetic look as she answered. "I'm fine, as I told you this morning. ... It's early, Karenne. ... Okay, I know, but yes.... He's right here with me, so if you don't mind, I'll call back tonight. ... I know that. ... I didn't hear you. The reception's bad. It does that in the mountains, you know. ... Does it matter where we work?" She sighed and moved farther from him, lowering her voice as she said something about letting her know...

Hank walked away, allowing the privacy she apparently wanted, but not far enough he couldn't see her. Gillian's back was to him and that bothered him but he tried hard not to let it bother him. He crouched in pretense of studying something on the ground, but it was more to stretch his legs and to do something other than standing around waiting.

"Sorry." She came back to him and he looked up but stayed where he was.

"Everything okay?"

"Yes. She's been acting like she thinks she's my mother ever since I let her know I'm expecting. I tell her to stop, but..."

"I guess we should be working instead of acting like this is a vacation." Hank eyed her, anxious for her response.

Gillian hesitated, returning the gaze, then touched his hair, smoothing her fingers back around his ear. "I don't know."

"You don't know? That is why you came back."

"You think so? Do you really?" Her gaze softened with enough moisture to make her eyes shine, but no more than that.

Rising to his feet, he wrapped a hand behind her neck, and lowered his face close to hers. "You walked away so I wouldn't hear you. Why?"

"I um... I let her run over me too much. I know I do. I guess I didn't want you to hear me doing it. How pathetic is that?"

His nerves eased. He was far too suspicious. Not a secret she didn't want him to hear, only something she saw as a character flaw, as though he didn't have plenty himself. "Gill, you don't have to hide anything from me."

"Maybe. Hard to break such an ingrained habit, though."

"Understood." Hank tried to think of a way to tell her she was safe to break that habit with him, but he didn't have the right words, so he kissed her.

Gillian wrapped her arms up around his shoulders and took him in, close enough he could feel the small swell of her child. And he knew, at that moment, he wanted them both. He wanted to help raise her child, for as long as he could.

Nearly breathless when she allowed a release, he spoke next to her ear. "How about you give up that habit with me and I'll give up my habit of suspicion with you?"

When she pulled back to eye him, he cringed inwardly. Not what he meant to say. Not what he should have said.

"You're suspicious of me?"

"No." He kept her from pulling away. "Of everyone. Had to learn to be. But not of you, not more than ... than habit."

She nodded, her lips pursed in thought.

"That didn't come out right."

"Okay, Hank. It's okay. I understand. You're waiting for story questioning, so maybe we should get that out of the way?"

Right. He was. Except she'd just hinted she hadn't come for the story. "Fine. Fire away."

"Now?"

"Why not?"

"I need ... my notebook, pencil..."

"You didn't bring them?" He glanced at the little tote bag over her shoulder.

"No." She noticed where he was looking and grabbed it to pull out a little book. "My journal. Observation journal. I use it for notes, yes, for ... well, for my new direction, other than the freelance stuff. Not for work, for the paper. This is for me. I didn't bring anything out here for the story. I don't even have questions written out as I usually do. Like I said, I'm not... I didn't come for that. I only let Karenne think I did. It's very dishonest, I realize, but..."

"New direction?"

"Writing. Fiction." She blushed and looked away. "Fact based. But fiction. I carry this everywhere in case I see or hear something I want to remember that maybe I can use sometime."

Fiction. The woman was writing fiction. Hank couldn't help the smile that came at the thought.

She walked away in a huff.

"Hey, hold on." He caught up and touched her fingertips, but she yanked her hand away, so he moved in front of her and took them both, making her stop.

"Don't make fun of me." Her face was red.

"Why would I?"

"I know. Everyone is writing a book these days. Everyone thinks it's so easy to just sit down and bang out a book and put it online and make a bunch of money. I know it doesn't work that way. I know it may be no good, or not interesting enough to anyone else. But just because I work in journalism doesn't mean that's all I am or can do. I may not do anything with it. Maybe it'll sit in a file somewhere and languish, but I enjoy the creativity of it and it helps my ... my..."

"Depression."

She stared. And then collected herself. "Karenne told you?"

"No. It was a guess."

"It's not an excuse. It's clinical. It just hits and nothing I do or tell myself stops it. I can't just get over it when I decide. Some days it's all I can do to get out of bed, but I do that. At least most of the time I can. I keep going. It's occasional, usually no more than a week or two at a time. And it's fine. I handle it."

"I know."

"I'm not nuts or anything..."

"I know." He released her hand to touch her face. "Gillian, I think you're doing fine with it, and I'm glad you found something that helps."

She stared as though trying to decide whether to believe him. "I've been writing for a long time. Not just for work. I didn't just read a book one day and think *I can do better than this* and pick up a pencil. I don't have some idea that it's easy and anyone can do it, at least well enough to sell big. I'm not fooling myself that I'll be the next Susan Mallery or Kristin Hannah."

"I wasn't suggesting any of that."

"Yeah, well, I know what people think. It's why I haven't told anyone, not even Karenne. So..."

"Gill, I think it's nice."

"Nice, like cute?"

"No. Pull back your defenses a bit. I mean nice as in I'm glad you have more than your work. Everyone should have. And I won't be at all surprised if it lands you a book deal."

"I'm not even thinking about that. I'm taking a creative writing class for now and seeing what I've been doing wrong and reworking things. So it's not even at sharing with a friend stage yet."

"Well, when it is, I'd love to be the first to have that privilege. Are you ready to go? I don't want you to get too tired."

"Or you're avoiding the conversation. About which? My depression or my writing? Because I'm aware that both make people roll their eyes."

"Neither. Actually, I'm tired. I hate to admit it…"

"Do you feel okay? Should you have come out here?"

"Only tired, Gillian. Even fully healthy people get tired. Truthfully, I haven't slept well since you left…"

"I'm sorry. I mean, about the way I left. It was partly the depression and partly starting to realize I was pregnant, and I got scared."

"Understood. It's fine. And we can come back another day…"

"I bet it's beautiful here at night."

The fast jumps in conversation left him befuddled. "Okay, how about one thing at a time? Let's head back and we'll choose a topic and stick with that."

She chuckled. "I'm a little lost, too."

"Glad it's not just me, but yes, it is beautiful here at night. We'll do that one of these days."

Gillian found it easier than she imagined talking to Hank about her depression and depressive episodes, which she had never talked about. To anyone. She handled it. Mostly, she handled it well. She'd yet to pinpoint any one trigger or to figure out whether there were several triggers. It just hit her suddenly, under different conditions. Her doctor, when she did mention it years ago, suggested it was hormones and normal. She was glad Hank looked annoyed when she repeated as much. She could have figured that out if it happened at the same time every month. It didn't. She could go months with no signs, and then bam, it would slam into her.

Sometimes it was fairly minor, only a general sadness she couldn't shake and didn't understand. Other times it was full blown and she couldn't get out of bed for days. She gave Karenne so much leeway since her editor had given her leeway for it more than once.

Hank sipped his warm green tea with local honey at the restaurant somewhere between Durango and Hovenweep, a quaint little place with its old-time beige and gold speckled veneer tables with red vinyl chairs, wood paneling painted the same beige, and gold picture frames sporting old posters that looked like they'd been there since the Sixties.

The server who recognized him was happy to see him again, and relieved, Gillian thought, that maybe he was still around to be seen. Or it could be her imagination. He didn't talk of his illness more than she talked about hers. How would the woman know?

"I dated her."

Gillian looked back at him from where she realized she was again watching the woman walk away. She was only partly watching her, though. Mostly, she was hoping their food would arrive soon since the place smelled strongly of burgers and fries and she was starving.

"You're wondering why she asked how I'm doing and if I feel all right, yes?" Leaned back, relaxed against the booth he'd chosen rather than a table, he took another swallow of tea.

"Yes. I was." She studied the woman, an older brunette, or at least a good bit older than she was herself, with shoulder-length curly hair that needed the help of a good conditioner, and caught a glimpse of a chef salad on another table. Gillian considered ordering that, too. "So." She took a good swallow of her iced tea, wishing she'd added sugar. "Serious?"

"And you mean am I serious that I dated her, or was it serious?"

"Yes. I mean..." She shrugged. "Not my business."

He grinned. "It was more of a close, casual friendship. I told her we shouldn't get serious because of my ... well, physical instability, and she agreed, so that was that. No hard feelings."

Gillian thought there might be a few hard feelings on his part, and she wouldn't blame him for that. "Is that why we stopped here?"

He laughed. "Think I'm showing off my new girl?"

"No, I..." New girl? "I meant so she can see you're okay. Am I your new girl?"

"Do you always jump conversations like this?"

"Often. So?"

"So." He leaned forward, crossing his arms on the edge of the table. "I think *new girl* doesn't sound quite right, not for you. And since it sounds like I jump around from one woman to another the way you jump around in conversation, I assure you I don't."

"Don't worry. Given my own history, I'm in no place to judge."

He grew suddenly serious with a soft nod and stared into his tea mug. "I stop here because I trust their food to be free of things I don't want, which is what got her attention since she's a naturalist, for different reasons. I'm not here to show you off, but I guess there's a part of me that enjoys ... well, at least the possibility of saying not everyone would be scared away, at least so far. And yes, I'd like to think of you as ... not a *new girl*, exactly, but..."

"As yours. *With* you."

"Yes."

"Okay."

"Okay?"

She reached for his hand and felt the heat from his tea. "If you can deal with me expecting another man's child, especially under the circumstances, I can deal with whatever happens with your health. I mean, none of us know, right? Life and how long it happens to be is all a guessing game. And I think you could very well outlive me, Hank Dennison. I know you could..."

"Don't say that."

"It's true. We never know."

He leaned forward and took her other hand, as well. "I don't want to outlive you, Gillian. As selfish as it might sound, I've done enough of the outliving people I love thing already. I've had about my fill of it and I would rather..."

"People you love?"

"My father, far too early. My brother, *younger* brother. My mother, also too early. I've outlived them all already and I'd rather not outlive one more person I love, since there aren't very many of them in the first place."

"Person you love." It was nearly a whisper and her eyes watered.

"Yes." He squeezed her fingers. "So you can't do that to me. All right?" His eyes watered as much as hers, which made her lose the control she'd been fighting to maintain.

When she wiped at her face, he came around to sit beside her and held her close. "I shouldn't have done that here. I'm sorry."

Her head shook and she grasped the front of his shirt. "I can't do the story, you know. It has to be objective and I can't."

He kissed her head and raised her face to his with fingers under her chin. "I want you to write whatever it is you need to write. Without bounds. If you think my story's interesting enough, do it, but not as an assignment. Because it matters to you enough to be worth your time. You can ask me anything and I'll answer you. Honestly, though, Gill, I'm far more interested in your fiction."

He would answer anything. But how could she ask if it was for a story? It didn't seem right.

She wanted to do Hank's story, but not as an assignment, as far more than that. A biography, maybe. His story was too big for one article.

Karenne would definitely have her head.

Twenty-nine

Gillian turned her phone off. Karenne wouldn't stop calling, to ask if she didn't have what she needed by now for the article, to constantly remind her she only had four days, and to ask, several times, if she was actually working or taking vacation. Aside from being annoying, she didn't want the distraction.

She was working. On his story. In order to appease Karenne, and as promotion, she would do the story for the paper as a segue into the book. She hadn't told Hank about her book idea. She planned to show him the article, which would come from parts of the book she had in mind, see if he approved, and then send it to Karenne with a hint about more to come. No one needed to know about the book until it was done.

Her novel in progress could stay in progress. She'd work on it in between. But Hank's story came first. Because that was what she wanted. For herself. For him. Because it needed to be out there.

He'd again refused to stay at the townhouse the night before after the long day at Hovenweep. But he'd lingered longer. Gillian loved how hard it was for him to make himself leave.

She had the day to herself. He had things to do, he said, and she needed work time. He'd broken down and bought a basic cell phone to keep not on his person, but nearby, so she could easily reach him. She'd hugged him and promised that, in return, she would use the house phone to talk to Karenne when the conversation needed to be more than a minute or two, even though she believed his concern was a little overboard. It made him feel better.

"Back to work, Gillian." As she'd promised him, she'd stepped away from the computer while she ate lunch, stretched her hands and arms and legs, got her blood flowing again. Her normal routine was to grab bites of a sandwich in between typing, and she'd told him as much. She couldn't even be irritated when he asked her not to do so, to get up and give herself a break for meals and now and then in between. He was the first one to worry enough about her to bother. How could she be irritated by that?

And it did feel better. Her flow was steadier. Her typing more smooth and natural. Of course, maybe it was her subject matter since she loved him ... loved it, her subject, her story, so much. Writing felt like playing whenever she hit on something she loved.

She did love the man.

She did.

Allowing herself a smile at the thought, she rubbed a hand over her abdomen as a way to tell her little one all was going to be okay, more than okay, and went back to work.

Hank took a break and rested his body while nourishing it with a glass of green tea steeped with ginger and a splash of lemon juice. Nearly time for dinner. Gillian hadn't called. She was busy working, he supposed. She hadn't asked him anything further for her article, although he wasn't sure there was any more to add or that his story was worth an article. Possibly she was working on her novel instead. He hoped she was.

Resigned to give her the whole day alone to work, rest, whatever she wanted to do, he'd thrown himself into his own newest project. He needed the time, as well. And yet, he considered breaking his own promise and calling to ask her to dinner. Just to be sure she was taking a good break.

Not true, of course. He wanted to see her.

Purely selfish.

With a deep sigh, he got up to grab the bag of grapes out of the freezer, poured some in a small bowl, and returned to his front porch to further replenish his system.

A beautiful day. He hoped she at least had the windows open to enjoy it. The black squirrels that had made their home among the ponderosa pines bordering the cleared land around his cabin romped through fallen leaves at the edge of the yard. Hank never raked the leaves; he let them shelter small critters until they became mulch. He'd tried hard not to disrupt the natural habitat more than necessary when he built the cabin.

When he chose trees to carve, they were either already part fallen or more than plentiful. He mainly used pine for his quick work, for random ideas, or for anything he planned to use indoors, since it was soft and easy to carve. The limited supply of spalted maple piled inside his storage shed became specialty indoor pieces. Hank loved the dark streaks within the normally light-colored maple, created from fallen trees that had started to rot but were still intact enough to hold. Neither stood up well outdoors over time, though, so for projects he cared more about, those meant to stay out in the elements, he used the more than abundant juniper. It was slower going, but the hardness allowed extra detail and it would last fifty years or so, protected by its natural oils. He loved the smell of them, as well. His fantasy carvings were made from juniper, but for those, he also added a protective layer of varnish.

Eventually, he would get back to working on them.

It was warm enough he didn't need a jacket and cool enough to work without sweating. The sky was nearly cloudless. It would be a nice day for a walk.

Also a nice day for the art festival. Hank considered going by himself for an hour or so, but she'd agreed to go in the morning, so he could wait. He had work to do. Work he was more excited about than he'd been in years.

Thirty

It was a good thing Gillian had been out walking with Gia so often. Otherwise, she never would have been able to keep up with Hank and his monument tour and then spend all day at the arts festival two days later. He'd wanted to be at the festival at ten a.m. when it opened and spend a couple of hours or so.

Now 4:30 with a half an hour until closing, they were still there wandering, sometimes sitting long enough to listen to local musicians or to grab something not terribly healthy that tasted wonderful, which he admitted he still did on occasion. Mainly, they looked at artwork and various crafts. There were nearly a hundred artisans and Gillian wanted to see them all.

He'd asked a few times if she was sure she wanted to stay, that he'd take her home and come back, but she was enjoying herself immeasurably. Now and then she stopped to watch young children involved in an art activity. A wonderful thing for the community, she thought, one she wanted her child to take part in. The thought startled her a bit. She wanted her child here, in Durango. She loved Denver, but Durango was growing on her fast. Or Hank was. Maybe both.

She stared so long at the group of kids that Hank rubbed her back and gave her a quizzical look. Since she didn't want to explain, she smiled and began walking, away from where she could too easily see her child running around enjoying the fun in a few years.

Denver had art events, as well, but she'd only gone to one, several years ago, as an assignment. It wasn't the same as wandering with Hank, a hand on his arm at times, and with him reaching out to block someone who got too close to her at other times, protecting her child.

It was so horribly sweet she'd actually kissed him once after he'd done so. Publicly. Just a small kiss. His expression said he hadn't minded. Now and then, he claimed her fingers while they walked instead of offering his arm. Far more intimate. And when he ran into anyone he knew, he introduced her using her real name, not the pseudonym he'd given Mrs. Whatever-her-name-was a few months ago.

Gillian loved hearing him introduce her because he sounded proud to do so. She'd never known that feeling. Ever. Her baby's sperm donor generally hadn't bothered to introduce her at all when they were out together, and when he did, it was reluctant.

He didn't matter. She only hoped her child was more like herself than like him, no matter how self-centered that sounded. In the least, she would raise Baby to be respectful of others, the way Hank was. If she had a boy, he would have an awfully good role model. Maybe she should start wishing for a boy.

Truthfully, she didn't care about the gender. She wanted healthy and smart and the rest she was happy enough to leave to fate.

But she did want him or her in Durango, with Hank, at least part of the time. She couldn't possibly think of a better role model.

Hank knew he'd pushed her limit having her out there all day, but he enjoyed it entirely too much to cut it short, since she didn't want to cut it short. He sat to rest more often than he needed in order to make sure she rested often enough. Since he hadn't let himself go see her the night before, although he'd considered it far too often, he went to see Susan at the health store to ask questions about pregnancy.

Could be he shouldn't have told Gillian's secret, but if she stayed, it wouldn't stay a secret for long. Susan would be straight with him and keep her mouth shut. The woman had five kids of her own, all natural. The perfect person to ask what he needed to know.

Walking was good for her. Gillian needed to stay active. He'd also picked up natural supplements to help with her energy and iron level. She didn't know yet. He'd yet to admit what he'd done. He felt better, though, knowing more about what to expect, about what was safe.

And he wanted her to stay. He wanted very much to be part of her child's life. Maybe he did have a reason to fight harder to stay around. Maybe, if the cancer came back at him, he'd be a guinea pig for the more extreme natural cures he'd read about and was helping to fund. There had to be a way. He couldn't let himself believe otherwise. Especially now.

"What has you suddenly so serious?" Gillian hung her sweater on the rack beside the front door and ran hands up his stomach to his chest.

"Thinking. Gill…" He didn't want to bring it up. Not that. "How about letting me cook?"

"That's not what you were thinking."

"No, but you've been on your feet enough today, so you need to sit and relax."

"I feel just fine, Mr. Overprotective. And it's my turn."

"I want to be here for you." He ran fingers through her breeze-blown hair, smoothing it.

"You are. That doesn't mean you have to do everything for me. I don't need that."

"That's not what I meant. Sit with me a minute." He claimed her hands and walked backward to the couch, pulling her with him. With a deep slow breath, he tried to let the right words form. "Before this goes further, I need to finish explaining why I've been so reticent about pulling you into this, about letting this … proceed."

"You mean you're thinking about staying tonight?" Her eyes sparkled, teasing.

His stomach tightened. "No." Also wrong thing to say, or the wrong way to say it, judging from her reaction, the way she pulled back. "Gill…" How did he say it? He couldn't. Hank couldn't look her in the eye and tell her. "You know what? How about we cook together? Will that work for you?"

"Fine. But what were you going to say?"

"It'll wait." He stood and went to the kitchen. She'd have to decide whether to follow. He couldn't do that conversation after such a beautiful day, after she'd stood there watching the children for so long, when she was so happy about her coming child. She'd want more than one, he assumed. How could he tell her that couldn't happen with him?

She tried not to let herself believe he would back away because of … which thing? There were so many she could guess. Her job. The story. Where she lived. How she lived. The baby. Her depression. How annoying she'd been the last time. She wouldn't even be able to blame him.

Watching him walk away from the conversation, again, Gillian sighed and considered sitting there on the couch refusing to move until he talked to her. The idea sounded petulant, though, and she didn't need to add to the list of reasons he already had.

A sudden heaviness moved in, faster than usual. Instead of giving in to it and sinking onto his couch, the one he let someone else choose for him, the rather ugly plain almost-black uncomfortable leather couch, Gillian went up to her room. He could cook without her. Or he could wait.

At least she knew the trigger this time.

Too much doubt. Self-doubt. Too much of a habit.

Grabbing Danskin workout pants that she'd started wearing at home for added comfort, a loose Metallica shirt she only used to sleep in, and undies – which did she want? a turn-on pair or comfortable? Gillian rolled her eyes at herself and went with comfort since he'd made it clear it wouldn't matter. Not having sex didn't matter to her. What mattered was that he didn't want it, or didn't want quite that much of her.

She shut the bathroom door a bit too hard. A long hot shower would help. Often it did. She needed it to help. He didn't need her stupid episode to deal with on top of his own issues. Or another reason.

Hank turned back to find her, but she wasn't on the couch, or in the living area. "Gillian?" A door slammed upstairs. With a sigh, he wondered whether to follow or let her be.

Deciding to give her a couple of minutes, he went back to pull out twenty different ingredients for a salad – not twenty, actually, but close enough – complete with hard-boiled eggs and a few slices of bacon to crumble over top for extra crunch and flavor.

When the eggs and bacon were both ready and cooling, he went to the bottom of the stairs and listened a minute. No sound. Was she napping? Possibly. Susan said she may need to nap now and then to regain energy.

Giving her more time, he returned to chop the fresh broccoli, red and green peppers, black olives, carrots, cauliflower, tomatoes, and mushrooms. He rinsed the baby spinach and lettuce well. Then he peeled the eggs. He kept everything separate in case she didn't eat any of the individual ingredients.

Still no sound, so he flipped on the computer from its hibernation and sat down to do some research.

Dandelion root tea. Hank shuddered at the thought. He'd tried eating dandelion greens for their health benefit but found them rather inedible. Canadian scientists had some luck with dandelion root killing, they believed, cancer cells quickly without other harm to the body.

A little hard to believe, he thought, but not impossible to believe. It wouldn't hurt to try. Just in case. He'd even eat the bitter leaves themselves if it might work, no matter how much he hated the taste. There was more than himself at stake now.

Checking his watch, Hank made his way upstairs to knock on her door, but it was open, so he stepped in ... at the same time she came out of the bathroom barely wrapped in a towel.

"Oh. Sorry." Her face reddened as her fingers clenched the towel more tightly. "I should've shut my door."

"I'm glad you didn't. You have beautiful shoulders. It's nice to see them again."

Gillian opened her mouth, then closed it and gathered herself. "Did I take too long?"

There was a mood change in her far too evident not to notice. "You're fine, time-wise. Are you otherwise?"

"What?"

"Everything all right?"

Her head shook softly, as though of its own accord, as though she hadn't meant to answer.

He moved closer, close enough to touch her shoulder. "We can talk while we eat. Okay?"

"Hank." She watched his fingers caress her skin. "Since you're not staying tonight, you really need to stop doing that and let me get dressed."

He froze. For a couple of seconds. Then he met her eyes. He

didn't want to stop. Or back away. Or let her get dressed. "Gill..." His own head shook. He needed to tell her. But ... but not now, he didn't. His body was apparently functioning just fine at the moment. The wanting coursed throughout his system as he slid his fingers up along her neck, up behind her ear, the beautiful un-pierced ear. He had to wonder why her ears weren't done like every other woman in the country, with at least two holes boasting studs or dangling pretty things. Hank ran his fingers over the unmarred lobe.

"Dinner can wait." Her voice was nearly a whisper.

He was definitely functioning just fine, other than an obvious lack of control. Unable to stop himself, he leaned in to kiss her.

Gillian wrapped an arm around his shoulder and her hand grasped the back of his head. They didn't need words. Not now. He kissed her beautiful bare soft shoulder, her neck, her jaw, in front of her ear. His conscience told him to warn her, but he couldn't say it. He wanted at least one time with her that she wouldn't be wondering if it would work or how long they could have this. He wanted her to think of him as whole, at least this first time.

She was an odd, beautiful combination of shy and aggressive. He exchanged her hand for his own where she gripped the towel and she let him unwrap it, move it away. Her expression was unsure, wary, but that sparkle was strongly in her eyes.

With a soft smile, he ran his hand first over her swollen abdomen. Her child. Part of her. It didn't matter that the child hadn't been conceived in love. He or she was well loved. She loved her child and it showed in her eyes, her protectiveness, her wariness.

And Hank loved the child because it was part of her.

He returned to her lips, trying not to rush although his urges tried to rush him. Moving things along, Gillian began undressing him, not slowly, pushing his clothes out of her way, kissing him both softly and aggressively.

Hank forced other thoughts, concerns, from his head as he took her to the bed, took her in his arms, as she took him inside, her fingers insisting, digging into his lower back. He loved her mix of tenderness and aggression. He loved the way she met his eyes at times and kept them away at other moments, how she let the tension always within her heighten and then dissolve, her eyes closed, her expression relaxed.

With a kiss to the top curve of her nose, he lowered carefully against her body, not enough to put pressure on the child, and enclosed her within his arms.

"I think I may have to move." Gillian ran fingers down his bare chest, over the dark blond curly hair between the hard roundness of the muscles he had tuned up so well. Wrong phrase, she knew, but anatomy had been among her most hated classes. She was better with mechanical terms. Karenne had jumped her more than once about it.

"You're not comfortable?" He kissed her head where it rested part on the pillow and part on his shoulder.

"What?" She looked up at him.

"You need to move?"

"Oh. I mean..." She shifted, up on her elbow, allowing her breasts to rest against his skin. "I mean move, as in to Durango. Out of Denver." Studying the mix of emotions on his face, Gillian had to wonder if she'd mentioned it too fast, but he'd said...

"It won't always be like this, Gill. I should have told you before, but I had trouble saying it."

"Like what?"

His chest raised hard and lowered softly, and he moved, turning her to her back, smoothing fingers along her face. "I hope you realize by now that I love you, and I want you to be happy. More than anything. More than my own personal needs. That matters."

The lump in her throat kept her from answering.

"So you should know that ... what I had ... have ... is pancreatic cancer. It's hard to cure. Survival rates aren't good, about seven percent make it five years, and I'm on year three. But there's growing research that says many foods and herbs can stop or slow it and I focus on those and I haven't had symptoms lately..."

"You're going to be fine." Gillian stroked fingers up through his hair. "You are. And it's not going to scare me away. In case you've been wondering. Whatever happens, I'll be here, if you'll let me. I'm strong enough to deal with it. You haven't seen much of that side of me yet, but I am. If … if it comes to having to fight it harder and you need help, I'll be here to help. Okay? Will you let me?"

His eyes moistened and he kissed her nose. "The surgery I had… Gillian, I can't have children. And some nights, I … get too tired or at least part of me is and I don't always… I may be unable, at times, no matter how attracted I am to you…"

"Okay." It was too hard for him to say, so she stopped him with a kiss. "It doesn't matter."

"Don't say it doesn't now just because this was … incredible. It was, but it may not be very often…"

"I don't care." She saw the doubt in his eyes. "It's funny, really. Maybe it's a fate thing or something, but, I can't tell you how often I've wished to just have a nice companionship, some cuddling and such, without the rest. I rarely want the rest of it. I'm being completely honest, so don't look at me like that. Really. It too often just feels like an intrusion I don't particularly want. I may be interested far less often than you're … interested, or able, or whatever. Is that going to work for you?"

"I love you, Gill." His voice was soft, shaky. So unlike the tough, sturdy Hank Dennison he always showed. "I'm willing to work around whatever works for you, for as long as I can."

"Don't say it that way. And I feel the same."

Hank's nerves didn't subside with her reassurance. It was all he could do to hide them while they ran through the shower together, dried and dressed, and went to eat a late dinner. He had strawberries and raspberries in the refrigerator and spooned some on top of a mix of plain yogurt and local honey, hoping she'd enjoy it. She'd piled every ingredient he'd cut up on her salad, which he'd found amusing. The girl liked to eat, and she wasn't particular.

And she loved dessert, as well.

But she was quiet through the rest of the night. Possibly because he was. He felt raw, open, too vulnerable. He needed time to himself, and so he still didn't agree to stay overnight.

She was offended, although she didn't say so. Hank couldn't blame her, but he needed time and space, to recover, and to work.

Gillian leaned back against the door when it closed behind him. She'd handled it wrong. Why else wouldn't he stay instead of driving all the way back out to the boonies?

She hadn't overreacted. She hadn't pushed him away or pulled away. She didn't treat him differently, other than the way things were always different after allowing someone in that far, figuratively. And literally.

She'd actually felt far more comfortable with him afterward, which usually worked the other way for her. She'd always wished they would just go home and leave her be after sex…

Maybe he was the same? Except she didn't want that with him. Gillian wanted, desperately, for Hank to stay the night; she wanted to wake up beside him. Still, if he felt the way she always had before, she'd rather he just go than try to fake wanting to be there as she always had.

Karma? Maybe she'd been unfair to pretend, although she was only trying to spare their feelings.

With the darkness trying to resettle in her soul, Gillian shook it away the best she could and went to the computer to work. She automatically pulled up his story but closed it again. She couldn't deal with that tonight. Instead, she opened the story she'd put aside since arriving in Durango. Her fiction. He said he was far more interested in her fiction than in whatever she chose to write about him.

There were parts of him in it, though. He was too much always in her thoughts to get around that.

Thirty-one

They'd fallen into the habit over the past two and a half weeks of having dinner every night, either at the townhouse or on the town, and otherwise staying apart. It wasn't her idea. Gillian wanted to see him more often. He claimed she needed the time to work, and he had a project he wanted to finish.

She couldn't help but think, though, that he might be having second thoughts after she practically pushed him into sex. He accepted a kiss now and then and he held her hand or offered his arm when they were out. Otherwise, he was more quiet, more thoughtful, more distant. After saying how incredible it had been, he gave off every sign that he didn't plan a repeat performance.

Gillian couldn't make sense of the man. She figured she might as well get used to that. He wasn't an easy-to-know type, which was fine. At least she wouldn't get bored. And she wasn't needy. A good thing, apparently.

Again ignoring a call from Karenne, Gillian gave in at the last second and answered.

"Decide to talk to me, finally?"

"I've been talking to you, but it's hard to work with the phone constantly ringing."

"Gilly, you know I don't believe you need that much time for one article. What's going on?"

She sighed. "Okay."

"Okay, what?"

"Okay, the article is done and I'll send it along to you soon."

"Soon? It's been done how long?"

"A week or so. And don't yell. I have my reasons and I'm not getting paid anymore, so..."

"You will when you turn that thing in."

"I realize that."

"So what's the delay?"

Gillian got up, a hand under her stomach for support, not that she needed the extra support yet, and went to the window. Leaves carpeted the yard. When a man had come to clean them up the day before, she told him to leave them there. She liked the leaves. She liked being able to traipse through them and hear them crunch. Hank had grinned when she told him why it hadn't been done and said he'd tell the guy not to bother.

"Still there?" The annoyance came through loud and clear.

"Yeah. And I'll send it to you tomorrow."

"Why not today?"

"Because I haven't let him read it yet."

"Let him read it? Since when do you let a story subject read an article before it comes out?"

"Since now. I won't do it otherwise, so don't bother to argue."

A long silence came over the line, silence with a filtered background of normal life at the paper. Voices. Drawers closing. Keyboards clicking. Sounds she used to love. And she still did, here on her own when she made them.

"So are you coming home after you let him approve your piece and send it in?"

"I'm... Um, no. Not yet. There's still something I need to do and this is working for me. Being here. It's ... inspirational, I guess." She wandered the other direction to the kitchen to find something to snack on since she'd been interrupted.

"Gillian, be careful..."

"Have to go, Karenne. I don't want to lose my train of thought. Bye." She hung up quick.

Okay, it was a bit of a lie. She just wanted off the phone. And she didn't want to hear any admonitions.

Truth was, she'd already lost her train of thought while thinking of him. Ironic, she supposed, since she was supposed to be thinking of him, but not that way and... "Fine. Time for a break." She grabbed a bag of trail mix, homemade trail mix he'd brought her the other day for protein and energy, he said, and decided she needed music.

Dancing to whatever came up when she asked for a hard rock and metal mix, bag in hand and munching at the same time, Gillian felt an odd kind of twinge in her abdomen and stopped to concentrate on it. She even shut off the music, although there was no reason to do that since it wouldn't help her feel anything any better.

Again. A flutter.

A flutter. Movement. Her baby was moving. Dancing, too? A silly thought. But maybe he was. They heard sounds very early, she'd read. Maybe he was.

Her eyes watered and she set her hand over where she felt it. Was metal rock good for tiny little humans? They wouldn't understand the words, but there was so much talk about Mozart for babies some time back, maybe she should do that instead.

She didn't want Mozart. She didn't know what she wanted.

So she put it on shuffle everything and let fate, or whatever electronic device made the choice, decide. Gillian kept dancing, the idea of whether a fetus would dance too intriguing to stop, but slower, with her hand in place, concentrating on her body, which she almost never did. Usually, she had a very good disconnect between her physical self and her mental self. She prided herself on it.

Maybe that was her big problem with sex. She couldn't connect the two well enough. It was just a thing. Sometimes okay enough. Sometimes pretty good for a few seconds or so. But just a thing.

Except with Hank. It was the mental part of it with him that was so thrilling. Maybe she would want it more often. Would she start to want it often enough to be bothered when he couldn't? Not likely. But then she tried to never fully discount any possibility.

Still, having that every now and then and actually wanting it would beat the repulsive thought of *having* to do that in order to keep a relationship going.

Gillian wanted to tell him she felt her baby moving. She wanted him there. She could easily work at his cabin, as well. The large battery recharged by his generator to run lights without the generator running continuously would run a computer, she expected, or at least her laptop. She'd gotten used to using his nice computer instead of her little laptop, but she could go back to that. At least he'd be around, even if he was out and about carving up some tree trunk somewhere.

She wanted to see him. More than for dinner. At least overnight. Even in different rooms, if he insisted.

When a country song started, it made her want to see him even more. She wondered if it was one he liked, a nice female voice she didn't recognize. Soft and slow and ... singing about home, finding *home* after nearly giving up.

Gillian cried as she stood and just listened.

With you I found my way...

It was her song, hers and Hanks. Maybe thousands of other women thought the same, but she didn't care. It was hers. And she was home.

She wasn't leaving.

Whatever he decided, however distant he stayed or however much alone time he needed, it was fine. She was staying. She could find her own place, maybe closer to his cabin but still with electric and running water that didn't need a pump. Or she'd stay in the townhouse if his offer remained valid.

Either way, she was moving to Durango.

Hank planned to take her out. It was easier to be out and about and keep things easy and uncomplicated than to be alone with her and do the same.

He was waiting. He'd let her in, told her what she had to know, and pulled what had to be just as raw an emotion for her out into the open. She didn't like sex much. Damn well could have fooled him.

When she opened the door, since he always knocked at the townhouse to respect her privacy, a savory scent drifted past. Even more seductive was her little black dress which covered her well but hinted both of her figure and of her pregnancy, which he found strangely sexy. Mostly it was her smile that pulled him in, an honest happy smile.

"Hi."

And her simple *Hi.* Luscious. "You look nice."

"Thank you. Coming in or standing out here?"

"Trying to decide."

"Yeah? Well, make up your mind. It's cold out there. I thought we'd stay in tonight."

"Apparently." He stepped in beside her and closed the door. "Smells good."

"Me or dinner?"

"Yes." He leaned in to set a light kiss on her neck. "Both."

"It's natural. An essential oil I bought from your friend Susan."

"Nice. But you don't need it."

"Thank you again." Her hand brushed against his leg. "So, I promised Karenne I'd send her the article tomorrow morning. I got tired of the phone calls. Want to read it before dinner or after?"

Read it? He hung his jacket up and turned to her. "I don't need to read it first. I trust you, Gill." She did that thing he loved by now where she started to speak and stopped, wordless. "What are we having?" He went to the kitchen because he needed to stay in motion and to take his eyes off her.

She followed, but instead of showing him whatever she had in the oven, she slid her arms around his waist to wrap around his stomach. "I'm moving to Durango, Hank. Should I find a place of my own or is it okay to stay here?"

Moving? He turned in her arms, studied her warm light brown eyes that still looked like she was trying to figure him out, or figure out where they stood, and waited.

"I'm home. Finally." Her hands drifted up to rest on his chest. "Whatever you do or want is besides the point by now. I mean, it's not, but I'm moving here anyway because it feels like home, like a real home, like I want my child to grow up here. I felt him moving earlier. It was ... so beautiful and ... I want the best for him or her. I want the fresh mountain air, the smaller more personable atmosphere, the clean mountain water where he can swim and go fishing and actually eat his catch, or hers, and ... I would really like him to know you, to be able to ... learn from you what he won't from me. I want to be as unwound for him as possible. So I'm staying. I'll tell Karenne after I send her the story tomorrow, but I wanted to tell you first. And I want you to read it before I send it."

Staying. She was staying in Durango. Of her own accord. He reached up to caress the strand of hair in front of her ear. "You might as well stay here for now. Since you're settled and all."

"For now? I should look for my own place? I will..."

"Absolutely not. But we'll have to discuss the arrangements, since I prefer the cabin and you prefer town."

"Arrangements? To stay together, you mean?"

"Do you think, Gillian Hart, that if you're staying in Durango, I don't intend to be right here with you? A part of your life, and your child's?"

"How much?" Her eyes sparkled, still hesitant.

"How much do you want?"

With a light grin, she grabbed the stereo remote and pushed play. Jo Dee Messina's voice surrounded them. "I found a new favorite singer today, and a couple of new favorite songs."

Burn. One of his favorites, also. One of the sexiest songs he'd ever heard. "I do, Gill. Burn for you. And I've been waiting to make sure you still can, and will, even knowing it may or may not work. Can you still see me the same as you did before I told you?"

She wrapped her arms around his shoulders and kissed him. "Oh, you silly man. I have wanted you here every night. I've had to work late every night to keep from thinking about how much I want you here, how much I want..." A deep shaky breath took over and her fingers slid from his neck back down to his chest. "I've even had thoughts of sneaking up to your cabin in hopes of finding you naked in that stream of yours, but I figured it was too cold by now."

Hank nearly admitted he'd been in that stream, naked, far too often, wondering if she might, hoping she might.

Instead, he fell to one knee and pulled out the ring he'd been carrying the past two weeks.

"Yes." Her voice was a whisper, tear-streaked. "And wow, that's beautiful."

"I haven't asked yet."

"You don't have to ask. Yes. And I'll sign anything you want, so you don't have to ask that, either."

"Sign what?"

"A ... contract or whatever. So you know I won't try to take everything you have and..."

"Stop talking, Gill. The *yes* was good enough."

"But I wouldn't blame you. I don't want you to think I want you because of..."

"Gillian." He smoothed a hand over her growing child. "Who else would I leave it to, anyway? The only thing you need to sign is the marriage certificate. Now give me your hand."

It shook as she offered it and he slid the diamond on and kissed her beautiful fingers. "Will dinner wait a bit?"

She wiped tears from her cheeks. "Yes. Have something else in mind?"

"The story. I want to read it." When she looked at him again as though she was going to speak and then didn't, he chuckled and pulled her down to sit on his leg. "What in the hell do you think I have in mind right now?"

"Well, I didn't want to assume, you know. *Oh*." Grasping his hand, she moved it to the side of the baby bulge.

He felt movement. Soft movement, but undeniably her child. His eyes closed and he followed it with his palm, felt her hand gently over his, guiding to the right spot as baby changed where he kicked, felt the soft kiss to his head. She was concerned about a prenuptial agreement for his money when she was giving him *this*, her child, allowing him to be a full part of it, a father? She hadn't quite said that much, but he would lead into it when the time was right.

He would gladly give her anything he had in exchange for this.

~ ~

Gillian held up her hand to watch the large diamond sparkle. A perfect moment. A write-worthy moment. She was tucked in against his naked body beneath the blankets, secure, loved, wanted. Engaged to Mr. CEO Hermit. And her child was going to have a real father, fully by his choice.

"What brought me here to you, Hank?"

He nuzzled his cheek against her hair. "Your story."

"No. Yes. But I mean ... I've done lots of stories and they were just..."

"Gillian." He smoothed fingers along her face and raised her eyes to his. "I mean *your* story. You needed to be here, for some reason. I needed you to be here, and I have no doubts left about that reason. You're here because you need to be here."

"You believe in that? Like destiny? We're just following a path already laid out for us?"

"No. I believe if we listen closely enough, we'll tell ourselves where to go and what to do in order to get where we need to be, even if we don't realize we're telling ourselves. We're led to certain paths, but whether or not we take them is up to us. We have to be willing to listen. And what we do on a path once we take it is our own choice."

"So if I'd found you and chose to stay in Denver..."

"I might have had to follow you there."

Follow her? "Would you have? After you went to such extreme measures to be where you want to be?"

"I probably would have tried it. Against my better judgment. To tell you the truth, I'd started looking at places on the outskirts. I'm much happier to stay here, though."

Her lungs expanded fast and released it. "I love you, Hank Dennison. And I think the cottage would make an incredible honeymoon spot. I'll gladly stay there with you until winter sets in. After that, I will need electric and a shower with hot water whenever I want it."

"Cabin, Gill. It's not a cottage."

"Maybe not yet." She grinned and kissed him before he could argue.

Thirty-two

With a sigh, Gillian went to grab her phone. She'd turned her cell off during dinner so they wouldn't be interrupted, as she always did when he was there, whether they stayed in or went out, and hadn't bothered to turn it back on. After dinner, he read the article while she cleaned up. Giving her a beautifully sweet approval, Hank told her to send it. She sent the email right then, before she lost her nerve.

He'd finally stayed the night and they lingered in bed when she woke to his stirring and the sunlight. In his room. They talked for some time and she mentioned maybe interviewing at a local paper. He suggested she not rush into finding a new job, that she should work on her own project and consider what she wanted for a wedding, when she wanted the wedding, offering anything she could dream of, with the only restriction whatever her pregnancy demanded.

After a late breakfast, he went back out to the cabin, leaving her to her own work. Although curious about what he was doing out there, she didn't ask, other than whether he needed help with anything. He only smiled and kissed her head. As soon as he left, she'd turned her phoned on and skimmed the missed calls and messages from her editor that said they had to talk. She'd tried twice to call back, but it went to voicemail. By now, it was nearly dinner time.

Gillian had to wonder if Karenne hated the article enough to need to make herself calm down before picking up the return calls or if she was only purposely make her wait in return. Gritting her teeth, she released the clench of her jaw with a quick deep breath, and answered as though not annoyed in the slightest. "Hey, Karenne."

"Hey? What do you mean *hey*? Gilly, that story... Are you sure that's what you meant to turn in? You wrote that?"

"Of course I wrote it. Think I'd steal someone else's work?"

"No, of course not. I mean, it doesn't sound like you. It sounds more like ... well... more adult."

"Really? Thank you." She rolled her eyes, and then smiled when he knocked. The man didn't need to knock. "Hold on a second." Putting the phone on mute while Karenne was talking, she went over to greet him, glad he at least unlocked the door and came in after knocking instead of waiting for her to let him in.

He noticed she was on the phone. "Your editor?"

"Yes. Hi." She kissed his neck. "Mm, you smell like fresh air. Give me a minute?"

Meeting her lips gently, slowly, Hank released them. "Take your time."

She watched him remove his jacket and shoes while she un-muted Karenne. "Sorry. So?"

"So? Are you kidding me with this article? What did you do? Let him write it for you?"

"Of course not. I just went back to my old style, the one you used to like."

"But this... I understand why you didn't take my calls after sending this. We need to talk."

"I tried to call twice today." She wandered over next to Hank when he pulled out two glasses and filled them with mountain water.

"Yes, well, I've been in the middle seat of a last-minute sold out flight because you wouldn't answer last night or this morning..."

"My phone was off. It was past work hours." Gillian played with his hair and realized what she'd said. "Wait. A flight? To where?"

"Durango, of course. I'm at the DoubleTree, overlooking the water, of all things; otherwise it's fine. How do I find you? Are you out at that god-forsaken cabin? Is there an address I can give a taxi driver?"

"You're here? Now?" She heard Karenne's reply, her irritated tone, and tried to pull her head together.

Gillian looked at Hank, wondering what she was supposed to do. She didn't want Karenne there. This was her territory. Hers and Hank's. It was a huge unwanted intrusion. She definitely didn't want her editor coming to Hank's townhouse and she had the sudden thought of having him take her out to the cabin so she was harder to find. Karenne could call Ernie and see if she could actually find Hank's place, which Gillian doubted. If she did, though, that was unacceptable. Too much encroachment.

Hank took the phone while Karenne asked if she heard what

she'd been saying. Introducing himself, he said they'd meet her at a restaurant downtown, close enough to her hotel she could easily walk.

She wouldn't, though. Gillian knew her editor would not walk the three blocks or so by herself in a strange town. She didn't walk anywhere by herself. Ever. Hank told her the hotel shuttle would take her and they'd be there in half an hour. If she needed more time than that, they'd wait.

He hung up and kissed her head. "Might as well get things out in the air since she's here. I'm going to run through the shower first."

"I'm sorry. I didn't expect her to... You don't have to..."

"Relax, Gill. It's fine. I've dealt with far bigger fish than your editor."

For a moment, Gillian could actually see the spark in Hank that could make him the ruthless CEO they said he was.

~ ~

He had to wonder why Gillian was so nervous to meet up with someone she called a friend. He had to disagree that Karenne was any kind of a friend to her based on what he'd seen and heard, but he didn't know much of the story and was willing to give the woman a chance.

His fiancée held his arm when he walked her into Ken and Sue's. She looked around at the place, getting her bearings, as Hank was used to her doing by now. The place was decoratively minimalist, which he appreciated, along with its friendly and earthy yellows and browns. A smiling greeter asked where they'd like to sit and he requested an outdoor table for three, letting her know they would be joined by another party soon.

Gillian answered when asked if the table was satisfactory. "Yes. Thank you." She let him hold her chair and he couldn't resist a kiss to the top of her head before he took the chair beside her rather than opposite the square table. "This is beautiful."

"I thought you might like it. Is sitting outside fine?"

"Of course." She cast her gaze around at the red brick half-wall planters full of flowers and small shrubs, and at the light strings hung around dark green canopies that sheltered the tables.

"Let me know if you get cold." She'd worn a long-sleeve jacket, but it was lightweight and cut in to barely go over her breasts, hanging loose and rounding back around to her waist, allowing her flowing, long but low-cut blouse to show well. The blouse was soft coral and yellow, the jacket deep red. She looked like a mountain sunrise. On a barely-there silver chain was a small pendant, a natural crystal of some kind, with a pinkish tint.

Hank couldn't keep himself from picking it up, allowing his fingers to touch her soft, pale skin. "A gift?"

"No. I picked it up on one of my work travels in Utah. It's a Lemurian crystal. They're supposed to emit light and hope and take away negativity. I'd put it away some time ago and forgot it until I spent some time deep-cleaning the apartment to make room for Baby."

"You wore it tonight to protect you from your editor's negative energy?"

She chuckled. "No. I like how it looks with this outfit. Why? Do you think I need protection from my friend?"

"I don't know, Gill. You're nervous about her being here. Do you?"

Starting to answer, she looked up at their server greeting them.

Relaying the specials of the day, the young woman offered a wine list. "If you haven't been here before, we're known for our large wine selection. I can help you decide, if you'd like."

"Thank you. Just iced tea, please, no sugar. I'll have to try whatever wine you recommend when it's safe." Gillian ran a hand over her stomach to show off the baby bump that her blouse concealed, and accepted congratulations with a smile.

"Should we start with appetizers until Karenne arrives?"

"If you'd like. And I'll trust your judgment."

Giving her a light grin, he ordered the Cajun scallops with aioli, mixed greens with dill, and lobster quesadillas, along with three plates.

Gillian laughed. "Three appetizers? How hungry are you?"

"I wanted you to have a good selection. Do any of them sound all right?"

"They all do, but..."

"If you can't finish your meal, it'll make a nice lunch tomorrow when I'm off working." He grasped the hand over her stomach and raised it to kiss her fingers. "Besides, you need to eat well."

"Oh. Should I have done that?"

He very much wanted to skip dinner by this point and take her back home. The thought was so entrenched in his head, he thought he might have missed something. "Should you have done what?"

"Made Baby so obvious. I wore this blouse because it still covers me fairly well, and I can still hide things a bit for now if you'd rather. But you know most servers tend to think there's something wrong with you if you order tea instead of alcohol. I shouldn't worry about what she thinks, of course, but..."

"No. You shouldn't. Either way. You should order what you want, not what you think you should based on what anyone else thinks of it. And as for your child, Gill..." He moved his chair closer and smoothed his hand over her beautiful new-life-protecting abdomen. "Why on earth would you want to hide something so miraculous?"

Her eyes watered. "I don't. I also don't want to... Well, we haven't known each other long and you know what people will say. They'll think... Well, what are we going to say about it?"

"Oh, Gillian. You worry too much. You need to stop that." He grasped her fingers again. "As far as I'm concerned, we'll tell anyone who bothers to ask when you're due and how excited we are and leave it at that. No one will ask details and they can think whatever they want. Unless you want to specify."

"Will Baby... I mean..." She avoided his eyes. "I guess what I say will depend on ... well..."

"Gill." He lifted her face to his. "What?"

"It's early yet, I know, but ... should I give him your name? If you'd rather I didn't, I'll completely understand. I mean, you don't even know the guy, and you have no reason..."

"Are you taking my name when we're married?"

"Oh, of course. If you want me to, not if you don't." She looked up at the server when she came back with the drinks, gave her a smile and a thank you, and then brushed fingers along the side of his head through his hair. "You thought I wouldn't?"

"As independent as you are, I couldn't be sure. I wouldn't try to insist."

"I absolutely will if you don't object."

"If I objected, Gill, I wouldn't have proposed." He nearly had to brush at his own eyes with the way she looked at him, and the way she was touching him. "Marry me before he comes and give him our name."

She smiled, a beautiful warm smile, and nodded.

"Thank you." It came out a whisper and he leaned in close. "For giving me the family I never thought I'd have."

"Oh Hank. You're giving us so much more..."

Instead of debating the issue, he kissed her.

He kept his chair close while they enjoyed the appetizers and talked about possible wedding dates. They both wanted to be sure Curtis and Gia could get there for it, and Susan. She would invite Karenne. Neither cared about anyone else being there. A small, very intimate, wedding, then. Possibly at the Strater. He could book a private room and they could take a long honeymoon anywhere she wanted, either before the baby came or long enough after she would be easily able to travel. Whichever... or both.

When he suggested both, she leaned in to hug him. While still accepting the embrace, he noticed an overly tanned woman with long dark hair streaked with dark red highlights come into view. She scanned the outdoor patio as though looking for someone. "I think your editor's here."

Releasing him, but not too quickly, Gillian waved her over and Hank stood in greeting, to which she raised her eyebrows with a toss of her hair. "I would suppose you're Mr. Dennison."

"Hank." He offered his hand. "It's nice to meet you, Karenne."

"Yes, and you." She only barely accepted the handshake and the chair he pulled out for her on Gillian's other side after giving her so-called friend a brief half hug.

Immediately after sitting, Karenne asked if she and Gillian could talk alone, assuming he would obey her command and leave. It was easy for him to see how she would intimidate Gillian and anyone else used to respecting authority, whether or not the particular authority deserved anyone's respect. But Hank was not one to be intimidated. Instead, he took his seat and ignored the request. "Help yourself to the appetizers. We haven't ordered yet."

"I hope the food is better than this place looks. Airplane food is crap, you know, even if you have to pay for it separately these days. Couldn't we have found somewhere quieter and more ... upscale than this?"

"Karenne." Gillian glanced at him as though apologizing. "This is beautiful. Look around."

"It's outside."

"The weather's perfect."

"No such thing. Air conditioning is perfect. That's why it was invented."

Their server interrupted and Hank asked her to bring a third menu along with Karenne's request for a nice dry wine. "I thought a casual conversation between the three of us might be a good idea."

"Is that right?" The woman pivoted in her chair to face her friend. "Gilly, since when did you start letting a man make your decisions?"

"What? He doesn't."

"No? And yet you wouldn't turn in your story before he read it, which we never do, and you're staying in his house because he suggested you should, and you turned in your resignation this morning when I know you want your job."

"My decisions. All of it."

"Of course." Karenne glanced at him like he was some kind of predator.

"Please. Can we just have a nice conversation without bringing work into it for now? I'd like you to get to know each other."

"I'm sure that's really not necessary. I came to talk to you."

"Karenne." Gill raised her left hand to show her ring. "We're getting married and I'm moving to Durango. That's why I turned in my resignation. I want to be here where my husband is. Fiancé at the moment, but husband soon."

"Husband?" Fire lit the editor's eyes and she nearly grabbed her wine from the server's hand to take a large swallow. "Well, so..." She glanced down at Gillian's middle. "That kid you said wasn't his..."

"Isn't his. As I said. I don't lie to you. But he will be Hank's, legally."

The woman started to say more, but his look changed her mind. He had no doubt she would say far more to Gillian as soon as she got her alone.

In the meantime, he did what he could to keep the evening relaxed, teasing about the caramelized bananas in rum sauce which she said was maybe the second most luscious thing she'd ever had in her mouth, at which Karenne spit out a bit of wine and drew the server's attention.

"I was talking about the steak, Renne. The one I had the first night Hank and I dined together. But since you mentioned it, I should knock it down to number three." She smiled and squeezed his thigh. "He is pretty luscious now that you've seen him in person, isn't he?" As her words sank in, she reddened again. "I mean... Hell. I'm going to stop talking now."

He pulled her in for a quick kiss. "Yes. I'd say that's pretty luscious, too." With a wink, he teased more about her dessert.

They walked Karenne back to her hotel since she didn't want to ride in Hank's truck and Gillian didn't see the need to call a taxi for three blocks when the evening was so nice. There was a crisp chill in the air now that the sun had set, but it was fresh and sweet and river-scented. She enjoyed the walk even if her editor didn't. Ex editor. Friend still, though, Gillian expected.

Durango sparkled at night. When the weather warmed, she'd ask Hank if they could take that walk up to the bluff as he'd mentioned over the summer, at night, so she could see it sparkling from above. By then, they'd have a stroller, also. An odd thought. It would never be only the two of them. They would always be three. It was a good number, though. She would be happy with three.

She suggested walking along the river a bit, as well, since it was right there running beside the hotel, but Karenne hated water and was tired from the "exhausting" flight.

The DoubleTree was gorgeous and Gillian nearly wished she

could stay there, also, to use the big indoor pool. The only thing marring the gorgeous night was Karenne bitching about everything. Her room overlooked the river, and Karenne didn't like rivers, or hotel pools, or hotels.

And she too obviously did not like Hank.

She grabbed Gillian's arm just inside the glass doors. "Would your *fiancé* mind if we had a little girl talk time? I'm only here for the night, so it's our only chance until, or unless, you decide to come back home."

"I am home, Karenne. And you're being rude."

Hank touched her face. "It's fine. I'll wander a bit and be back soon. Stay inside until I'm here, okay?"

"Yes, but..."

He kissed the side of her head. "Have a nice girl chat. How long should I plan?" He asked Karenne.

"Oh, I don't know. Can't she call you? Or do you have her on a schedule?"

Gillian wasn't sure whether to laugh at the thought or yell at the rudeness.

"I think you're giving me far more power than I've ever had. Or you don't know her as well as I'd thought." Hank rubbed a hand down her back. "I'll check back now and then."

He didn't bring his phone. Gillian knew he didn't. She handed him hers. "Karenne's number is in there so you can call if you get restless or I'll call you. Are you sure it's okay?"

With another kiss to her head, he whispered not to let herself get upset and nodded a goodbye to her friend, with a polite *nice to meet you, have a safe trip home*. He was hardly out the door when Karenne started in.

"Have you lost your mind?"

"What?"

"*That* man? Why would you marry *that* man? I know you're in a bind, but Gilly, this isn't the answer. I can help you. I'm around if you need help. You don't have to do this to yourself on top of what you've already done."

"Karenne..." She was so taken aback by both accusation and tone,

Gillian didn't even know how to start answering.

"Come on. We'll talk in my room in case he has spies listening."

She felt herself being dragged toward and into the elevator and down the hall and was in too much shock to fight against it. Behind the closed door of a gorgeous room with a gorgeous view, Gillian just wanted to call Hank and tell him to come right back.

"So tell me." Karenne plopped down onto a chair. "How did he make you think this is a good idea?"

Staring, Gillian suddenly wondered if her so-called friend actually knew her at all. Did she come off as that easily manipulated? Maybe she did. She'd sure given in to her editor, ex-editor, often enough. And she had the nerve to accuse Hank of the same?

"Gilly, come home with me. Tell him you need time to ... I don't know, plan your dress or whatever. Some distance will help you see what he's doing."

"What he's doing?"

"The guy's nearly twice your age and probably has a string of former fiancées out there broken-hearted because they figured he'd take care of them and he just dumped them like he dumped his employees..."

"Did you not read my article?"

"Of course I read it. Did he write it for you? Or have someone write it for you in almost your voice?"

Her head shook. "You're unbelievable. I can't believe I didn't see it before. You can't be happy so you don't want others to be happy, either. How many times did you say there are no happy endings? Well, you know what? You're wrong, and you won't ruin mine."

"Happy ending?" Karenne laughed. Loud. "You think you'll have a *happy ending* with that cold, manipulative business exec? You're smarter than this, Gilly. It's your hormones interfering, or you're scared and wondering how to do this on your own." She glanced at her stomach as though her child was alien demon or something.

"You're wrong." Gillian heard her voice shake. Shock. Sadness. Her only friend in the world, other than Gia, and Hank, couldn't be so ... so evil. Even if she did gloat about being promoted over Gillian, about being able to give her assignments she didn't want, about being well taken care of by a husband who was never home to be in her way but provided whatever was needed. She meant she didn't have a happy ending, so no one else could, either. "You're very wrong. I had myself covered fine. My copyrighting is going well. I have more job offers than I have time to take."

"And how much of that is his doing? You think he wouldn't? You think those offers will continue once he stops wanting you to work to focus only on him?"

"Wow. You're seriously delusional." Gillian went to the door and turned back. "I feel sorry for you, Karenne. You should try to let yourself be happy. You should also act like a real editor if you want that paper to keep going and do real stories with the flat-out truth, whether people like it or not. You're not helping anything trying to act like everything is sunshine and daisies when you don't even believe it yourself. Get some help. As for me..." She ran her hand along and under her beautiful baby bulge. "As for us, we are going to have our happy ending with a good, honest, decent man who loves us. He does, whatever you want to believe."

"You are so gullible, Gilly. You know you're gullible. Don't take it out on me because you're in a mess and believing what you need to believe so someone will fix it for you."

"No, I'm not gullible. And I fixed my own mess. I'm a good writer, better than you are, actually, and you know it. That's why you've tried so hard to hold me back. It won't work anymore. And Hank... Hank is a want, not a need. I want him. And I love him."

"Love." She rolled her eyes. "Come on, Gilly. It's time you grew up, isn't it?"

Grew up? She was so fully more grown up and aware of what was real than Karenne had ever been. But nothing she said would matter, as Hank often told her. The woman's mind was too set. She wanted to be listened to, not to listen. It just wasn't worth it anymore. "Goodbye, Karenne."

Gillian's hands shook as the door closed behind her. What an idiot she'd been. Not anymore. Maybe she did fight depression, but at least she wasn't fake about it. She wasn't the one who needed help, as Karenne always said she did. Hank was right. Everything he said...

Unsure whether to laugh or cry, Gillian pushed the elevator three times before it came, anxious to get back to him. He was right about everything. He'd tried to warn her. Gently. Letting her make her own decisions...

The man knew how to guide, to lead. By suggestion. Through empowerment, not force and not by being demeaning. He made her feel smarter than anyone else had. No wonder he was so good at what he did.

A lady in the elevator asked if she was alright and Gillian nodded, thanking her for the concern. He wouldn't be far. She'd use the desk phone to call him and he'd be there within a few minutes.

But he was there. In the lobby. And he came to meet her.

Relief surged through her system. "You didn't wander far."

"No. I thought you might not be long." His head tilted as he studied her face. "Everything okay?"

She held him. "Thank you for believing in me. I think you're the first person in my life who really has."

He kissed her head. "The first of many, Gill. Just have to get you in the right crowd. Curtis says they'll be here whenever they need to be and Gia wants to help you any way she can. I used your phone. Couldn't wait to tell them. I think Gia was actually jumping up and down in the background."

She chuckled against his shoulder. "Let's go home, Henry."

Thirty-three

Gillian stretched her fingers and her neck and then continued typing. The book was flowing much faster than she'd expected. Hank's comment about her being there for *her* story had changed the direction, turned it from a biography into a double-memoir, not that there was such a thing, but she figured she could do it that way if she wanted.

Her article about Hank had struck big. Mainly, they were trying to discredit her and the story since it didn't fit what had already been put out about him. But too many facts came out from those still willing to be honest, and those who cared one way or the other were fighting among themselves about who to believe.

Gillian didn't answer any of it. When Hank was bothered in town, he veered around them without saying a word unless they disparaged her, and then he jumped them full force, verbally, which of course became a story about his temper. They expected the controversy would only fuel book sales when she had it done, and then they could argue whether or not her defense of him, or rather, the truth about him, was true or not. It wouldn't matter. She'd already decided to put her fiction out under a pen name and keep it separate from her non-fiction work.

The biggest thing that slowed her progress, both on the memoir and her novel, aside from the copywriting she still did for her own spending money, were the luscious distractions. She and Hank often took nice long walks when the snow wasn't too high and the temperature wasn't too extreme, on one of the area trails or off-path up in the mountains, when they were both up to it and needed the break. They also spent days at a time in his cabin just talking, or working side-by-side. Much of the memoir, she was writing on paper with pencil, the way she used to write. When they worked late and Gillian was too tired for the drive back to the city, Hank tucked her into his bed, under three blankets since it was cold at night as the fire died away, and lay beside her on top of two of them, using only the top layer to cover himself.

On rare nights, they pushed the blankets aside for a time and warmed each other. Gillian had yet to notice any difficulty on his part in keeping up with her, but then she was often tired and glad to be able to do no more than sleep beside him, so she wasn't all that hard to keep up with, as he'd teased more than once.

She was five and a half months along and not showing too awful much yet. Her big hips, she figured. Susan told her to expect a girl with the way she was carrying. Hank believed his friend enough that he'd gone right out to pick up a few pink frilly newborn girl clothes. He said if she had a boy instead, he'd donate them somewhere.

Either way, the fatigue often got to her. Gillian found herself going to bed much earlier than normal and she allowed herself the indulgence rather than fighting it off as she normally would.

At times Hank stayed with her at the townhouse, in her room, at least part of the night. She'd more than once woken to find he'd gone to his own room at some point. Gillian didn't bother to ask him why. She was fine with it, although she knew most people would raise their eyebrows at the idea of him doing so or at the idea that she didn't care if he did. It worked for them. She saw no reason to question it. She also would not include anything that personal in the book, so who was to know, anyway? It was easy enough to do things the way you wanted privately as long as you kept it private.

She smiled from the computer chair, a well-cushioned ergonomic chair he'd found for her after she'd said it was hard to sit long enough to get any real work done, when she heard him come in the front door and call her name. He'd been out all day and his voice was a beautiful respite from the voices in her own head that spoke as she wrote, sometimes loudly, other times as a near whisper she had to decipher before transcribing them.

"Ready for a break?" He came up behind her and rubbed the shoulders she hadn't realized were so tense.

"Two minutes. Okay? I don't want to lose this thought."

"Of course. Should I leave you alone?"

"No." She reached back to squeeze his hand and went back to her keyboard. Gillian knew he read over her shoulder at times. Usually that would drive her crazy, but she didn't mind with Hank. She even managed to work through the back rub and kisses to her neck long enough to get her thoughts down.

"Okay. I've had enough for today." She saved her file on both the computer and her jump drive and shut it down. "What do you want to do tonight?" Gillian turned the chair and stroked a hand down his chest to his stomach.

"I've had the smoker going all day with a nice pork roast and a few things I'll bring back here to throw in the freezer for quick meals. How about packing an overnight bag? Weather's supposed to be decent tomorrow. We can do a short hike in the morning if you're up to it, before I bring you back."

The thought of pork in the smoker, the large smoker she'd thought was an outhouse, made Gillian think she was suddenly famished, although of course she wasn't since she also allowed herself the indulgence of snacking whenever she felt like it, almost always on healthy stuff for the baby's sake, and for Hank's, so he wouldn't worry so much.

She reached up to touch his face. "Do I get to see what you've been working on up there yet?"

"Yes." He helped her to her feet. "It's time."

Hank pulled into the circular driveway full of fresh gravel and lined with the carved stumps she'd found behind his cabin that worked as a privacy fence on the outer side with his carvings facing the house. He stopped in front of the porch.

Gillian turned from looking at the carvings to the house. "This place is beautiful. Are they friends of yours? You made those carvings for them? How can you bear to part with them?"

"Want to look around?"

"Are we allowed?"

He chuckled and went around to open her door with an offered arm. Supporting the little life inside her own had slowed her, but not nearly as much as he would have expected. A sturdy woman, his city girl. She always raised her eyebrows when he said as much, but he needed sturdy. He loved that she was sturdy. Yet she gladly accepted his help when he offered, and if she needed it and he didn't realize, she had no qualms about saying so. The girl knew by now she had nothing to prove, especially since he gave her the same consideration and willingly leaned on her on his bad days. Fortunately, they were fewer and fewer.

He led her up two wide steps to the large front porch bordered by a low picketed railing and unlatched the gate that would keep a young child from falling down the stairs. She went straight to the handmade birch rocking chair, stained light to show its grain and sealed well to protect it from the weather.

"It's beautiful. Oh Hank, you made this?" Gillian fingered the etching of a water nymph sitting on a flat stone in a stream across the top of the chair, above the thick cushion covered by heavy fabric in a water print that Susan had made for it and then protected with a stain guard, for baby spit ups and toddler spills and such, she'd said.

"Thought it might come in handy in a few months." He lifted a hinged panel on top of one padded arm that folded out to reveal a cup holder and one on the other arm that had an open rectangular tray. "I figure it'll hold a bottle or pacifier or other little baby things you might want to have within reach. When you don't need it for that purpose, you could throw pencils and erasers in there."

"But..." She looked around at the large front yard as though waiting for someone to jump out and yell. "Are they holding things for you?"

"This is part of my property, Gill. Told you I owned a large bit of it. Come inside."

"There's electric here." She'd noted the porch light.

"Yes. And normal indoor plumbing, with a generator in case the power goes out so you can still have a warm shower instead of joining me in the cold stream."

She was quiet while he led her through the house with birch floors throughout, all tongue and groove with a few well placed nails and no glue. The walls were all painted a soft sky blue with dark green wood blinds and light green valances over the windows. The kitchen cabinets and island were bamboo since she liked it so much in the townhouse. The guest room and main bath were only sparsely furnished so far, as was the large master bedroom with private bath. The spacious office with big windows was well-equipped and looked out over the swimming pond, but so far, he had the blinds closed so she didn't see it.

"Now this looks like you."

He rubbed her back. "Do you like it?"

"Of course. Like I said, it looks like you. You designed it?"

"I did, but I'll admit to hiring out building help, as well as the electric and plumbing work. I did want it done right. Come here." He took her to a door that led from the office directly into a smaller room.

Her jaw dropped as she surveyed the little nursery with the crib that would convert to a toddler bed in time and a dresser and changing table, all with different engravings of fantasy creatures. He'd moved a couple of small tree trunk carvings in, also, to serve as stools or low tables, one beside a second rocking chair.

The chair featured little fairies across the back. The tree stump beside it had been turned into a fairy with long hair, holding a flower, with a wistful, independent look on her face. A small table was behind her back and wooden pegs extended behind the flower. One held a bib, another a small cloth.

"It's beautiful." She walked over to the crib and ran her fingers over the carvings along the top of the back rail. Sprites playing with baby animals.

"There's no bedding yet. Thought you might want to pick that out, along with the decor in the other rooms. We'll go do that whenever you're ready."

Her eyes were moist when she turned to him. "Our house? This is ours?"

"It's a cross between living in town and living in the cabin. A compromise. Does it work for you?"

"Oh, yes."

"Good. I put a lot of planning into it to try to make it as perfect as possible. By the way, this door goes directly to our bedroom." He opened the one on the opposite side from the office door. "To make it easy to check on her during the night or while you're working. The office is yours."

"Oh, Hank..."

"There's more." He took her hand and led her back through the house to the back porch, a screened porch overlooking a wood-gated pond-style swimming pool, complete with waterfall. "It's heated. And that path you see?" He pointed beyond the pool to a gravel road and small shed covering an ATV. "It leads to the cabin. I'll use it as a workshop and keep the sawdust and noise away from the house. It gives us both our private work spaces and our together space."

"I don't know what to say."

He skimmed a hand over her head down along her face. "Say you'll list me as your child's father. I had Curtis track down your sperm donor and he readily signed paperwork giving up his rights, which..."

"You what?"

"I didn't want issues."

"What did you do?"

"Curtis took him paperwork, with a lawyer at his side, and said you wouldn't ever bother him with the child or ask for support if he'd sign. It wasn't hard. He said it probably wasn't his, and..."

"He said what?"

"A few other things not worth repeating, but we made it very clear and simple and he read through it and signed away any rights he might have had. They did it in Curtis's favorite diner where plenty of people could see he wasn't forced or intimidated or anything of the sort. Not that he would, but I like to have my bases covered from all angles."

She turned away and went back into the house.

Following, he found her in the nursery running her fingers over the engraving on the crib. "Gillian." Hank stopped just behind her. "Did I overstep boundaries? I should have asked, but I didn't want you to worry about it until we found him and took care of it. You said you wanted nothing to do with him..."

"No. I don't." It was nearly a whisper.

He moved around to see her face. "Tell me the truth if you're upset with me."

"You're already her father, as far as I'm concerned. I'm not sure I wanted him to know..."

"It'll come out, Gill. There are too many who know we haven't been together that long. As I said, I didn't want issues. He was going to find out. Not that I wouldn't have paid him off if needed, but I hate to give in to someone trying to make a buck that way. Curtis told him the lawyer was yours and that he was your friend doing it for you because you didn't want to see the guy's face again. He apparently believed it."

"Of course he did, because he knows I don't. You ... you were smart to do it that way, because he would have taken whatever he could get if he found out who you are. But ... you didn't meet him?"

"No, although I was tempted out of curiosity. Curtis said he could see why you were attracted, but he still thinks you're better off with this old man than with that young Atlas type. I hope he's right."

"Of course he's right, and you're not old." She wrapped her arms up around him. "Thank you. And yes. I would love to put your name as her father. I'd thought about it so often, but I couldn't quite ask."

He kissed her as relief swelled through his chest, through his heart.

Gillian melded in against his body, making him feel every bit the Atlas type more than an old man as she caressed him, then took his hand and led him through the little doorway to their bedroom. "How about we break this in?"

"Not until our wedding night, Gill."

She drew back to see his face, questioning whether he was serious.

"We can head to the cabin, though. I need to pull the meat out of the smoker by now."

She chuckled. "That's one way to put it, Dennison."

~ ~ ~

"You know..." Gillian grasped his arm before he rolled out of bed, away from her.

"Good morning." Hank turned back with a grin and ran fingers along her face. "I didn't know you were awake."

"Hm, I felt you move."

"Sorry. Go back to sleep. I'll start breakfast." He kissed her nose.

"Huh uh, you're not escaping this conversation again." She slid a hand up under his arm along his warm skin to grasp the back of his shoulder, as though she could actually hold him there if he wanted to move away.

"Were we having a conversation? Was I awake for it?" His eyes teased with only the slightest upturn of his gorgeous lips.

"There is something I still need to know. Why fantasy creatures?"

"Ah." His chest rose and fell with a large deep breath.

"I think if I can give you my child, by all rights, you could probably tell me why you're so engrossed with things that don't exist."

"You're turning this baby into a bargaining tool?"

"No, I ... That's not what I meant. I mean I trust you that much, with the most important, most precious thing in my life, other than you, of course, but I mean..."

"I'm teasing." He cuddled in close and kissed her head. "And I realize your child comes before me, as she should. I wouldn't have it any other way. Nothing in the world should come before your child."

"Glad we have that understood."

He grinned and stroked a thumb along her face.

"Why fantasy creatures?"

With a deep breath, he moved the blanket aside and traced fingers over the swell of her child. "Because sometimes believing in fairy tales and fantasies and other things that seem impossible is the only way you can deal with reality. The impossible has to seem possible. At least at times. I have to believe that what they say can't happen *could* actually happen, that maybe they don't know as much as they think they know. Maybe those creatures are real and we simply don't see them. Does that make sense?"

Gillian felt her eyes water. Such a poet, her hermit CEO. So beautiful inside. Such a determination to live, to fight. To stay with her and their child, despite the odds. "It makes perfect sense."

"Good. Because I plan to read fairy tales to this little girl. I want her to believe in the impossible, to believe she can do anything."

Feeling herself nod, Gillian ran her fingers through his gorgeous dark blond hair, so thick... "Is it me or is your hair actually getting thicker?"

"I think it is. A good sign, so I've read." He grabbed a quick deep breath and sat up. "Come help me make breakfast since you're awake, and we'll go for a walk before I take you back to town."

As he pulled on the lower half of his sweats, Gillian got up and slipped into her robe and wrapped her arms around him. "I think I might work here today and maybe the next few days if you don't mind. Will I be in your way?"

"Gill, you're going to be my wife. You think I'm worried about you being in my way?"

"Well, you did set up two different work spaces."

"For your convenience, not mine."

"Oh. So are you going to show me how to drive that little thing out there beside the path so I can invade your space when I want?"

"That's the plan. We'll have to fit it with a car seat, though."

"Careful, Henry. You may not get much work done until I get used to having you around all the time and need space again."

He closed in, sliding his hands inside her robe and up her naked skin, planting kisses on her neck. "These days, work keeps my hands busy only when they're not otherwise occupied. It doesn't take precedence. I'll let yours do that instead and I'm always willing to fit in around it." He raised his mouth to hers and whispered against her lips. "I love you, Gillian. I love that you're making me a husband and a father. Let's do this. Time to make it official."

She nodded, brushing her face against his.

"What do you think about a Christmas wedding? Curtis and Gia will come out and spend the holidays here if you agree. They'd love to stand up with us, unless you have someone else..."

"I don't. And I'd love that. All of it. Yes."

Thirty-four

To his surprise, she stayed at the cabin for five days straight. They walked every day but one when the fatigue hit her and she couldn't make herself go out, and she carried her camera every time.

He was showing her his carvings, those he remembered how to find, and she took pictures of each one, sometimes several photos from different angles. It didn't matter how often he assured her he had photos already. She kept taking them.

After their late morning walks and a good rejuvenating lunch, she grabbed her notebook and a pencil and curled up on the couch to work. Not the memoir, she said, and not her novel. Something else that had come to mind during their walks. She wouldn't say and he didn't press.

Hank loved their non-invasive private relationship. It was easy and comfortable. They didn't have the intensity some couples had, but they were both fine with that. They'd both had their fill of intensity in other areas of life.

And they were plenty intense enough on nights, and sometimes mornings, when their physical needs took over. No question there. So far he hadn't had issues, but he'd stopped worrying about whether he would. She wouldn't make a big deal of it. Hank knew that by now. She'd shrug it off and go to sleep and likely tell him she was happy enough to simply go to sleep. At his side.

When she worked during the afternoon, he left her alone and went out to carve or simply wander. Unless he was tired and then he'd pull out a book and kick his feet up on the ottoman and sneak peeks of her working intensely while he read. Even when she sat, pencil in hand, staring out the window, he knew she was working and didn't interrupt.

December twenty-first couldn't come soon enough for him. They'd agreed on the date. Curtis and Gia had plane tickets reserved. Gia would stay in the townhouse with Gillian for two days before the wedding to help with any final plans and Curtis would stay in the cabin with him, just for the getaway, his friend said. On the twenty-first, Hank and Gillian would move into the house, their house. No more back and forth visiting.

They were delaying their honeymoon until the summer when it was better travel weather and when Baby was old enough to travel. Gillian wanted to see the east coast since she'd never been out of the west other than barely into the Midwest. He'd offered anywhere overseas, but with things as they were in the world, she wanted to stay in the States. They would travel mainly by car, after flying out to Maine, starting in Acadia, and then work their way down to Florida.

He truly looked forward to the trip. These days, he truly looked forward to everything.

Gillian looked up from her current Forest Nymphs story in progress to find her fiancé watching her and gave him a smile. "Yes?"

"You're beautiful."

"In other words, you want my attention?"

"No, it's all right. I don't want to interrupt."

She knew the tone for what it was and set her work aside to go sit on his lap with an arm around his neck. "You can, you know."

"I know." He stroked hair back from her face.

"I need to head back to the townhouse tomorrow. Okay? At least for a few days. Some of what I need to do will be harder from here."

"After our walk or before?"

"After is fine." She loved how much it meant to him that she was willing to go walk around in the trees at his side. She'd even learned not to worry so much about the crawling, wriggling, slimy things. Now and then he picked one up to show her, not too close, not trying to scare her, just to show her and to explain its function in nature. They weren't really so bad, she supposed. At least she didn't jump anymore when one crossed their path. "I'm done working for today. What do you want to do? Beat me at chess again?"

"Actually…" He stroked her face and let his fingers slide down her neck as his mouth met hers.

"Hm, nice. Is that an invitation?"

"It is, but you know I'll take a rain check."

Melding into him, she slid her fingers under his shirt. A hard kick against where her stomach pressed into his made them both laugh.

Baby girl often kicked at her daddy when he got that close. Gillian smoothed her hand over her quickly growing child. "Not going to work. You're going to have to share nicely."

Helping her up, Hank led her to the bedroom, pulled her shirt over her head, lowered to his knees, and kissed her roundness with his hands lovingly supporting each side. "Don't worry, sweet little angel. I'll never come between you and your mom." Rising again, he took her face in his hands. "I just want to help keep her happy now that she is."

"Back at you, Henry." Gillian kissed him hard and took him to bed where she thought she might try to keep him until breakfast.

Epilogue

Gillian leaned back against the rocking chair, closed her eyes, and listened to Hank read her third published Forest Nymphs story to little Henry Curtis Dennison. Only three months old, their son had no idea what Daddy was saying, but he always peered up wide-eyed and lay still when Hank read to him. Unlike little Miss Never-sit-still Hannah Jill. She was much more her father's child than her mother's with her constant insistence in running her little legs off or climbing on the furniture or drawing with Daddy's sketch pencils. Her own regular pencils weren't good enough. Hank always gave in despite Gillian's insistence the girl should learn boundaries.

Her picture book series inspired by Hank's tree carvings were doing surprisingly well. She wrote them under the pen name she planned to use for her novel when she bothered to finish it, but whisperings were starting to spread that she was the same author of *that CEO memoir* which was still being both praised and slammed.

Hank often asked when she would finish her novel, but Gillian was too busy enjoying the fantasy and fun of taking his carving creations and turning them into stories. With each book, she sent photos of his work to a local pastel sketch artist she'd hired after seeing her at the arts festival. Every time she saw a finished drawing, Gillian's eyes misted. They were all just perfect, so intricately detailed and vibrant. Hank said the artist's work was far better than his. Gillian always told him they were equally good, only different, with a hint to their past backgrounds they still often teased each other about.

Hannah was her mom's biggest fan. Her copies got so worn out, Hank had laminated the pages of one of each book to let her "read" as often as she wanted on her own without destroying them.

Gillian couldn't believe their daughter was two years old already and she now had two children. She'd had major doubts when Hank called her to come into town that day three months earlier. A newborn boy had been dropped in front of the police station with a note to say sorry, but she just couldn't deal with the crying and didn't know what to do with him and had no way to take care of him well enough. The note was barely readable, as though it had been badly texted instead of written.

Over the past couple of years, Gillian and Hank had become local fixtures. Someone let it slip that he'd been anonymously donating money to Durango's community shelter, and that led to offers to be on the board, which he refused for a long time until he stopped refusing. Gillian signed up as a volunteer, went through the security check, and had already stepped in to mentor a young woman and her child escaping a bad situation. So when they needed someone to take care of the three-week-old baby while things were sorted, they called Hank. As soon as she picked the boy up and he cuddled into her, Gillian knew she was in it for the long run.

It didn't take long to find the very young, frightened fifteen-year-old mother. To ease her mind, they took her to lunch, told her she wasn't in trouble and they'd help her if she wanted to keep her child. The girl cried and shook her head. No family support, she said. She was staying with a friend's family, but they threw a fit about the crying and she'd left school to care for him, and she loved him but didn't know what to do with him. She and her boyfriend both readily signed adoption paperwork when Gillian and Hank promised they could stay in touch and see him now and then. They'd already been to the house several times, visiting. But when the girl held the baby and he cried, she gave him right back.

Gillian had the feeling they'd adopted little Henry's parents, as well, since their own families were too busy or uninterested and they both leeched onto any guidance offered. So far, with advice and mentoring, they were staying with separate friends and were still seeing each other, but they'd stopped the risky part of their relationship. She'd gone back to school and worked part time for Susan, and her boyfriend was working full time along with helping Hank around the place now and then.

Gillian had barely slept since the night Henry came to live with them. The boy wouldn't let her out of his sight or away from her side without screaming, except when Hank read to him or walked him around outside. The up side was that her depressive episodes had waned down to almost non-existent. They'd disappeared when Hannah was a baby and needed a lot of cuddles, started to return when the girl became independent, at least in her own mind, and disappeared again while she held Henry. Hank teased that he'd have to keep watch for more babies in the future who needed someone to sit and rock them.

"Go on to bed, Gill. I'll wrestle the little wild things to sleep."

She opened her eyes and gave him a soft grin. "How about we both wrestle them to sleep and then do a little wrestling ourselves?"

"Are you up to that?"

"I am if you are, mister."

"It was my skinny dipping earlier, wasn't it?"

She chuckled. "Only you would not only swim when there's snow on the ground, but in the buff."

"The pool's heated."

"Enough to make it just above freezing instead of frozen."

"I might have to add a winter cover around the pool. That was a little extreme even for me." He set the book aside when the baby fussed.

She went to get him and cuddled him in. "Shh, baby. It's bedtime. Tell your sister to pick up her toys and come on."

Of course Hannah started a little hissy fit. She hated bedtime. Gillian left her to Hank and went to make a bottle for little Henry.

While she rocked him, she looked out over the snowy mountains surrounding Durango and a scene came to mind. For her project. Her novel. Her new direction that would have to share its path with her family. After she made love to her luscious husband, she would take a few notes so she wouldn't forget the scene and then curl in beside his warm body and let the thought simmer overnight.

Her Hank got stronger and less tired as time passed. They both worried less about it. Some days, she looked at him and caught her breath at his beauty and at the way she loved him, her eyes moistened, and she sent a prayer up for his health.

No matter what his coming checkup told them, though, Hank Dennison aka Henry would live and breathe forever. She would make absolute certain he did.

EllaMKaye.com

Dedication

To those fighting and to those who have lost their fights with mental or physical illnesses. Also, to the loved ones trying to help hold the pieces together.

Acknowledgements & Author's Note

I'd like to thank my own local natural health source of both information and natural, organic supplies. To Heather Rust-Murray, who, after years of employment in the conventional medicine industry changed paths and now works to help support local farmers and local organic produce, along with encouraging those of us looking for other options.

As always, thank you to my beta readers and editors. <3

Also, a huge thank you to the ridiculously talented Tommy Craggs, Tree Sculptor, from Co Durham, England, for permission to use the beautiful little fairy carving that graces the cover of this book. Find his work here: http://www.treesculpting.co.uk

This is a work of fiction.

The debate between conventional/modern medicine and natural medicine has been ongoing for centuries. This story brings light to the current trend of restoring natural, holistic healing, but it is a story, the author is trained in creative writing, not in medicine, natural or conventional, and nothing within the story is intended as medical advice. There is a plethora of research available and easy to find from both sides of the aisle, and it's a very rare thing that only one side is right while the other is wrong. It's nearly always, if not always, somewhere between the two. If the notion interests you, please do your own research and make informed decisions.

Music Mentioned in the Story

(I do not own any rights to any song/album/artist listed. All are used fairly under US copyright law. Permission for use is not implied.)

Zac Brown
Metallica/ James Hetfield
Gabriel Fauré
JoDee Messina: *Burn, Feels Like Home*

About The Author

Ella M. Kaye uses her art and psychology background to create contemporary love stories with mental health issues set around the creative arts. Each of her novels and novellas fall under one of three series: Dancers & Lighthouses, Artists & Cottages, and Songwriters & Cities. Kaye has been writing romantically inclined literary fiction that branches into straight mainstream in both novel and short story form under the name LK Hunsaker for more than two decades. After many moves as a military spouse, she and her husband are settled in western Pennsylvania where she enjoys the abundant foliage, recreational lakes, and hilly vistas, as well trying to keep up with her hectic handful of gorgeous grandchildren.

EllaMKaye.com
LKHunsaker.com

Other Books by Ella M. Kaye

Pier Lights
(Dancers & Lighthouses 2013)

Caroline was a relevé away from becoming prima ballerina when, partly due to her own actions, she was damaged enough to never be allowed en Pointe again. Returning to her hometown area, she finds a grittier dancing job and determines to land on top this time.

Dio hides away on his farm near Charleston, South Carolina, and ventures out only when he can be in disguise. He uses his swordsman skills to work out aggression and connect with others while he maintains distance. When the two collide on the beach in the glow of the lights from the pier, their personal scars push them away, and pull them in, just as the ebb and flow of the Atlantic.

Shadowed Lights
(Dancers & Lighthouses 2014)

When her sister loses her house to Hurricane Sandy, Delaney Griffin welcomes the family into her home. Months later, with five noisy kids and an overbearing brother-in-law threatening her sanity, Delaney spends much of her free time at the wildlife refuge, which also works as her refuge. Still, the lack of privacy, along with space to dance, her only passionate release, causes her debilitating social anxiety to escalate.

Eli Forrester has come from small town Indiana to Barnegat, New Jersey with his company to help restore the coast. A high rise worker who loves new people and new places, he fears nothing, except water. When he accidentally kicks one of the sea critters Delaney is trying to help rescue, he is drawn to the quiet New Jersey girl. Unwilling to take her cues to leave her alone, Eli is alternately put off and turned on by her odd behavior.

Under shadow of devastation, fear, and forced separation, Delaney and Eli search for their own rescue light.

Pieces of Light
(Dancers & Lighthouses 2014)

When her niece is diagnosed with autism, Emma Turner chooses to support her sister, a single mom, and is served divorce papers by her possessive husband who doesn't actually intend to let her go. Moving from Boston to Provincetown, Massachusetts, Emma teaches fifth grade during the week and takes care of Patty on weekends. That changes abruptly when her sister's health fails and Patty needs more than weekend care.

Fillan Reilly has taken a summer job on Cape Cod teaching ballroom dance. A Galway, Ireland native, Fillan uses the change of scenery to try to clear his head and decide his direction after his long-term girlfriend leaves him, unsure whether she'll return. With pressure to enter the family business and push his dancing to the sidelines, he expects an easy relaxed summer to think things over.

As fate brings them together, Emma and Fillan must determine whether joining their lifeboats will provide an even keel or throw them further off-balance.

Shadows of Greens & Memories
(Artists & Cottages 2015)

Francis Barrett returns to her hometown of Storm Lake, Iowa to take care of the family holdings after her father passes. While turning his garden shed into a small but livable cottage, she runs into an old flame she admired from afar but never dared speak with during their high school days. Using her secret passion of oil painting to unwind from long days of clearing out the mess, Francis finds her father also had a secret passion and left behind a tale of a man she didn't truly know.

George Frederick McKenry never left the Midwest town where he was born other than brief travels with his four children, who he now has custody of since his ex moved into a condo with her new boyfriend. Running into the one girl from school who rebuffed him when he asked her out, G.F. can't help checking on her and making sure she's getting along alright. False assumptions and past resentments fade as Fran and G.F. let down their guards in order to create new memories.

A Melody in the Dark
Singers & Songwriters: a prequel novella (2017)
published by Fire Star Press as part of the *Music of the Heart* anthology.

Meladee Lerner, a single mom and struggling songwriter, moved to Pittsburgh to escape a marriage she didn't want. It's 1979, just after the big snow storm that paralyzed the city, when they run into Niall Dillon, a hard-working young Pittsburgher with strong Irish roots. Niall is making plans to travel the US on his own, but one eventful night gives him second thoughts.

~~ ~~ ~~

Watch for more Artists & Cottages books from Ella M. Kaye, as well as the continuing Dancers & Lighthouses series, and the new Songwriters & Cities series, soon to come.